Royal Disaster

ALSO BY PARKER SWIFT

Royal Affair

Royal Disaster

A Royal Scandal Novel
Book 2

PARKER SWIFT

FOREVER
YOURS

New York Boston

Copyright © 2017 by Parker Swift
Cover design by Elizabeth Turner. Cover copyright © 2017 by Hachette Book Group, Inc.

Forever Yours
Hachette Book Group
1290 Avenue of the Americas, New York, NY 10104
forever-romance.com
twitter.com/foreverromance

First published as an ebook and as a print on demand: April 2017

Forever Yours is an imprint of Grand Central Publishing. The Forever Yours name and logo are trademarks of Hachette Book Group, Inc.

The publisher is not responsible for websites (or their content) that are not owned by the publisher.

The Hachette Speakers Bureau provides a wide range of authors for speaking events. To find out more, go to www.hachettespeakersbureau.com or call (866) 376-6591.

ISBNs: 978-1-4555-9807-6 (ebook), 978-1-4555-9806-9 (POD edition)

To ER again, because always.

Acknowledgments

Thank you to Megha Parekh, Lexi Smail, and everyone at Forever Yours for helping to continue Lydia and Dylan's story.

There will always be unrelenting, enormous, supersized gratitude for my agent, Kimberly Brower, who continues to make me a better writer. Thank you, Kimberly, for telling it like it is, indulging my bizarre questions, and continuing to make me feel like any of it, all of it, is possible. I'm so glad to be on your team.

Finally, as ever, none of it would be possible without Ethan. Two writers and two kids and two jobs is an impossible task, and yet you have a way of making it feel not only possible but imperative. Thank you for being exactly the person you are.

Lydia

Chapter 1

It's bloody arctic downstairs. Thank god we're staying at my place tonight," Dylan said, climbing back into my bed and handing me coffee.

The clock read 6:45 a.m., and the early Monday morning sun was just peeking through the light layer of frost on the windows. He pulled the duvet up over his bare chest and wrapped his hands around his own coffee mug.

"Aw, poor baby," I teased. "Are your aristocratic toes too delicate for my unheated floors?" A cold front had come in, and late October had arrived with a vengeance.

Dylan looked at me with playful revenge in his eyes, put his coffee down, and slid closer to me under the covers. Suddenly I felt a sharp shock of cold on my warm legs as his frigid feet pressed against my skin. I shrieked and quickly put my coffee down before he wrapped me completely in his chilled body.

"Dylan!" I yelled into his cool chest and laughed as he tried to maximize my exposure to his freezing-cold limbs. In no time he was on top of me, tenting me with his body and the duvet.

The heat between us built and the warmth returned. He brushed my hair from my face and kissed me sweetly on the lips while nudging my legs apart with his knee.

"You know, damsel," he started, punctuating his thought with a seductive kiss to my neck, "if you would just move in with me"—a kiss to my collarbone—"Molly would make the coffee." His head moved farther south, disappearing beneath the duvet. He kissed me between my breasts, and suddenly I wasn't cold anywhere. "And your toes would always be warm."

I fought off my arousal enough to grab his face with my hands and pull it up to my own, kissing him sternly on the lips. "My toes weren't cold," I pointed out, smiling smugly. "As much as I adore your housekeeper, my *boyfriend* made me coffee. And we've been over this—it's too soon."

"One of these days I'm going to get you to say yes," he said with an evil gleam in his eye, and he resumed his attack. He bit down gently on my nipple, and I was a goner. That familiar heat pulsed through my veins, and my attention was limited to the physical sensations at every place our bodies touched. My hips thrust up to meet his. Our toes were warm. My coffee was forgotten.

* * *

It was quarter to nine by the time we were dressing for work, and Dylan looked at his watch, sighing. "We have to get out of this habit," he said. "I used to be in the office a half hour earlier before you came along." He said it as though he wasn't one hundred percent responsible for our delay, and I gave him a skeptical glare that said as much. Plus, he may have been *trying* to mean what he was saying, but he had his hand in my panties and was pulling them off of me while he was saying it. "No. Knickers."

"This was entirely your fault," I replied as I pulled the black lacey thong back over my heeled brown boots, up my legs, and swatted away his hand. "I have a meeting today with Hannah and a potential investor. About the store. I'm wearing a skirt. I need underwear."

"What time is the meeting likely to end?" he asked, alternately holding up two ties to his neck—one a rich burgundy, the other a trendy olive color. He was looking over my shoulder into the full-length mirror behind me, deciding. I took the silky olive-colored tie from his hand and draped it around his collar, and he promptly started to knot the fabric at his neck.

"It's a lunch thing, so probably two?" I turned around so he could fasten the clasp on my skirt for me, which he did without looking. When I turned back around, I tweaked the fabric behind one of his cuff links, straightening it.

In no time at all we'd fallen into these little habits, habits that involved touching each other when there was no earthly reason why touching each other would be necessary. As if I'd never fastened my own skirt before. As if he couldn't straighten his own cuffs. We were unabashedly in the thick of it. Touching each other. Looking at each other. As though these things would sustain us during our workdays. As though they were the very things that kept us in love.

"Perfect," he replied, and I looked at him quizzically. "I'll come round at quarter past and remove them for you."

I rolled my eyes and laughed despite myself as I left my bedroom, Dylan following right behind. When we landed in the kitchen, reality hit me like a force field. Frank Abbott, my new bestie, was waiting for me, offering up a second cup of coffee in a travel mug. Frank had been my shadow for the last couple weeks. His official title was security, but I'd been calling him *honey* because it irritated Dylan.

Ever since that email had arrived two weeks ago, the one that still made me shudder when I thought of it, Dylan had been urging that it was smart to hire some security for when he wasn't with me. First we had a blowout fight, wherein I reminded *him* that I could obviously take care of myself and he reminded *me* that he actually had experience with this kind of situation. In the end, as much as I hated it, I acknowledged that I *didn't* have any experience with this, and we agreed to hire Frank, at least for a little while. It felt weird and excessive—people in my world just didn't hire bodyguards—but until we knew this cyberstalker didn't mean any real harm, I had to concede that it also felt smart.

That email had added an ever-present thread of stress to our otherwise honeymoonish lives.

LIAR. CRIMINAL. TRAITOR.

Those were the words scrawled across the intimate photo in the email. A photo that should never have been taken, of a moment that no one should have seen. We had been at Dylan's hideaway in the country. A place surrounded by wilderness, where we should have been safe from prying eyes. But the photo was clear enough—my arms tied high above my head, my chest bare, Dylan's lips against my skin, our naked bodies flush against each other. A moment so private that seeing it through a stranger's lens made me see myself differently, made me see just how open I'd become with Dylan, how raw, how close.

The photo made me feel violated. And the threatening words were, apart from entirely confusing, *menacing*. The subject of the email had been *He's not who you think he is*, referring to Dylan presumably. But I kept trying to tell myself that this email proved nothing, apart from the fact that someone had been out to get us. Him. Me. Whatever.

When it had arrived, I hadn't known what to do. I hated to think of it, but my first instinct had been to believe the harsh words and to not trust Dylan. I'd only just started trusting him enough to let him back in. We were on the heels of the whole Amelia nonengagement/engagement fiasco, which had been spurred by the tabloids, and it felt like too much. Like the relationship gods were putting me through my paces, throwing one too many damning pieces of evidence my way.

So for two endless days I'd said nothing. I'd avoided him. I'd retreated slightly at his touches.

That night we'd been lying in his bed, me flat on my back, eyes staring into space, and him wrapped completely around me. We'd just made love, and I knew he was deep in his post-coital hazy cuddle-Lydia-into-submission phase, which I normally would have reciprocated. But I was distracted, half somewhere else, anxious that I was wrong about him.

"Baby," he said, followed by some question about whether I'd liked what we'd just done.

"Mmm-hmm," I replied, not a hundred percent sure I knew what I was replying to.

Before I realized what was happening, he sat up against the headboard and hauled me across his lap, so I was straddling him. Before I had a minute to even register what his intentions were, he had his huge hands braced around my body, forcing me to look at him.

"*Enough*," he said. "What is going on with you?"

I didn't say anything at first. I was stunned that this was the moment of truth. I should have known better—he could always see right through me.

"If you think for a second I haven't noticed your one-word distracted answers over the last few days, you're mad. I know every inch of you," he said, confirming my suspicions.

I sighed and dropped my gaze to his chest, but Dylan promptly lifted my chin with his finger.

"What?" he asked, with notable restraint. I knew him well enough to know he wished he could dive into my mind and just take what he was looking for.

I sighed deeply and began. "I got an email a few days ago."

He looked only curious at this point. "From whom?"

"I don't know," I said, and his curiosity became tinged with concern. "The sender was a series of numbers and letters, and it disappeared when I tried to forward it." I sighed before deciding the best thing was just to be honest. "Look, I wasn't sure I should tell you, because, well, honestly, I didn't know what to make of it."

"What do you mean? Lydia, what did the email say?"

This was going to be the true test. He'd either look guilty, indicating the truth of the words in the email, or he'd looked shocked, displaying his innocence. "There was a photo. Of us," I said, and Dylan's eyes widened slightly. "At your house in the country. In the bedroom." His eyes widened more and became tinged with something darker. "My arms..." I trailed off, not really able to say it out loud, and instead raised my arms them above my body, mimicking the position I'd been in in the photo. "My breasts," I said, and I could hear the vulnerability in my voice, the discomfort at having been photographed that way. "Your mouth, your naked back, your profile." Dylan's eyes were narrowing now, lining themselves in anger and worry. "The photo was a little grainy, black and white, but it was clear it was us. Clear as day."

Dylan straightened in the bed, almost going into business mode, ultra-protective mode, a mode that was laced with his concern for me. His friend Grace, who'd committed suicide after being hounded by the paparazzi when they thought she and Dylan were dating, was all of a sudden present in the conversation—his terror that something like that could happen to me. But that's not what this was about—this hadn't been paparazzi. It had been a *threat*. And, I guess, maybe that was worse.

"Dylan," I resumed, and I told him about the incriminating words scrawled across his back in the photo, about the accusatory subject heading.

As soon as I told him, just saying the words out loud, I knew in my gut that I had been wrong to mistrust him. And as soon as he wrapped his arms clear around me and pulled me into him, I was able to release the tension I'd been carrying around for days. He held me like that for longer than I probably realized, rubbing my back.

"I'm so sorry, damsel. You shouldn't have to deal with this kind of crap."

My head flew up. I had been expecting righteous anger, shocked fury, fear that someone was out there directing their evil intent our way. But apart from his initial concerned reaction, he was mostly calm. "Why aren't you surprised?" I asked.

"Lydia, this crap is just part of my life. People—in the press or in private—say things that aren't true about me on a daily basis," he started and then exhaled with sorrowful resignation. "They'll start saying them about you too before long." He stroked my cheek with his fingers, and I could see the distaste for these intrusions in his eyes. I thought back to his "engagement" to Amelia and realized just how true this was. I thought back to him telling me how his phone had been tapped and how the police had actually *assisted* the paparazzi in that situation. He was used to being targeted.

I leaned into him, sighing deeply, inhaling the comforting scent radiating from his warm chest, and he ran his fingers along my spine.

"I'm afraid, baby, that this isn't uncommon. There's never been a photo used in one of these personal attacks, and I'm concerned that they were able to get *that* photo in particular," he said, and I could hear his brain turning, trying to work out who might be behind it. "But now that you're here," he added, squeezing me for emphasis, "they have a new way to get to me. My personal life has always been somewhat unavailable."

A particular Dylan brand of protectiveness and frustration was running through him—I could feel it. It was like concentration paired with barely tethered energy. "You must understand that when money and position are at stake, people will go to great lengths…I will take care of this," he said reassuringly. "I have a good sense of who the likely culprits are."

"Who?" I'd asked.

"I don't want you to worry about it. Hale Shipping has its own set of…complicated relationships in the world. Or my father has, anyway. This is likely a retaliation for something. I will find out and make sure it's taken care of." I looked up at him and could see the determination written all over him. I had no doubt that he would have this wrapped up by sundown the next day given the energy in the room. "I don't want you to worry, but, baby, this needs to be taken seriously until I know for sure who is behind it and that it's an isolated incident."

I met Frank the next day after work. Dylan reassured me Frank would be necessary only for a little while, until he knew for sure that there was no threat, but he didn't give any indication of how long a little while was.

Dylan stood, frustrated, as I explained that this new security plan was all well and good, but I hoped Frank enjoyed taking the Tube and walking to work. I had waited a long time to live in London, and I wasn't about to be trapped in an isolated car when I could be out, in the city. Walking and taking the train made me feel connected to London, like I could breathe it in, become a part of it. Dylan knew me well enough to know not to argue, and I knew him well enough to know he admired me standing my ground.

Now, here I was, two weeks later, entering my kitchen and seeing Frank's now familiar face smiling back at me.

"Morning, honey," I said to Frank, walking fully into the kitchen and popping my hip in an exaggerated flirtatious gesture. He laughed at my little act of defiance.

"It's not getting any funnier," said Dylan, grabbing his keys from the counter.

"Oh, sure it is. Right, schnookems?" I batted my eyes at Frank, who was not my type at all. Big, bald, bearded, burly, with an elaborate tattoo peeking out of the collar of his pressed white shirt. He couldn't have been more than thirty-five, and if you had a thing for ax-wielding, rugged Alaskan types, he'd be your man. Even in a suit, he looked like he'd be more at home bear tracking than driving the Jaguar. I'd been surprised, expecting Dylan to hire only the most refined-looking staff, but when I'd raised an eyebrow after meeting my lumberjack one-man security team, Dylan had simply shrugged and said, "He's the best."

"All right, all right," Dylan chided, and he gave poor Frank a firm stare. Then he turned back to me and pushed me against the counter in the kitchen, digging his hips into me, leaning his face over mine. He hovered his lips near my ear and whispered, "Remember, damsel. You're mine. Be good, and I'll reward you later." Then he kissed my ear so gently it almost tickled, but instead it stoked the fire that hummed under my skin any time I was near him.

When he pushed back from the counter, allowing space between us, I suddenly remembered we weren't alone—he had a way of making the world disappear, even if just for a moment. And when he cleared his throat, I knew he'd been affected too. He smiled mischievously and said in a more audible tone, "You've got this, baby. You're one hundred percent right that Hannah should open a brick-and-mortar store. It's a brilliant plan, and I have no doubt you're the woman to do it. You're going to be stunning today." He was driving his gaze into my own, making sure I heard him, and I nodded. "Take the car—" he started.

"Already planning on it, smarty-pants," I said with victory. I knew he'd been preparing to go all dominant on me and insist. "I'm going to have Frank take me to the meeting. I don't want to risk being late."

I caught the chuckle in Dylan's voice as he shook his head slightly, clearly amused at my beating him to the punch.

"I love you," he said, flashing me one of his killer smiles before heading out the door to where his driver, Lloyd, was waiting for him in the long, sleek, silver Mercedes-Benz.

I took a minute to catch my breath. He didn't say *I love you* often—he was, after all, still a stoic, proper Brit—but when he did, god, well, he must know what it did to me. I tried to shake it off. I grabbed the coffee from Frank's hands, thanked him, and said, "Sorry about that, buttercup—I hope I didn't get you into too much trouble."

Frank laughed and closed the door behind me. "Not at all, Lydia. Not at all."

Chapter 2

Once safely at my desk for the morning, I tried to focus on the mountain of work that had piled up over the weekend and get my head in the game for the lunchtime presentation. In the weeks following the fashion show, business had been booming.

Apparently the combination of a well-received, much-touted spring line and a blockbuster news event including one of the gowns (oddly, worn by me) provided a significant push for Hannah's business. Princess Caroline had worn another one of her gowns when meeting the president of the United States at a summit in Berlin, and the influx of requests for fittings and appointments at Hannah's private studio was mounting quickly.

Thankfully Hannah had allowed Fiona and me to hire an intern to help cover the spillover, but even with the intern the work was feverish. It had occurred to me at some point between fielding phone calls from eager socialites and hopeful shoppers and scheduling Princess Caroline's next fitting that we might be able to streamline things if Hannah would consider turning the private studio she'd been planning on opening into a full-on brick-and-mortar shop.

I had eventually floated the idea by my friends. Fiona, my fellow assistant, had been skeptical, or maybe just surprised. I had a feeling this wasn't in line with the subtle British caste system—it wasn't exactly standard protocol for the new girl to come barging in suggesting a major business change. But Josh, our fabulously gorgeous and gay receptionist, had been enthusiastic, although I was pretty sure it was mostly because he wanted something juicy to gasp about around the coffee station.

But when I finally summoned the courage to approach Hannah about the idea, bracing myself for her shock at my impertinence, she'd been intrigued and was now allowing me to pitch it to an investor. It felt like a gesture of trust on her part, but in reality it was a test, a test I'd been hankering for. I craved the responsibility, and I was determined to carve my way into the fashion world. This was an opportunity to demonstrate my independence, my ambition.

I'd been preparing for the presentation nonstop for the past two weeks. Deirdre Rocker, the president of the British Fashion Council, had offered to meet with me after Dylan had introduced us at Fashion Week—a meeting I had been unable to get on my own. And, even though her intentions had been to offer me a job as *her* assistant, I had ended up agreeing to the meeting so that I could pick her brain about opening a designer's flagship store.

And it wasn't only Deirdre who had seemed to pop out of the woodwork. The attention had been startling—no one seemed to care about my credentials or background, only that I was front-page news, only that I was on the arm of the city's hottest bachelor. I'd never realized how gutting that could feel. What a stark indicator it was that your worth was entirely encapsulated by your romantic relationship, by your ability to hold the public's attention, by your ability to sell newspapers. Dylan's star status was the result of being the shockingly good-looking and mysterious future seventeenth Duke of Abingdon. For me it wasn't even that—it was simply being on his arm.

I now understood why he felt the way he did about his title. He was always slightly disgusted when people reminded him of his position or ingratiated themselves to him. I doubted that anyone who didn't know him could tell, but there was a little twitch of his lip when someone called him *my lord* or *Lord Abingdon*. People could praise him to the hilt for his design and architectural accomplishments, and he would open up, engage, possibly even lecture you on the role of sustainability in modern architecture until you elbowed him in the ribs. But the title, *Lord Abingdon*, closed him down. And I was beginning to see why. It felt dangerous to let it define you, and it was concerning when others defined you that way, because really, at the end of the day, it had nothing to do with who you were.

So I was determined to use every opportunity this new weird Dylan-fueled situation afforded me, but on my own terms.

When I received a phone call from a menswear designer, I had met with him, promptly turned down his offer to model neckties in my birthday suit, and instead laid the groundwork for a potential collaboration that might benefit the new Hannah store.

When I received an offer for free shoes in exchange for telling every journalist that the brand was my favorite, I had politely declined and then parlayed the connection into asking them how quickly they expanded from one store to two and how that affected their approach for online sales.

So when I walked into the restaurant to meet Hannah and the investor at the upscale boutique hotel 45 Park Lane, I was ready. I was armed with a memorized presentation, folders of information, contracts with vendors ready to be signed, and countless statistics and figures, and I knew my ideas were good. I could do this, and I had the pitch deck to prove it.

We were calling it *lunch*, and by lunch they meant I had an hour and a half and one meal to demonstrate that this whole thing was a good idea, that Hannah's brand was ready, and that we'd be able to make use of the money if it was given. My textbooks from the one business course I'd taken in college had been dusted off, and I was ready with words like *market share* and *brand awareness*.

"Lydia," Hannah started as she and a fit older man rose from their seats to greet me. "This is Giles Cabot." I firmly shook his hand, took a hopefully unnoticeable deep breath, and we were off and running.

For an hour and a half I did my thing. When he reminded me that we were on the heels of another designer's failure to launch, I reminded *him* that other designers hadn't had production lined up in advance—we did. When he suggested that perhaps it was too soon for Hannah, that we should wait another season, I pointed out that both Diane von Furstenberg and Vera Wang had had their first shops at similar stages in their careers. Not only did I know every figure to the exact pence, but I was pretty sure I'd charmed the pants off good old Giles. Apart from the one embarrassing five-minute period during which I was pretty sure I had ketchup on my cheek, I knew I'd done the best I could.

So by the time dessert forks had been placed down and my folders put away, I felt confident. Not certain by any means, but confident—I'd given it my best shot. I stopped talking, probably for the first time during the entire meal, and I saw Giles give Hannah a generous smile.

"You're quite impressive, young lady." He was folding his hands together over the tablecloth and looking between me and Hannah.

I knew it was technically premature, but the corners of my mouth were already rising. He raised his glass towards the middle of the table. "Congratulations," he said in his thick posh accent, and Hannah and I looked to each other and then raised our own glasses towards his. "To Hannah Rogan, the woman, the brand, and the shop."

Inside I was screeching one of those foot-stomping, excited, could-barely-breathe screeches, but on the outside I was managing to keep it all cool and say things like *thank you* and *I'm really look forward to working with you* in a reasonably calm tone. It was really going to happen, and I was going to be responsible for it. I knew the holy-shit-what-have-I-gotten-myself-into freak-out would come later, but for now, I was still in the glowy oh-my-god-I-did-it phase.

As he launched into a story about the early days at his investment firm, a waiter tapped me on the shoulder. "Miss Bell?" he said, and I nodded. "I was asked to deliver this to you," he continued as he handed me an envelope.

Hannah and Mr. Cabot were cheerfully discussing something in voices tinged with middle-of-the-day glasses of wine. I discreetly opened the small envelope on my lap and pulled out a shiny keycard to a room at the hotel with a Post-it note stuck to it. In Dylan's unmistakable handwriting:

ROOM 35, I'M WAITING. X

I felt my pulse quicken and cheeks flush. He'd said he'd meet me after my meeting, and by this point I should have known he never joked when he said things like that. I tried to stop myself from smiling stupidly and rejoined the conversation just as it was entering that slightly awkward die-down phase. We all quietly beamed at each other with the energy of people who were about to embark on an artistic business venture together, and I tried not to rush the closing remarks the way I silently wanted to.

When I was finally freed from the meeting, I quietly explained to Hannah that I had to run an errand and would be back in the office soon. Then I texted Frank and told him I'd be another hour. And then I basically sprinted across the lobby, my heeled boots clicking along the shiny floor.

* * *

"There's my girl," said Dylan as he swung open the door. "Well?"

I was still standing in the doorway, taking him in, his expectant gaze and open posture. He was shirtless, wearing only his suit pants, and his lean, muscular body spanned the doorway. I knew the smile on my face must have made me look like a kid. I was giddy. I was giddy because my deal had just gone through and because the glorious man in front of me was just about to make my afternoon a hundred times more interesting.

"Well what?" I asked, not able to stop looking at his abs.

"How did it go?" His blue eyes were studying me, expectant, hopeful. "You got the money?" I smiled widely, and he beamed back at me, leaning in to sweep me into his arms. "You got it!" He spun me around.

"I got it!" I jumped and danced a little as he put me down, letting my excitement take over.

"I'm terribly proud of you."

"Thanks." I sighed and dropped my bag on the floor. "I can't believe it's going to happen. I'm heading up the opening of Hannah Rogan's first store. In *London*." He looked at me with a sweet smile and a slight shake of his head. "What?" I said.

"You. I can't remember the last time I felt about work the way you do now. About you? Absolutely. Work? Well..."

"Babe, you've just been so busy. Between all these meetings with your dad and wrapping up the Athens hotel and the other projects... You just need a break. Or to start a new design, something you feel passionate about."

He sighed and then looked back to me and nodded, cutting off that thread of conversation. "Will you tell me who the investor is now?" His hands were on his hips, all businesslike, as though he were prepared to take the gloves off and fight me hard if I continued to refuse him the information he'd been wanting for weeks. I hadn't wanted to tell Dylan details about the deal on the off chance that he would stick his nose in. I wouldn't put it past him.

"Giles Cabot. Have you heard of him?"

Dylan's arms fell to his sides and he stepped closer. He raised his eyebrow. "I have. He's a good man. He might seem a bit chummy, but the man does not part with his money easily. He's very discerning. You must have impressed him, damsel."

He placed his hands on my hips and walked me backwards until I was leaning against the caramel-colored leather desk. I felt so warm, so perfectly happy—I was sure the smile wrapped clear around my head. I finally took in the luxurious hotel room: warm, dark brown accents; sea-green walls; and an endless expanse of crisp white sheets spread against the bed behind Dylan.

His warm hands untucked my silky red blouse from my pencil skirt, first in the front and then in the back. I automatically raised my arms and he lifted it above my head.

"Giles said that—" I began as he continued to undress me, but Dylan placed his finger over my lips, slowly shaking his head.

"I want to hear about it, but right now I need you to be quiet." I sucked in my breath. "I'm going to make you come, and then," he said as he reached between my legs and pulled his hand up, bringing my grey pencil skirt with it, "I'm going fuck this sweet cunt of yours." My eyes locked with his, and I nodded in a daze, unable to focus as all my blood sailed from my extremities to the aching knot at my core.

"How?"

"However I want. No talking," Dylan replied with that rakish smirk. His hands roamed appreciatively over my ass, smoothing over my cool skin. "God, you're like silk." He reached behind me and unfastened my skirt, lowering the zipper and shoving it past my hips so it fell to the floor. He pulled off my boots and dropped them to the side. To see him in the bright afternoon light, in this beautiful but foreign room, felt like such a wanton secret. It's not that we hadn't made love during the day, but it was always on a weekend, buried in the sheets of one of our beds, indulging in our limited free time in private. But this felt naughty, stolen.

I was now only in the black lace La Perla panties and bra that Dylan had given me. I was not even sure why he'd bought me the panties, since I rarely wore underwear these days, per Dylan's "no-knickers rule," which I protested for good measure but not-so-secretly loved. My hair was still in a soft, clean bun at my neck, my bangs swept aside. Dylan's hands slid into my panties. Both his hands cradled my ass, the ribbons of the thong holding them to my skin, and then the panties were sliding down my legs.

"There. All's right with the world again," said Dylan, as he shoved the tiny black scrap of fabric into his pants pocket. I rolled my eyes and gave him a playful, mocking look. He gave me an equally playful look of warning and lifted me onto the desk, pulling me forward by the backs of my knees until I was barely perched on its edge.

Dylan sank to his knees and firmly pushed my legs wide, spreading me open before him. I shivered in anticipation and let my head fall back, bracing myself on the desk surface behind me, arms locked. The room was so bright, and I strangely felt so exposed—not by my nakedness or the gorgeous man between my thighs but by the high windows, the bright afternoon light streaming in, the sound of traffic outside, all the reminders that we were playing hooky.

Dylan gripped my inner thighs, holding them apart, as he drew his nose along my leg.

"Ahh, Dylan. Please, please get there." I exhaled breathily as I said each word, and my eyes flung open when I felt a sharp sting on my inner leg. Dylan had bitten me. Hard.

Right.

No talking.

Dylan worked me deliberately, carefully, masterfully. I could feel everything—his midday whiskers brushing against my inner thighs, every flick of his tongue, every rough stroke against my clit. Each gesture drove the energy inward, coiled my body tighter, and each goddamn retreat made the sweet ache deepen, made my chase feel more desperate. I grunted in frustration, nearly ready to pull his head up to my own, to try to kiss him. To attack him the way he was attacking me. He was driving me crazy, and he knew exactly what he was doing. He always did.

My nails were digging into the leather-covered desk so hard I wouldn't have been surprised if we ended up with a bill for damages later. Then he finally delivered on his promise and sent my head flying backwards, my breasts aiming for the ceiling, and my body collapsing under me. I came once, and then when I was sure I was too sensitive, too tightly wound, again.

Fuck, my boyfriend was good at that. Whenever he tore me apart that way, there was a tiny voice, a voice I wanted to hurl off a cliff, that whispered there was a reason he was so good at it. How many girls, exactly, had he gone through to get that good?

The air moving over my damp skin brought goose bumps to the surface, and I involuntarily shook slightly, still raw from my orgasms. Dylan must have stood, because his hands were now firmly placed at the sides of my face. "Open those brown eyes for me."

I looked up into his stunning smile and marveled. This man was mine. He was so sickeningly beautiful. His hair had grown out a bit in the past month. He needed it cut, but secretly I hoped he wouldn't do it. This roguish hair looked more like the Dylan I knew—slightly wild, a little less stiff.

I gave a lazy smile back as I ran my fingers through it. "That was almost as good as winning over Giles Cabot down in the dining room."

He raised his eyebrows. "Almost?"

I smiled bigger—there was nothing more fun than winding him up. He reached beneath me and lifted me, practically throwing me on the bed behind him, and I skirted around the shifting fabric as he hastily removed the duvet. "On your knees, you ungrateful little thing."

I rolled over immediately, desperately. Yes. This was going to be—*swack*.

His palm. Right across my right ass cheek.

"Yes," I said, inviting him. In an instant he was behind me on the bed, his bare thighs resting against my ass. He must have dropped the trousers. His hands roamed and groped as I was presented before him on all fours. They stroked my legs, smoothed over my back. He unclasped the bra I was still wearing and roughly shoved it down my arms so it rested on the bed below me. My breasts filled his hands, and he rolled my taut nipples between his fingers, kneading them.

I don't know what in the hell he was waiting for other than to torture me—I was so blissfully ready for him, but bliss would soon turn to agony. He wanted me writhing.

"This is for you, my impressive, business-minded, smart-as-fuck girl," he started, his hardness barely grazing my entrance, taunting, teasing. "And you. Are. Going. To. Take it." The heels of my palms dug into the sheets, and I nearly collapsed with the force of him entering me. He hit the desire in my belly square-on, and I called out in needy satisfaction.

Dylan's firm muscular legs met my ass with each thrust, and as he rolled back and hit me in just the right place, I squeezed around him, desperate to hold on to him. "Fuuuck, Lydia. Do that again, and I'll deny you...Oh, fuck it—please do that again!" I smiled and couldn't help but let go of a breathy giggle as I complied with his request.

Dylan fucked me like he meant it. He always meant it, but since our over-the-top confession of love at Primrose Hill, every time we'd made love, no matter how adventurous, kinky, or brazen, the reverence of our feelings for each other was always there, making it deeper. But this time, we were in it for no more than the fun of it. It was sex as celebration. Our feelings were by no means forgotten, but they weren't the point. This—this was a reward, not a profession. This was strictly *fun*. I was pretty sure that when I came I screamed his entire endless aristocratic name: Dylan William Lucas Hale. And when he came a moment later, I don't think what he screamed was even words, or if it was, it wasn't English.

My body collapsed beneath his and sank into the luxurious mattress. He fell next to me and stroked my back. We lay there for several moments, catching our breath.

"Baby, look at me," he said. I had been facing the window, away from him, my eyes closed in recovery. I turned, and my hair fell in front of my eyes. He promptly brushed it to the side. "I'm so proud of you."

"You said that."

"I meant it."

"Thank you," I said, basking in his pride. "So you got an expensive hotel room to celebrate my success? What were you going to do if we didn't have anything to celebrate? What if I hadn't gotten the money?"

"Then I would've done the same thing, only to make you forget." I looked at him staring back at me, and I was floating. I was completely blissed out, in love, gazing starry-eyed at my perfect boyfriend. Then I had the misfortune of catching the time on his enormous gold watch: 3:25 p.m.

"Shit. I have to get back to work," I said and let out a sigh. "I wish I could stay here with you all afternoon and do what we just did again and again." I was already standing, pulling on my boots.

Dylan sighed and stared at me appreciatively. "As do I."

"Where's my blouse?" I asked, now stalking the room in my boots and bra, holding my skirt in a viselike grip. Dylan rose and helped me look. I was standing in the middle of the room, the tingly post-orgasmic feel quickly being replaced by anxiety at my need to get back to work. Then I saw the red silk poking out from the garbage can by the desk. I pulled it out, only to find one side smeared with what must have been Dylan's lunch. "Curry?! You dropped my blouse in a curry?!"

"Shit, baby. I'm sorry. I was distracted." He glanced down at the blouse apologetically. He was stroking my shoulder, giving me these adorable and seriously smoldering puppy-dog eyes. I sighed in resignation.

"Do you have a spare shirt in your car?" I asked. Dylan always kept spare clothes handy—he was constantly going from meeting to meeting, and he was Captain Prepared. He nodded. "Good, then give me yours." He looked at me, eyebrow raised, but clearly didn't dare disobey.

As Dylan texted Lloyd to retrieve a clean shirt, I stood in front of the mirror and tweaked, stretched, fussed, and pulled at his bespoke pale blue button-down. I somehow managed to twist it into a kind of collared wrap shirt that tied at the small of my back. I rolled up the sleeves into tight cuffs above my elbows and layered my necklaces over the shirt, hoping they'd distract anyone from noticing that I was clearly wearing a man's dress shirt.

"Impressive," said Dylan, standing behind me, his hands resting on my hips and looking into the mirror with me. "Are you sure you're not interested in the design side of fashion?"

I turned around and settled into his arms just as a knock at the door announced Lloyd's delivery of Dylan's shirt. I waved at Lloyd with a smile before he let the door close, leaving us alone in the room once again... "I should have taken the clean one," I said, eyeing Dylan as he unboxed the freshly laundered shirt.

"No. This is better," he replied, looking at me sternly as he put on the shirt. He pulled me back into him, buttoning his shirt one-handed so he could keep me trapped. "This way you'll smell like me the rest of the day." I hid my smile in his warm chest. "Come on, let's get you to work."

We stood outside the hotel for a moment, both of our cars behind us, ready to take us to our respective workplaces. He brushed his fingers under my chin, and I reflexively looked up into his waiting eyes. I got one sweet kiss, a deep pressing of his lips onto mine, and we parted.

I wasn't a half a block from the hotel before my phone rang.

"Miss me already?" I answered.

"Always." I could hear him smiling. "But that's not why I'm calling. I forgot to mention that I won't be home until late tonight." It was Monday, and we'd settled on weekends at mine and weekdays at his—I couldn't deny the advantages of a house-keeper, especially on weekdays.

"Oh? What's going on?"

"A meeting with my security team, and then I've got a dinner. Might go late. You'll be in my bed when I get home, damsel?" He wasn't usually so vague, and actually I'd been accompanying him to these dinners lately. I was quiet.

"Do you want me to come with you?" I asked, but as soon as the words were out of my mouth I regretted asking. If he wanted me there he would have asked me.

He was quiet for a moment. "Tonight is business. You'd be bored, trust me."

"I'll just go to my place—we can see each other tomorrow night." It didn't make sense for me to go to his place if he wasn't going to be there anyway. Plus, the little nagging part of me that wasn't quite ready to move in with him was getting its turn at the microphone. Sometimes I felt this little tug-of-war in my brain—one side saying to never leave Dylan's side, the other hastily retreating to my own independent world.

"Lydia." He was using his I'm-the-boss tone, which was sexy as hell in the bedroom but drove me crazy outside of it.

"What, Dylan?"

He sighed deeply on the other end of the line. "Christ. I'm having dinner with my father. It's about family business…He's been impossible lately."

"Oh."

Three weeks after seeing his parents at the party, and I still knew next to nothing about them or Dylan's relationship with them, except that it wasn't exactly rosy. I knew he'd been seeing his father a lot lately—he'd referenced lunches and weekday meetings, and I knew the difference I saw in him in the wake of these encounters. He was tense. Frustrated. Cold. He emerged as the hardened Dylan I saw with other people. The ruthless, closed-off, my-way-or-the-highway architect and businessman. I'd asked him a few times, probed gently for him to tell me more, but I never got more than a vague huff or disgusted grunt.

"I'd really prefer to come home to you than to an empty bed," he said in a way that, even if I didn't know the details, somehow spoke to everything he wasn't saying about the dinner.

"I'll be there." I could almost hear the weight on his shoulders lighten as I said the words.

Chapter 3

I expected the remainder of the workday to be uneventful. I probably could have told Hannah I'd finish up the emailing and phone calls I had to make from home—she probably even expected me to hide away somewhere and regroup after the pitch meeting with Giles Cabot. The truth was, I only went back to the office for two admittedly selfish reasons.

The first was that one of Hannah's apprentice designers was doing some final tweaks on a dress I was borrowing for an event that Friday night with Dylan. Hannah had been incredibly gracious three times already, letting me borrow and alter dresses from The Closet. The sad truth was that I couldn't afford *one* dress that would be appropriate for the kinds of parties and dinners Dylan took me to, let alone several. The first few times I'd figured out ways to dress up things I already owned, but I quickly ran out of options. And the salary of a second assistant didn't exactly allow for the purchasing of designer clothes. For the party Dylan was taking me to that Friday, Hannah had offered me something she'd been working on for an upcoming collection. Hence, the extensive tweaking.

And second, Josh had just come back that afternoon from a vacation in Marbella, Spain, where he'd been for two long weeks. I was dying to see him. Fiona and I had received one cryptic postcard at the office with a picture of a beach at sunset on the front and the words *Sand EVERYWHERE. XO—Joshy* on the back. We needed the story.

At that moment the three of us stood in The Closet while the apprentice designer tweaked, Fiona and I riveted by the play-by-play Josh was giving us, down to detailed descriptions of every tropical-themed cocktail imbibed and outfit worn.

"Blimey," Fiona responded once Josh had finished his retelling. "I mean, you're a massive whore, obviously. But well done, you."

"You don't understand, Fee. Fernando is *hot*," replied Josh, closing his eyes as if remembering at that moment. "The most ravishing tosser I've seen. He's *Dylan* hot," he added, looking right at me, just daring me to judge him in light of this new information. I blushed on cue. I mean, I wasn't going to argue with him. Dylan *was* hot.

As we stood there gossiping, Hannah's apprentice was re-sewing a thin strap onto the emerald-green satin silk cocktail dress I was to wear. It was a 1920s boudoir–inspired dress—simple, clingy, brilliant green silk hitting above my knees, strategic pin tucks around my hips, with bejeweled broach-like clasps linking the thin straps to the bodice. It was basically backless, the fabric coming into a deep curve that hit just above my derrière. It was, without a doubt, the most unique and startlingly sexy thing I'd ever worn.

"Well, if that's true"—I laughed at Josh while trying not to move my shoulders too much—"then it couldn't be helped. And I'm certainly not in any position to judge."

"Seriously, lovey," Josh said, rolling his eyes at me. "Have you agreed to move in with that scoundrel of yours yet?" Then he quickly added, "Fuck all, that dress is slutty. I mean classy, but slutty. Lydia, you look ferocious in it." I giggled in response, so thrilled to have his exuberance back in-house.

But when I thought about his question, I gazed at the floor and shook my head, hoping this line of conversation would end. It hadn't taken long for things to get weird at the office in terms of the whole me-dating-an-aristocratic-celebrity thing. Or maybe it was just that I felt awkward about it—I couldn't forget that stunned, stargazing look that had appeared on Fiona's and Hannah's faces when I'd first told them I was dating Dylan Hale. Ever since, I'd felt keenly aware, probably too aware, that it was a *thing*.

I felt I had to walk a fine line—if I said too many good things about how it was going with Dylan, then I could be perceived as bragging. If I didn't say anything at all, then it looked like I was haughty. So I tried to keep it light or blasé, didn't dwell or go into details. When I'd told Josh and Fiona that Dylan had asked me to move in with him right after we'd made up from our fight, they'd both been shocked—as they should have been. It's bonkers to move in with someone you've been dating for a few weeks. But it was more than just the craziness of the idea. Dylan's world was full of new territory—it was a world where people went starry-eyed at the mention of his name, a world with archaic social rules and where people with cameras hid behind bushes, a world where I had to keep secrets about threatening emails. It wasn't a world I knew, and I didn't like not knowing. I felt like I had to get a grip on it all before I went moving in with anyone.

Keeping the balance between the Dylan world and my old

just-Lydia world was frankly bizarre. As it was, I was standing before them getting fitted for a gown designed by our boss, not for a work reason, but because I was attending the year's biggest art-world party at the Serpentine Gallery—an event whose guest list had been locked in place six months earlier and which was promised to be covered in *Vanity Fair*'s "About Town" column. There were people who'd give their left arm to get into this party, but because Dylan was Dylan, he'd simply called and told them he'd be bringing a date. It was like I was leading a double life—by day I slogged away over email, feverishly trying to make it in the early stages of my career, and by night I was chauffeured by Frank in a Jag. The contrast made my head spin, made me feel like I had to keep track of who I was.

As I stood there, I realized I hadn't yet told Josh and Fiona about the store—I'd momentarily forgotten one of the details I *should* be sharing with them. Josh would be thrilled. He was always enthusiastic about Hannah expanding the business—it helped quell his constant fear of "getting sacked." And while Fiona hadn't said much about the idea, the plan would benefit us both—less crazy running back and forth to Hannah's studio for fittings, less one-on-one interaction with the likes of Amelia Reynolds and her posse of posh, snobby socialites. I was about to tell them when Fiona piped up.

"God, I'm so jealous of you two twats," she said quietly, picking lint off of her sweater and not looking either of us in the eye.

Hannah's apprentice had finished with the dress, and I was sliding back into my clothes behind a Japanese screen. I peeked my head out. "Fiona? What's going on? Aren't things going well with you and Ben?" I could see now that she was fighting off crying. She was a pro at holding back emotion and burying it under her Yorkshire wit, but I could see it.

"Ahh, it's fine," she quickly said, straightening. "He's just being a plonker, is all. You'll have to take my word for it, Lydia—guys who are our age and don't have heaps of money can be right idiots."

I wasn't imagining things. I definitely heard the subtext—somehow I wouldn't understand because my boyfriend was older, rich, and supposedly perfect. "Well, I'm happy to listen, if you want to talk?" I said, to which she shook her head slightly, picked up her bag, and headed back to our office.

By the time I sat at my desk to wrap things up for the day it was nearly seven. Hannah had ended up sending an office-wide email about the store, announcing that as soon as I found retail space, I'd be moving to work from there. Fiona, who'd been quiet the rest of the day, had left shortly after, leaving me in a quiet office, checking things off my to-do list.

Knowing Dylan was out for a work thing and dinner with his father, I hadn't rushed, and there was a lot to tie up after the presentation. I was about to shoot off a thank-you message to Mr. Cabot when I heard the familiar ping of a new email waiting for me. I saw the new bold line in my inbox, and I immediately got chills.

The sender was once again unknown—a series of jumbled numbers and letters—and the subject line read: *Don't be fooled.* When I opened the email, I saw only one line of text: *CAN YOU TRUST HIM?*

Below the words was a crystal-clear photograph of Dylan outside a restaurant with a man in a dark suit and long dark coat. I recognized the restaurant—a pizza chain in Trafalgar Square, not at all a place Dylan would go with any of his friends or clients. It looked like they were in a heated exchange, and the man was pressing a large envelope into Dylan's hand. If it hadn't been for the clear date stamp on the photo I wouldn't have thought much of it. Dylan out to dinner with some other business dude? A person who looked less than pleased with whatever Dylan was saying? That was pretty much Dylan's life when he wasn't with me. But the date was a night when he had said he was in Amsterdam for a meeting about a new building. A Thursday. I remembered it well because it was the first night we'd spent apart since we'd said *I love you*. I'd seen him that day, and he'd been wearing the tie I now saw in the photo in front of me, a tie I'd given him.

He'd lied to me.

* * *

I stared at the screen and noticed my chest rising and falling rapidly. My breath quickening. A pit settling in my stomach. My immediate instinct was to feel like a fool. I'd been here before—on the receiving end of a message from the world that Dylan was lying to me, that he wasn't who I thought he was. The gut punch of finding out he was engaged to Amelia.

But then I remembered: I'd been here before, and the world had been wrong. Dylan hadn't lied to me then, and I needed to give him the benefit of the doubt now.

I immediately took a screen shot of the email, suspecting that, like the last one, if I tried to save it, it would simply disappear. I attached the screen shot to a new email to Dylan with the subject line: *Another email.*

My phone rang within the minute.

"Baby, when did you get this?" Dylan asked as soon as I'd answered.

"Just now," I said. I heard him tell someone else in the room with him that I'd just received the email; then it sounded like he was stepping away from that person, moving.

"I have my people looking at it—it's perfect timing. I was meeting with my security and IT." Dylan was speaking to me as though we were on a fact-finding mission together, like we were Mulder and Scully solving mysteries, one disturbing clue at a time. That somehow there was such a thing as the "perfect timing" to get an email like this. Only the information I needed at that moment was not going to come from his IT or security people. And it was less about who had sent the email than what the email contained. I needed him to show me that I wasn't a fool for giving him the benefit of the doubt.

He read my silence immediately.

"I did go to Amsterdam that night, Lydia."

"Okay," I said slowly, trying to work out how to say I needed him to explain more, but he cut me off before I got the chance.

"I had an impromptu business meeting that evening, and it went late. I flew out later. I didn't tell you, because it didn't change anything. I might as well have been in Amsterdam as far as you were concerned. The whole thing was rushed. I barely made it that night—the pilot, who had been expecting me to fly out at four in the afternoon, had been awake for too long. If I'd gotten there ten minutes later, he would have been unwilling to fly me at all. I promise you, baby—there's nothing here you need to worry about. Someone is just trying to fuck with me."

"Except they're fucking with me too," I said, hearing the surliness in my voice.

"Damsel—"

"Don't 'damsel' me, Dylan. Even in the best of circumstances it's a shitty feeling when someone knows something about your boyfriend that you don't." I realized as I said this that I actually had no idea if this was true. Dylan was my first boyfriend, and this was the only circumstance in which this had happened. "And it's even worse when that something looks like a lie."

"I'm not bloody lying, Lydia." Great, now he was getting frustrated with me.

"Who's the guy in the photo?" I asked, hoping that some basic information, if not his willingness to provide it, could defuse the growing tension between us. I heard him sigh deeply on the other end of the line.

"No one important. It's someone from the government whom I'm working with on something."

"A building?"

"What does it matter, Lydia? Don't get out of sorts. It's just work. Don't let whoever is sending these emails get to you, okay? Please, let me handle this."

I didn't say anything. I had been taken off guard, and I was pissed. I was the one getting threatening emails, but I didn't feel like I had the power to do anything about it. And now suddenly we were in the middle of a fight.

"Lydia?" He waited, but I just didn't know what to say. In my gut I knew this wasn't his fault, or at least his story wasn't completely implausible. And I knew that he and I were on the same side, but I didn't like it. I didn't just want to be on the same side; I wanted to be in this *together*.

"Baby, listen," he started sweetly. "I know this feels shitty. I've been there. This guy is encroaching on your space. You feel out of control. You want to retreat, to get a grip on what you can count on. But, Lydia, if you let this degenerate, whoever he is, get to you, then he's getting what he wants. This person obviously knows I care about you, and he's trying to get to me through you. Don't let him."

"Dylan—" I felt like a petulant child, wanting to dig my heels in.

"Damsel," he whispered, and I could hear a door shut on his end of the line. "I just don't want you to have to deal with this. I'm on it. I promise. If I have any solid information on this guy, I will tell you. Goddamn it—I *should* have solid information by now, and I'm sorry I don't. I haven't a clue what's going on, actually—it's never taken this long for my team to nail something like this. It's like every lead we have disappears before our eyes." He sounded so frustrated, so angry with himself, but I didn't like just waiting.

"What can *I* do? I don't like to sit on the sidelines."

"Baby, you're doing the most helpful thing—sending me that email immediately. I'm used to this. I have the resources. When there's something to tell, I'll tell you. Trust me."

Why did I feel so unsatisfied with this arrangement? He was right—I didn't know the first thing about hunting down cyberstalkers.

"I love you, baby. I'm sorry this is on your plate at all," he said, and I could hear the deep regret in his voice. And also his sadness that we were fighting about this. And in my heart I *did* trust him. This wasn't actually about whether or not I believed him, I realized. It was about feeling powerless, which I did. I took a deep breath. It wasn't another picture of him with Amelia or some other woman. It was business. Classified business. I summoned the inner reserves to let it go and vowed to figure out how to deal with this better going forward.

We both sighed audibly at the same time, like a wordless truce. "You'll be in my bed when I get home?"

"Don't get your knickers in a twist. I'll be there," I replied, bringing humor back to myself too.

"Watch it, damsel," he said in his husky bedroom-boss tone, behind which I knew there was a smile. I heard noise and voices and general work chaos on the other end. "Must run, baby. I'll see you tonight. And, baby? Please be careful. Let Frank drive you."

"Frank took the car home after dropping me off."

"Baby, please." I heard him tell someone near him he was coming, and he said goodbye before I had a chance to reply. I could hear the plea in his voice. Not demanding. Not trying to be bossy. He was *worried*. I didn't know how to argue with that. I didn't even know if I should.

Chapter 4

Unless he was willing to throw me over his shoulder fireman style, there wasn't much Frank could do when I insisted on taking the Tube home that night, in spite of Dylan's plea. I knew Dylan was worried, and there was an unfamiliar tingling of guilt knowing this would make him worry more, but I just needed to be in the midst of people, around the London buzz. Sometimes it was actually easier for me to think when I was part of the city, when I was moving, when there was a crowd.

Frank and I stood next to each other in the packed train car. He managed not to sway while holding onto nothing; meanwhile, I gripped the yellow pole for dear life as the train made a curve. Frank was protective, and while it irked me that he needed to be there, I had to admit he came in handy, and after today I felt pretty comforted by his presence. One time, a few weeks earlier, a man had "accidentally" bumped into me and then let his hand linger a little too close to my ass for a little too long. Frank hadn't hesitated to physically remove the man's hand and essentially shield my body from other passengers the rest of the ride. The amazing thing was that I don't think one passenger other than the offending guy even saw it happen. Frank, despite his obvious desperation to be chopping wood somewhere, was seriously smooth.

I thought back to the conversation with Dylan about this latest email intrusion. He *did* make me feel safe—I didn't doubt for a second that he was doing everything he could to catch this guy. I knew that a big part of the stress I saw in Dylan lately was the fact that it seemed to be taking him longer than he'd expected. But I also thought about the content of that email. More accurately, it was now clear to me that Dylan had huge swaths of this life—with his father, family, and apparently, business deals—that he kept to himself, that he had no intention of including me in. And maybe that was fine, expected even. We hadn't been together that long, and I wasn't experienced in relationships. How did people figure out this balance? Of when to push and pull? Of when to trust and let go?

This was where my mind was when I felt my phone buzz in my pocket. My body was exiting the Tube stop and walking down the street towards Dylan's house with my umbrella in hand, my bag slung over my shoulder, and the comforting sound of Frank's steps behind me. I looked at the bright screen and saw it was Michael, my neighbor.

I hadn't seen Michael apart from the odd passing each other on the street or taking out the garbage, but he texted occasionally—once asking me if I needed anything from the store, once commenting about our neighbor's odd dog, and once with a picture of some plant in his garden, asking me if I thought it was mint or a weed. This, however, was the first time he'd called.

"Hi, Michael, how are you?"

"Oh, fine. Sorry to ring—hope it's not a bad time. I just got home and the postman's been, and it looks as though he's left a parcel for you. Did you want me to bring it in? I know you get in quite late often, and it's raining, and well…" he mumbled.

"Oh, that's so kind of you. Um, sure. Yeah." I was rattling my brain for an alternative to Michael taking it into *his* house, but I couldn't. "I'll, um, come get it tomorrow or over the weekend, if that's okay?"

"Of course. Maybe I can come by with some of that mint from my garden, and I could bring it or…" He trailed off.

"I'm so sorry, Michael, but I'm just swamped this week. Hey, how was the date you had last week?" He'd mentioned to me a blonde from his office.

"Oh, wasn't a date—nothing really," he said emphatically, like he wanted to make sure I knew.

I exhaled with slight frustration through my lips, making them flutter and catching Frank's attention. It didn't seem possible that Michael didn't know about me and Dylan—everyone else, from the barista at the local Starbucks to the mailman, knew about my love life. But then why would he keep dropping hints? That night at the club when he asked me out flashed before my eyes, quickly followed by the memory of Dylan's red-hot possessiveness. If Dylan could hear this conversation now, I had no doubt he would want to pull the phone from my hand and make it clear to Michael in no uncertain terms what my relationship status was. Thinking about how frustrated he would be when I would let him do no such thing made me laugh a little, but Michael's voice snapped me back to the present.

"Hello? You still there?" he asked.

I coughed to stifle my chuckle. "Ah, sorry. Um, I'll call you about the package in the next few days. And thank you so much for looking out for me and my mail."

"Of course. Another time then," he replied sullenly.

"Yes, definitely," I replied. "And hey, I think you should ask Blondie out again. Persistence counts, you know," I said cheerfully, approaching Dylan's front door.

"So they say," he replied quietly.

"Talk soon," I said and let the call go. My mind was on a glass of wine and my book. Maybe TV.

Frank held open the door for me. "I can fetch your parcel for you, Lydia," he offered, shrugging apologetically for having eavesdropped.

"Oh, you don't have to do that. I'll get it."

"I suspect Mr. Hale would prefer I do it."

* * *

That night I fell asleep reading in Dylan's bed. I'd eaten a full serving of Molly's cottage pie and enjoyed a healthy-sized glass of Cabernet in front of the fire. I'd nearly drowned in his bathtub and then sank into his soft sheets, planning to wait up for him. Clearly that hadn't happened.

I heard my own moan before I was aware of anything else. I had been in a deep sleep, and as I came to semiconsciousness, the first thing I noticed was the cool, broad hand between my legs.

Then the warm lips against my cheek, then against my neck. I was so warm—I could feel Dylan's fingers stroking, coaxing. I moaned again and rolled, partly frustrated at being woken from my heavenly sleep, still in my dreamworld, and now partly from the oncoming desperation between my legs.

"Shh, baby," he calmed me, gliding on top of me and stretching my arms above my head, attempting to subdue my desperation but also fueling it. Somehow I'd gotten naked. Had I fallen asleep that way?

He played tormentor and rescuer in the same moment, and made the tension thicker, sweeter. He pinched my clit lightly, and my back arched off the sheet, exposing my breasts to the night air.

"Let me make you feel good," he whispered.

I moaned again, louder, and was met with another hushing from Dylan. My legs fell open for him, and I rolled my head from side to side, trying to relieve the tension somehow, somewhere, if not where it mattered most. I was still half in a dream state and half awake, which made the sensations pulsing through my body feel surreal, exquisite.

Dylan had me pinned now, his hips firmly above my own, one of his arms holding my hands down above my head, and the warmth of his breath hot against my cheek. He continued to work me with his fingers, splitting me, finding me, fucking me perfectly. By reaching into my slick opening and strumming the front of me from the inside, he demonstrated his terrifyingly perfect knowledge of the female body. Was it only me he could play this way, or was it every woman? I turned my head into the pillow, eyes still in sleep, and moaned louder, in frustration.

"No, no, baby, not yet," he chided, withdrawing his fingers at the precise moment I started to contract around him. I growled at him, eyes still closed, still groggy, and he chuckled against my neck. "So impatient. So greedy."

I raised my own lips to his neck and bit him, hard. I was lost to him, to feeling him.

He hissed and sucked in a breath. "You little devil. For that, you may not come at all." I bit again. Harder. I wriggled my arms and pushed my hips up into him, driving his fingers farther into me and searching for the real friction I needed. I could feel him smile against me. "Tsk, tsk."

We continued like that—me begging with my body and him almost giving in. Dylan was always bossy, always possessive of my pleasure, liking to dole it out in his measure, but this was beyond intense. He was taking it further, retreating more, bringing me closer, even more than usual, and yet always pulling back.

With each stroke, the pinpricks assaulting my core got sharper. The anticipation was a serrated blade carving me up. But I let him go on, trusting him, waiting for him to deliver. But he didn't. And it was torture. Had he been serious about not letting me come?

"Dylan!" I finally pleaded in a pathetic, shrieking tone, my eyes flying open in frustration, the room so dark I could barely make out his form above me. I was shocked by how desperate I sounded. "Please! Fuck me!"

He stilled, and I took in the dark room in the middle of the night, took in his lost face. He looked into me; for all I knew it was the first time he'd even looked at my face since he'd begun his assault. He looked like he had been somewhere else and, despite using my body like an orgasmic punching bag, was just now arriving.

He looked sorry.

I wriggled my hands free and reached between my legs—I needed to come. He had brought me to an agonizing place of need. "No, baby," he said more sweetly this time, "let me. I did this—let me make it right." He moved down the bed, pulling my legs over his shoulders as he went. I could see only his dark head and broad shoulders when I had the strength to lift my head and take a look.

He slid his hands, palms up, under my bottom and tilted me

towards his mouth. He kissed me. He kissed me like he'd kiss my mouth, devouring me. His soft, wet strokes spoke right to the intense heat that he'd built, and with a flick of his tongue over my raw, hard clit I spiraled out into my orgasm. My legs clamped around his head as I tried to cope with the searing contractions. I could feel my arousal pouring over his tongue, my muscles clamping down on themselves, hungry to be clamping down on him. And then again. He'd created so much tension, and it was being released in waves.

I was panting, heaving, damp with sweat, when he returned to me. "That better?" Dylan asked.

I smiled up at him—well, as much of a smile as I could muster in my haze—and I could see something in him I'd never seen before: need. Not just lust or possessiveness, but a deep desire to know that I was okay, for me to make him okay too.

"Now let me," I said. He needed to work something out, and he was working it out with me, on me.

I held his face in my hands for a moment, looking right into his eyes, and kissed him. I could have urged him onto his back and rode him, or given him a blow job. I could have gifted him orgasms that were all about me giving and him receiving. But I realized in that moment that was not what he needed. He needed to lose himself in me, to take me of his own accord. I could see it, written all over him—he needed to own me that night. I returned my hands to their position above my head and spread my legs just a little wider for him, inviting him. He saw my invitation for what it was, and he took it.

* * *

Dylan's head now rested on my belly, his arm wrapped around my waist, his legs gripping my own between them.

"Hey," I said softly, running my fingers through his hair. This time it was me trying to coax him.

He didn't look up at me but kissed my belly instead.

"Hey," I said more insistently. "Everything okay down there? I don't usually get wake-up calls quite that…determined."

He released himself from his viselike grip on my body and took up a position on the pillow next to me. "I'm…sorry about that. Not sure what came over me." Except I was pretty sure that he did know.

"Is it about the email?" I asked.

Dylan gritted his teeth and rolled to lie flat on his back, eyes now glued to the ceiling, and I curved onto my side so I could see him. "Baby, I can't stand that my crazy life is creeping into yours," he added, driving his fingers through his hair. "I hate that I can't confirm who the bastard is that's doing this."

"You can't control everything, Dylan."

"Apparently not," he said, eyebrows raised. "The Tube?"

I shrugged. I wasn't going to apologize for that.

"I just want you…I just want you safe. You know that, right?"

"I know, but like I said—"

"I can't control everything. I know," he said, sighing. "This isn't about the Tube," he added, wrapping an arm around me and pulling me against him. "Not that I don't want to spank you silly for that." He rubbed my ass with his hand, as though he was actually thinking about it, but then he exhaled again. "I might actually be able to catch the asshole, if only my fucking father would lay off me and actually *help* me."

"Your father?"

"He could help me do something to investigate one possibility for who's been sending these emails, but he's so caught up in his own tiny self-serving world that he won't. He's apparently determined for me not to press him. He just wants me to roll over like a puppy." Dylan was getting worked up, I could feel it in the rapid rising and falling of his chest. "He's a complete arse. A complete. Fucking. Arse. Worse than that—he's a greedy bastard with no regard for social progress, for running a company with any morality whatsoever. And being a father? Fucking forget it. The man belongs in the clink with Satan for a cellmate."

"Okay," I said, taken a little aback by his vehemence and the turn in the conversation. "Care to elaborate? Did he say something awful?"

"Oh yes. He can be counted on for that at least." He rolled onto his back again and threw his forearm over his eyes. "I don't want to talk about it, Lydia." I lay on my side looking at him, and I reached over and ran my fingers through his hair again, pulling gently at the short strands. "I refuse to be him, no matter how he tries to make me in his mold."

"He wants you to be like him?"

"If he had his way," he replied, "I'd sell the firm, forget architecture ever existed, take control of Hale Shipping, get married—preferably to a friend's daughter—and devote my life to producing heirs, having others do my bidding, and living a quiet family life riding horses, extolling the virtues of the peerage, and reminding everyone of their proper station in life. He's doing his absolute best to straight-out demand it." He was practically spitting as he spoke. "None of that is ever going to happen."

I curled myself into his side, letting him wrap his enormous arms around me and pull me in closer. "None of that is you. You'll never be so cold or heartless," I said before realizing that I had just called his father cold and heartless. "I mean, I shouldn't say that. I've barely even met him—"

"No, you're absolutely right. He's awful," he confirmed and rubbed his face with his free hand. "Do you know he's been cheating on my mum since I was a teenager?"

I looked up at him, dropped my jaw. "Really? With who?"

"His secretary," he said, huffing incredulously. "Can you believe that clichéd shite?"

"Have you met her?"

"You mean them? There have been seven of them."

I laughed, not because it was funny, but because it was outrageous. "Seriously? And they're always his secretary?"

"Every. Single. Time. You'd think he could at least be original."

"Yeah. Is it just me or is it somehow more disrespectful to your mom to have predictable clichéd affairs? Like, sure, maybe a little extramarital action is accepted in the aristocracy, but have some imagination for crying out loud. Like, maybe his proctologist? Or a member of Parliament? Oooh, or like one of those mimes in Covent Garden." I felt Dylan smile into my hair, and then chuckle, and then really chuckle.

"I can see the headline now," he said, his chuckle growing into a full-on belly laugh as he rolled onto his back. "'Your place or mime? Sixteenth Duke of Abingdon beds silent street performer.'"

His laughter was contagious.

"'Geoffrey Hale snogging outside the box,'" I said, laughing through my words and doing the classic mime box move with my hands.

"'While his mistress performs in one!'" Dylan was gripping his sides from laughter, and he could barely get the joke out.

"'"The Duke of Abingdon is all mime" mistress is thought to have said,'" I said, giggling and trying to act like a mime, making exaggerated expressions that no one would ever be able to interpret.

We were literally rolling over from dumb puns and slowly letting the silliness lie between us. Somehow we'd just ended up in a fit of laughter over his father's infidelity.

"By the way," I said, "I don't care if you are aristocracy. If you ever cheat on me, I'll put your balls in some kind of medieval torture device—I'm sure there are lots of options in the Tower of London, and I have connections."

"I'd never dream of it, baby. Why would I need to? The perfect girl is already mine."

I ignored the *perfect girl* part of what he said and just affirmed the important thing. "Yours."

"Don't forget it," he said, looking firmly into my eyes. He leaned in and kissed me sweetly on the lips. We stayed like that for a moment, the tension uncoiling, Dylan relaxing into our comfortable, safe world. Into us.

"Thank you," he whispered as we settled back to sleep. "Thank you for making me laugh. Thank you for letting me…" He didn't finished the thought. He didn't need to.

Chapter 5

That night was the most we were able to talk for the next four days.

On Tuesday, we only spoke in the morning before he ran out the door to an early meeting. He mentioned how "those fuckers better watch their back," and I had to admit—the vengeful side of Dylan was kind of a turn-on.

On Wednesday, he woke me up with a kiss and a latte but left before I could unearth any intelligible words. We had dinner plans that night, but he cancelled because he was at risk of being overdue on a project for Sir Richard Branson. Dylan Hale didn't do overdue—he was methodical, but I had come to understand that the amount of time he was spending with his security team trying to figure things out and his father because of family business was unprecedented and not something he'd planned for. He *was* sweet enough to have the restaurant deliver what he said was the best thing on the menu along with a card on which he'd drawn a rough sketch of a person, presumably him, delivering a dome of food on horseback.

On Thursday, I only saw him during a cocktail party for someone at his office. We stayed just a half hour, and then he'd had to fly up to Edinburgh to participate in the opening ceremony for a new building for the university's school of architecture. When he dragged me to the restroom so he could personally remove my panties, taunt me for my egregious error, and then fuck me with my back against the stall door, I somehow managed to ask about any progress on my cyberstalker. He huffed, paused contemplatively, and then simply brushed the hair away from my forehead, kissed it, and said I shouldn't worry. In these moments, it was as though he were trying to distract me, like he knew if he seduced me I'd stop pressing him, stop asking. And each time it happened, it felt more and more like Dylan was subconsciously somewhere else, trying to figure this out. Oddly, I missed him more when we were having sex than when we were actually apart.

Now it was Friday, I was midway through my workday, and Dylan was supposedly on a plane, returning to London. I had no idea how busy Dylan had been before we started dating, but he said it had gotten worse since our going public. No one could get enough of a love story, and ours was the one of the moment. The media attention had amped up, as he'd always said it would, and along with it interest in Hale Architecture and Design. It was as though all of London suddenly wanted an architect's—a very specific architect's—input on their home's redesign or wanted Dylan to speak at their club's annual dinner.

Occasionally I saw him wince when we'd catch a photographer watching us as we walked from the house to the car or when he'd see our picture in the paper, and I knew he was thinking about Grace, about what the media attention had done to her. So far, all of the pictures, apart from those in the emails, anyway, had been innocuous, banal even, but I knew he was fearing the worst. I could feel the tension radiating off of him whenever the paparazzi made themselves apparent.

And the media couldn't be avoided at that night's event. We were going to the annual showcase party at the Serpentine Gallery, and it had become increasingly clear that this party was a big deal. A really big deal.

If it hadn't been drilled into me by Fiona and Josh a gazillion times, then Hannah's excessive attention about her dress being photographed on me that night would have told me everything I needed to know. She had called me into her office not once but twice to remind me to wear nude heels with the dress. "Higher the better." And a third time to give me a sparkly black clutch from her own closet to take with me. Message received: *Don't trip on the red carpet or in any other way embarrass Hannah Rogan while out with your boyfriend.*

At that moment, with two hours to go until Dylan would pick me up from my place, Fiona gave me a rundown about who I was likely to see (apparently both Sting and Guy Ritchie had been there the year before) and we tried to figure out if I was supposed to curtsy in front of Caroline and her brother, Prince Richard.

"I mean, there must be some kind of rule," I argued insistently, "about not having to curtsy if your boyfriend used to date the person, even if she *is* a princess. It just seems wrong for me to have to curtsy to my boyfriend's ex!"

"I know you've got the passport, Lydia, but you're not much of a Brit if you can't remember that she's not just Dylan's ex. She's the future queen. I mean, according to the future history books she doesn't have any exes. You might have to suck it up," Fiona said while searching online for the rules for greeting royalty. She was being very matter-of-fact about this whole thing.

"Ugh, but they slept together!" A fact that made it a hundred times more difficult to think about curtsying to this woman, even if, as Dylan said, it hadn't meant anything. "I mean, Dylan didn't bow to her at the museum. Isn't there some royal rule about how if you've had sex with a member of the royal family you're exempt from bowing protocol?"

"Well, first, men don't bow. They just nod their heads," she started.

"So unfair," I pleaded, and she nodded, commiserating.

"Also, remember, love, he's a marquess. You, I'm afraid, are nothing."

"God, Fiona. Harsh."

"Sorry. I didn't mean you're nothing. You know what I meant. You don't have a title, and you're basically an American," she said apologetically as she swiveled in her chair and looked at me. "Look, you should just talk to Dylan about it. Ask him."

I sighed, probably louder than I should have. "Yeah, I will." I could ask Dylan, and I probably would, but not knowing this stuff just reminded me how different our worlds were. We spent the next fifteen minutes watching YouTube instructional videos on curtsying while Fiona critiqued my attempt with helpful advice like "Don't stick your arse out so much" and "Can't you go any lower?" and "Not that low! She doesn't need to know the shade of your nips, now, does she?"

When I wasn't laughing, I was wincing at the discomfort of the whole thing. "Since when does my dating life involve enacting scenes from *Shakespeare in Love*?"

"Since you started dating the aristocracy." Fiona was looking down at her feet as she said it, fussing with the laces on her lace-up boots. "And that scene where Joseph Fiennes unravels Gwyneth Paltrow's boobs and they make sweet love doesn't seem so bad," she offered unhelpfully, although little did she know that my sex life with Dylan actually did involve a fair amount of tying and untying knots around various body parts. I smiled to myself, wondering if Dylan would break out that silky rope again soon.

Just then Hannah came into our office in a panic. "Lydia, what are you doing here?" she asked, frantic.

"Um…" I looked at her blankly. Had I forgotten something?

"You're supposed to be at the studio. I called Stephen, and he's going to spiff you up." Stephen was Hannah's go-to hair and makeup consultant for her shows, and he had recently been deployed to make me look less average whenever I was wearing one of Hannah's dresses to an event with Dylan.

"Oh, Hannah, I didn't know. I still need to swing by home and find a pair of shoes—"

Hannah cut me off. "No. You go to the studio," she ordered. "The dress is there, and Stephen is waiting for you. Fiona," she said, turning to face her, "please go to L. K. Bennett and pick up a pair of nude patent pumps for Lydia. Tell them they're for me."

Oh god. Fiona's eyebrows shot up, and her gaze flashed to me, as though it had been me who just asked her to do this. "No, no, no, Hannah. Fiona shouldn't have to do that." The last thing I needed was Fiona running an errand for me. All of this gown borrowing and special attention from Hannah was bad enough, not to mention the fact that my idea for the brick-and-mortar store had been green-lit. If I wanted even a remote chance of protecting my friendship with Fiona, she could not slide into the role of my assistant.

"I'll just call the store and have my driver pick them up. It's fine." I realized as soon as I said *my driver* that I probably hadn't helped my cause. God, this was so complicated.

"Fine," said Hannah, visibly relaxing. "But, listen, Lydia, the dress you're wearing marks somewhat of a departure for me—people will notice. I need you to look perfect."

"I know. I won't let you down, Hannah. I promise."

When I looked back to Fiona, her gaze was firmly on her computer screen.

* * *

As I sat in Hannah's studio while Stephen pulled, straightened, tweaked, plucked, and brushed, I found myself spacing out. I'd had this tiny icky feeling lately, a rough pit in my stomach. About the emails. About how suddenly my life was open to scrutiny. About how I'd become someone who was sitting in this chair, getting ready to wear an expensive dress and extremely high heels. What I couldn't stop thinking about was that not being a secret may have closed one big gulf between us—that between our public and private lives. Everyone knew we were a couple now. But somehow it had cracked opened another. It had brought into relief how much of Dylan's private life—his family, his work, what he wanted for himself and for us, how to even navigate any of that—was still a mystery. When I was compartmentalized into the "secret sex" part of his life, not knowing had seemed normal, expected. We'd had strict rules about intimacy, rules that we'd ended up throwing to the side. But as his girlfriend, we were supposed to have more, weren't we? Somehow I knew, by the way he looked at me, by the slips of intimacy, the zipping of skirts and the fastening of buttons, that he was mine, that I was his. But it also somehow made what I didn't know about him so much more obvious.

Stephen tilted my chin up to his and carefully applied a thick coat of coppery eye shadow. He scolded me to snap back to attention, and then he proceeded to explain to me why I should be using a different skin care line and to chastise me for going to sleep with my makeup on.

Thirty minutes later I stood in Hannah's studio in the dress, wearing the new heels Frank had dropped off, and coiffed within an inch of my life. My hair was sleek and pulled back into a low bowlike bun at the nap of my neck. My bangs had been pinned to the side. I looked around the studio and scrounged up a handful of gold bangles, piling them onto my slim wrists.

I went to grab my coat—I could actually hear the cold wind outside the old building's windows. It sounded frigid out there, and I was basically wearing a handkerchief. But as soon as I lifted the thick navy peacoat and saw it against my slim, elegant dress I knew it was a no-go. The coat had seen me through college and with jeans looked worn in a purposeful, cool kind of way. But with shoes that cost five hundred pounds and a gorgeous, wispy dress, it just looked college-student grungy. I left the coat behind and braced myself for the chill.

Dylan's Mercedes was parked right outside the building, and he stood by the door, waiting for me, looking sharp, clean, and devastatingly perfect in his sleek modern tux and overcoat. As soon as I left the building, the cold fall air blasted against my bare skin, making me shiver and scamper towards the car.

Dylan rushed to me and pulled me against his warm body as he ushered me into the car. "Lydia," he asked, sounding worried, "where on earth is your coat?" The wind picked up as he said it, proving his point that I needed it. I ducked into the car as quickly as I could and soaked up the heavenly heated seats.

"I didn't really have one that was appropriate for this kind of thing," I said, shrugging. "I'll only be outside for a total of forty-five seconds. I think I can handle it. It's not like anyone will even notice."

"First," he said, looking down at my chest, "I think people might notice."

I looked down and realized that my nipples were hard against the thin satin of the dress. I hadn't been able to wear a bra, which Hannah had said was fine, but now I was wondering what the hell she'd been thinking. It looked obscene.

I covered my breasts with my palms, praying the warmth from my hands would improve the situation. I looked at Dylan, who now had an evil look of lust on his face. "They'll go away," I insisted.

"That would be a tragedy," he said, sliding closer to me. "You look bloody edible, Lydia. I mean, that dress. Christ." He turned towards me and pulled me over his lap so my legs draped over his, and he could rub his large warm palms down my bare arms and back. His hand continued and slid down the bodice of the dress, moving over my bare legs and back under the skirt of the dress as he took me in. The warmth of his hands clashing with my cool skin sent a shiver running down my spine.

He was speaking softly as he warmed me. "Lydia, you must let me buy you the clothes you need to go to these things with me. And for Christ's sake, you need to be warm. This is ridiculous. You know there is an account set up for you at Harvey Nichols, and the personal shopper is on call for you. Use it."

I pulled back from him, and he gripped me tighter. He wasn't going to let me pull away from him when we talked about this. Again. "We've been over this. I don't want to be a kept woman, Dylan. You can't buy me a wardrobe."

"I'm not talking about a wardrobe. I'm talking about a few things so you don't have to worry about attending these events with me. You're being ridiculous. You're so stubborn."

"No. This isn't stubbornness. Me refusing to go running the

other morning was stubbornness. This is principle. And maybe, you could argue, pride. But it's important." I looked into Dylan's eyes, and he was clearly skeptical. "Look. You grew up with all this, and I appreciate that to you it seems silly or needless for me to go without these luxuries when they're so easy for you to give. I get that," I said as I slid closer to him, higher on his lap. If I was going to get through to him, closer would be better. "But think about it this way." I added a seductive tone to my approach. "Why do you need architecture?"

"It's mine," he said, half-distracted by his view down my dress.

"Exactly. You enjoy being independent."

His lips twitched, and his thumb was stroking my back rhythmically. "And why do you admire that your grandfather built Hale Shipping on his own merit?" He saw where I was going with this, and I saw his certainty that he would win this argument begin to crack. "I'm not saying I won't accept gifts or I'll never let you buy me things," I said, kissing his cheek lightly, intimately, and leaning in closer to his ear. "If I recall, I wore some lingerie you bought me last weekend quite happily." I smiled and saw his eyes lose focus as he remembered how I'd looked, wrapped in plum-colored silk. "But things I need? The clothing on my back? I need to procure that on my own. Okay, knighty?"

"It's not the same thing, baby. But I don't want to argue. I want to enjoy you," he said, looking me over.

"I've done okay on my own so far, haven't I?"

He pulled me closer and gripped my thighs against his abdomen. "Bloody perfect," he said huskily, his lips suddenly hovering just above mine. He kissed me once, firmly pressing his closed lips against mine. He released me for a moment and looked firmly into my eyes. "So bloody independent," he mused, part frustrated, part turned on.

I bit my lip and nodded slightly, loving the way his bossy side was never far off and could fan the fire under my skin in a nanosecond. He smoothed his hand up my lap and under the weightless fabric of my dress. He pulled me against him, closer, as he reached to his side and pressed the button to raise the privacy screen between us and Lloyd. "We'll be there in a moment, but I need to feel you before we face them," he whispered, like holding me was allowing him to exhale for the first time all week.

He avoided kissing my mouth again because of my makeup and instead gently kissed my exposed neck as his hands wandered lazily over me, caressing, comforting, holding. He reveled in the slippery silk and how it slid over my small breasts, my stomach, my sensitive sides. I loved the way his touches somehow both woke me up and lulled me into a calmness, like some kind of special drug. We'd been so rushed, so far away from each other all week, and I could feel Dylan just trying to find me, to revel in me, in us. And I was doing the same. I felt the tension leave our bodies, and I suddenly wished we were heading home, not out for a night on the town.

I kissed his cheeks, noticing that he must have shaved in the afternoon—he was so smooth and clean. Then slowly he pulled away, kissed my shoulder, and straightened the bodice of my dress. I opened my eyes and realized we were pulling into the park. I reluctantly slid off Dylan's lap and he eyed my chest. "Better," he said, looking down. I followed his gaze and saw that my nipple issue had gone away. He gave my hand a gentle one-two squeeze that was better than a hug, more intimate, and for a second I could see the foreign world on the other side of the car door—the princesses, paparazzi, and perfectly coiffed socialites—not just as a series of land mines and learning curves but simply as the life of the man I loved.

Chapter 6

Dylan quickly ushered me out of the cold and into the Serpentine Gallery, the beautiful modern art museum housed in Kensington Gardens near the Serpentine Lake. So quickly that there was no way the photographers outside would have been able to get a clear shot of the dress. I'd have to get photographed inside, if I could, which I realized as soon as we entered wouldn't be a problem—I could see the occasional flashbulb even from the coat-check area. The party was already buzzing.

Just two years prior, Dylan had been honored there with a similar soiree and exhibit, but tonight was in honor of an emerging British artist, from whom Dylan had commissioned a painting for his hideaway in the country. The space was gorgeous, lit softly for the party but with the artwork still on full display. Although I wasn't sure how long I'd be able to stand and look at the paintings—the heels Hannah had purchased for me were too snug in the toes and, as promised, very, very high. I had no idea how I would make it through the night.

Dylan looked at me and then at my feet—we both felt how

odd it was that my eyes were now level with his chin instead of his chest.

"Well, hello there, tall girl," he said. "Have you seen my girl-friend?"

"Why, yes. She is back at the pharmacy, stocking up on the Band-Aids she'll need at the end of this night," I said, looking despairingly towards my feet.

"Plasters, you mean, from the chemist."

"Band-Aids, pharmacy."

"Plasters."

"Band-Aids."

"Baby," Dylan said, shaking his head, smiling at my obsti-nance, and leading me into the crowd by my hand, with me trying not to wince with every step.

We mingled, sipped Champagne cocktails, and I tried not to ap-pear completely classless as I surreptitiously followed around the waiter who was passing out mini crab cakes. They. Were. Amazing.

"Oh bloody hell," Dylan said under his breath after taking a sip of his cocktail.

"What?" I asked, following his gaze across the room. I saw a medium-sized guy with overly coiffed brown hair coming our way and raising his glass to Dylan.

"Tristan," Dylan acknowledged the man, without a hair more warmth in his voice than was strictly necessary so as not to ap-pear downright hostile.

Tristan, whom I'd heard about a few times before, turned to me, and it was immediately clear he was slightly drunk. "So this is the delicious thing that's kept you too busy to return my phone calls lately, eh?"

I cringed, partially because calling me a *delicious thing* was ridiculously offensive and also because I knew it would piss off

Dylan to no end. Sure enough, the crease between Dylan's eyebrows deepened considerably.

"I'm Lydia Bell," I said, reaching out my hand and intervening. I didn't care who this jerk was or what he thought of me—I wanted to have a nice night with Dylan, and I was happy to defuse the situation.

"Tristan Bailey," he said while literally eyeing me up and down, as though he were pricing me for an auction. This guy made my skin crawl.

Dylan immediately tightened his arm around my waist and then spoke to me directly. "Lydia, darling, Tristan works for my father. His right-hand man, if you will." He said the words with a subtle distinction, and I heard his commentary—his father choosing a guy like *this* to be his right-hand man was yet another indicator of how despicable his dad was.

"It's a pleasure to meet you," I said, summoning my politeness.

"Likewise," Tristan said with a healthy dose of smarminess. "You let me know if this cad doesn't treat you right, *darling*."

"I don't think that will be a problem," I said. "But thanks for the offer." I turned away from him, towards Dylan. "I think I need to find the ladies' room, Dylan. Can you show me where it is?"

Dylan nodded and then looked to Tristan again. The frosty fury on Dylan's face was frankly terrifying. "If you need my approval on something, Tristan, send word to Thomas. I'm sure he can get you what you need. Have a pleasant evening."

We were halfway across the room before he stopped. He grabbed two more drinks from a tray, handed me one, then planted one long kiss on my lips and took a swig of his drink. "I fucking hate that prat," he said, taking another swig. "But I fucking love you."

I smiled up at him. "That guy's an asshole," I said taking a sympathetic swig of my own drink. Dylan chuckled and grabbed my hand, pulling us back into the middle of the party. Tristan had reminded him of all the stress with his father in a two-minute conversation. And with one kiss he was back to me. I relaxed into his side and took another look around the room—the party had really filled up since we'd arrived.

"Is that Thomas?" I asked, squinting through the lights where I was pretty sure I saw Dylan's assistant by the bar ordering a drink.

Dylan nodded. "One of the perks of the job—he gets tickets too, when he wants them."

"Who's that?" I asked, gesturing with my glass to the tall, rail-thin man standing next to Thomas. The two of them were wearing slim charcoal-grey suits and looked incredibly hip, and actually gorgeous. I hadn't realized how handsome Thomas was before, probably because every time I'd seen him he was on the phone, chasing after Dylan, or bracing himself for a classic Hale explosion about something firm related.

"His boyfriend, Alex."

"Thomas is gay?" I asked, somehow totally taken by surprise.

"Mmm," Dylan affirmed just as the two men approached us.

"Sir," Thomas said, nodding at Dylan. "Lydia," he added, kissing my cheeks. "Lydia, this is Alex."

Alex and I chatted for a moment while Dylan and Thomas went over something work related. I could hear Dylan's tone go all cold and efficient, as it did when he demonstrated just how immovable he was on some feature of a design. I heard him say, "If he wants hippie modernism tell him to call in Behrens. I'm not designing a geodesic dome or a sixties flight deck. He knows what he gets if he comes to me, and if he has half a brain and a pair of balls he'll make the right decision. Tell him *no*." I glanced at Thomas, who seemed remarkably cool. A month ago Thomas would have been sweating his ass off in the face of Dylan's stubborn business arrogance. Now he took it in stride.

Just as Alex was telling me about the vacation he and Thomas were planning to Provence, there was a familiar stirring in the doorway. A moment later Caroline's swanlike frame emerged from the crowd the way someone might emerge from the mist in a music video from the eighties. Tall, elegant, as though the very lighting and air quality had been adjusted to make this one woman look profoundly beautiful and perfect. Immediately behind her was her younger brother, Prince Richard, whom I recognized from the tabloids, with his hand snugly around his willowy girlfriend, Jemma. The flashes became rapid-fire as the approved photographers captured the trio's entrance.

I leaned into Dylan's side and spoke towards his ear. "I meant to ask you—am I supposed to curtsy?" He grimaced and twitched.

"As an American, no. But since you're a British citizen, then, technically, yes. But these days the formality isn't required." Clearly this whole thing was making him uncomfortable too. I was grateful I didn't have to attempt the formality, but I took note that several people *did* bow or curtsy as she passed them.

"Thank god," I said, tightening my grip around his waist, letting him hold my body tight against his, and just then I saw Caroline's gaze land on us. Richard caught sight of us and lit up, half dragging Jemma behind him.

"Dylan," said Caroline, gliding in to give him a gracious kiss on each cheek. "Won't you introduce us?" She looked down towards me. Even with the increasingly torturous high heels she was taller. I expected to look at her and feel coldness or indifference, but her eyes were warm, kind.

Dylan chuckled and put his broad, warm palm against my bare back. "With pleasure. Caroline, this is my girlfriend, Lydia Bell. Lydia, this is Her Royal Highness, Princess Caroline." Dylan emphasized the title in a teasing way, and Caroline rolled her eyes at him in a way that spoke to their familiarity with each other, their closeness.

I didn't say anything—I was pretty sure I wasn't supposed to say anything until she spoke to me first. This was kind of crazy—I was meeting a *princess*. Even if I was technically supposed to be rageful with proprietary jealousy, this was crazy cool. She had a lovely warm smile on her lips and was generously holding her hand out. I recovered quickly and gently shook her hand.

"It's so lovely to finally meet you, Lydia," she finally said.

"Likewise. It's an honor, Your Royal Highness," I replied, surprising myself that I was able to speak at all.

"Please, call me Caroline. Dylan tells me you're from New York."

"That's right."

"Do you miss it?"

"Rarely," I said as images of my Brooklyn apartment, my college life meandering around the Village, and of course my dad flashed before my eyes in a moment. It was amazing how little I'd managed to think of New York lately. I felt Dylan give my hip a squeeze. "I've felt very welcomed," I added, smiling and looking up at Dylan.

Caroline looked genuinely happy—she looked at Dylan with so much fondness, which somehow conveyed a deep friendship but nothing more. "I'm going there next week actually. I've only been twice before on state visits, but I'd like to do some more exploring this time. Any recommendations? Something off the beaten path?"

This woman was a surprise.

"Something a princess might not come across on her own?" I asked, unsure if my familiarity or reference to her title was a total faux pas. I could feel Dylan smiling beside me—his hand resting heavily on my hip—and had a feeling this was going just fine. He was being possessive, and his position let me know in no uncertain terms that he and I were a unit. No one could have mistaken him for being with anyone but me. I knew it was purposeful, and as much as I hated to admit it, it was appreciated.

I proceeded to tell her about some of my favorite haunts, and the longer we chatted the easier it was to forget she was a princess. She was a pro at making people feel comfortable—she'd clearly been raised knowing how to miraculously and effortlessly maintain her princess-ness while putting those around her at ease. She didn't blink as the photographers captured our conversation, and she didn't fidget. At all. If it hadn't been stunning to watch, I might have almost been creeped out by it. Despite all my intentions to grumpily feel competitive with her, I felt brought into her fold.

Prince Richard joined the conversation just as Caroline gracefully excused herself. He had a bouncy, energetic jocularity about him. Floppy blond hair, twinkling blue eyes. He was a mischief-maker but kind. It was clear that his role as the younger sibling, the third in line to the throne, afforded him a more relaxed life. He spoke to Dylan with informal admiration, like Dylan was a cool older brother figure.

And he was clearly eager for Dylan to meet Jemma—Richard was beaming as he introduced her, as though seeking Dylan's approval. When Dylan reached out his hand, I saw Jemma blush, and at first I thought it was what women blushing around Dylan normally was—just taking in how domineering and handsome he was. But when I caught Dylan's expression—his mouth in a firm line, his brow slightly furrowed as though he was trying to communicate something to her—I knew it was something more.

Holy shit.

She was blushing because she was *remembering*.

* * *

"So when did you sleep with her?"

We'd been in the car for five minutes, and I still wasn't touching him, my ass firmly planted on the other side of the car. I was sitting on my hands, and my nails were digging into the leather. I was so mad at the situation I didn't quite know what to do with myself.

Part of my mood was about those horrible shoes, which were clearly a size too small and which I had removed as soon as we were in the car and out of the photographers' sights, but ninety-five percent was about the obvious look of lustful nostalgia on Jemma's face.

"What? Who?" he asked, looking at me warily, loosening his tie.

"Oh, please." Somehow I'd left this incredible party full of positive feelings for the gorgeous member of the royal family he used to date but completely annoyed about the bouncy, doe-eyed Jemma. "You think I didn't see the way she looked at you? Like she was remembering the best sex of her life?"

Dylan exhaled, loosening his tie even further and turning to me. "Would it help if I said she didn't even come close to being the best sex of my life? That no one could hold a candle to you?

That I honestly couldn't remember her name before Richard reintroduced us?"

"Ugh," I said with a look of disgust. "Your prior self is kind of repulsive." He looked sad when I said that, and part of me wanted to apologize, but I was too pissed. I knew he had a colorful past full of countless ex-lovers, but I didn't normally think about it. Somehow I'd convinced my conscious self—the one who actually went through the world day by day—that he had been celibate during all of those years between Caroline and me. If you'd asked me to discuss the topic out loud, outside the fantasy land of my brain, then obviously I would admit that wasn't true, but I'd found myself remarkably capable of avoiding that reality. Until now.

"How many?" I asked.

"How many what?" He looked at me quizzically, pulling my hand out from under my ass and gripping it, trying to pull me towards him. I glanced out the window, and I knew we were only a few moments from my house, but I wanted to talk about this now. I needed to know. I gave him an incredulous look that said *Think about it for two seconds, douchebag.*

"Oh," he said, realizing. "God, Lydia. You really want to talk about this?"

"I can't believe we haven't talked about it already." I raised my palms and slapped them back down on the seat for emphasis.

He sighed in frustration. "Loads."

"How. Many?" I asked again. He was dragging his long fingers through his hair, then he reached over and gave me another tug. "If you're going to make me talk about this, can I at least do it with you on my lap?"

I didn't move.

"Lydia. On my lap. Now." I rolled my eyes and began to

move towards him, but I hadn't moved more than an inch when he just hauled me over him. "If you're going to force me to think about other women, I want my hands on my woman." He pushed the skirt of my dress up to my hips. He tucked his fingertips under the side of my thong and moved his whole palm underneath it. I could feel the short hair there, just growing in, against his palm, and the sensation made me shiver. I needed to focus before he successfully sexed his way out of this conversation.

I gripped his hand to stop him from moving. "Don't get distracted."

He sighed again. "Fine, but we need to get you waxed again soon."

"Dylan!"

"Fine! I don't know," he said, his eyes flashing closed for a moment with what emotion? Was it embarrassment?

"What?"

"I didn't exactly keep a tally, Lydia."

"Guess."

"All right," he said, sighing in resignation and looked to the ceiling of the car, as though the answers were written there. "Well, it's been seven years since Caroline. And it was about two months after our breakup that I started sleeping with other people, and that was June, so we're talking almost exactly seven years until I met you. I'd say I was having sex about two or three times a week, and there are fifty-two weeks a year. I only did repeats occasionally, so I'd say somewhere between…" He started to try to do the math in this head, but I beat him to it.

"Over a thousand women," I said, astonished.

"That's not possible."

"Well, if it was three times a week, and no repeats."

"But if it was two times a week, with some repeats—" he objected.

"That's still over seven hundred women!"

"I did go on holiday with my family. Occasionally. It couldn't have been *all* fifty-two weeks of the year," he protested, but I looked at him with a skeptical look of shame.

"Fuck me," he finally admitted.

"Apparently," I scoffed, pushing myself off his lap.

"No. Get back here," he said, pulling me so I was straddling him, my dress gathered between us. We'd been parked outside my house for a few minutes, but I knew he wouldn't let us out of the car until we'd sorted this out. He firmly planted his arms around me, wrapping me, pulling me into him. I rested my forehead against his shoulder, and I could feel his lips in my hair. I hit him in the arm.

"Ow," he huffed, but he knew he had to take it. "How many men?"

"Dylan—" What was the point of even asking?

"Just answer me. How many men?"

I sighed in defeat. "Three before you."

He breathed into my hair, kissed my head, and pulled me even tighter into him.

"The best I can offer," he continued, "is to tell you that none of them meant a thing to me, as evidenced by the fact that I didn't even remember Jemma's *name* when I saw her. It wasn't me who was with any of them—in fact, being with them helped me *avoid* being me, to protect myself from the utter chaos of being a real person with anyone."

I scoffed again audibly, but he continued, "You know, in a way I'm grateful for those years."

"What? Why?" I asked, lifting my head to look at him.

"I wasn't ready to be myself with anyone. This probably makes me an asshole, but I was using them. I can only hope they were also using me." He paused for a moment and started to loosen the pins holding back my hair. "Plus," he continued, "by the time you came along, I knew well enough how to make you come in under a minute." I couldn't stop my small smile. He was right. He could. "And if that had anything to do with my being able to trick you into loving me back, then how on earth could I regret it?"

I rolled my eyes. "You are so annoying." I pushed against his chest.

"Who? Me?"

"I'm not supposed to get stupidly jealous about how many *hundreds* of women you've been with only to have you commandeer the conversation and turn it into some kind of sweet profession of love…and have it *work*. You're too good at this." He held my face in his hands, his fingertips weaving into my loosened hair, and he placed a long slow kiss on my lips.

"I'm taking you inside now," he said, no room for arguing. "I'm going to bring you upstairs into your frigid bedroom and bury you under the covers. When I have you nice and warm"—he kept talking, now rubbing his hands up and down my bare arms and across my bare back—"I'm going to make sure you fully comprehend that no woman before you meant a thing. And I'm sure as fuck going to drive the memories of those three other men so far into oblivion that you won't be able to remember their names either."

With that, my legs wrapped around his waist, my arms wrapped around his neck, he carried me inside. All thoughts of previous lovers, his and mine, disintegrated into the cool night air.

Chapter 7

By eleven thirty the next morning, Dylan had proved two more times that he could fuck the memories of other men right out of my brain. We'd taken breaks for coffee and croissants while sitting in front of the fire in my living room, and I'd proved to Dylan that his girlfriend could beat him at Scrabble. In fact, he had yet to beat me, even if I was six years younger and hadn't gone to Cambridge.

While I leaned back against his chest, our legs spread out on the floor in front of us, and his hand playing with my hair, I tried to remember the last time we had just lounged together, doing nothing other than reveling in each other. We had all day, and I was in a state of complete and utter euphoria at the prospect of those hours.

Until his phone rang, and he got up to get it.

I could tell immediately, based on his facial expression alone, before he even said his formal "Yes, Mum," that it was his mother.

"No, today won't work. I haven't seen Lydia all week, and I'm spending the day with her."

Silence. Dylan pursing his lips.

"Mother, you have no idea what my weeks are like, and I assure you I'm not gallivanting around town. Just ask father. He's the one who has me at the HS offices about six times more often than I agreed to." He was curt, frustrated. The second he'd picked up the phone, his whole body had become rigid with tension.

And now he was pacing.

"What on earth are you going on about?" he asked her, his hand tense on his hip.

"Yes, we were there, but—" he said in a skeptical tone and reached for my laptop, bringing up something on the screen, clearly something to which his mother was referring. He stopped cold. What was it?

"Mum…Yes, I understand…You hardly need to tell me—"

Silence and possibly the most pissed off expression I'd ever seen on Dylan's face. I half expected steam to come out of his ears.

"She had nothing to do with it, and I won't have you implying that she set this up—" He was actually gritting his teeth. "That's exactly what you were implying."

I stood and came up behind Dylan and wrapped my arms around him, wanting to comfort him. I had no idea what was going on, but I wanted to be part of what made him feel better. And then I saw it, over his shoulder.

The website for *HELLO!* magazine.

Two pictures of me, side by side.

In the first photo I was walking into 42 Park Lane, dressed in my red silk blouse and trim skirt, hair neat and tidy, folder under my arm—I could still summon the anxiety, the anticipation of making my pitch to Giles Cabot as I walked into the lobby. And in the second, I was standing in Dylan's arms, his lips were on mine, and I was wearing the same skirt, but my hair was askew, and I had on what was very clearly a men's dress shirt. The headline read:

Dylan Hale Has a Quickie in Midst of Unrest at Hale Shipping

It was bad enough that they were right—we had been having sex in that hotel. It was worse that Hannah would also now know that I had been having sex with my boyfriend when I told her I'd been running errands. And the worst thing about this was that apparently Dylan was coping with problems at his family's company, and this media attention possibly made those problems worse. I suddenly felt lost, like I didn't have the map I needed to navigate all of this.

I was no longer listening to Dylan's conversation with his mother. I was scanning the article for whatever I could see. I caught the words *sordid fling* and *different shirt*. I'd have to read it later to see how they were spinning this, but I could at least tell that none of it felt accurate, except for, you know, the fact we had indeed had a quickie.

"I told you. No. I'm spending the day here," he continued into the phone, then listened. More listening. A gruff, throaty, complain-y sound. "Fine...Hello, Father..." Dylan sighed deeply then said, almost shouting, "*Fine.* I'll come. No. I'll be there at two, no sooner." He hung up his phone and closed his eyes in frustration. Then he called Lloyd, telling him to bring a bag of clothes—presumably wearing his rumpled suit from yesterday wouldn't work for an afternoon with his parents.

When he hung up for the second time, Dylan turned towards me. I was in a partially catatonic state and barely registered that

he was pulling me towards the sofa in front of the fire and haul-
ing me onto his lap. I was wearing one of his button-down shirts,
not dissimilar to the one in the photograph, and nothing else,
and he arranged me so I was straddling him, his hands across my
lower back. I didn't feel like dealing with this. The trouble these
photos seemed to be causing made me feel like the ground was
shifting beneath me.

"That photo looks bad. I need to get smarter about this," I said,
feeling unsteady about the whole thing. I felt naïve, like such a
rookie, like Dylan was dragging around a girlfriend who had no
idea how to do the things she needed to know how to do in order
to *be* his girlfriend. It was like that first day of college, when you
reveal that you don't know what the mascot is or where the library
is—your every action reveals just how new you are, how far you
have to go before you belong. Then again, he'd been at the hotel
too. In fact, he was the one who'd gotten curry on my shirt.

"You have nothing to be sorry for, baby," he said, reading
my mind, reassuringly running his fingers through my hair and
pulling my head up, so I was forced to look him in the eye.
"Look at me. Are you okay?" He searched my face, as though the
article might have physically scarred me.

"I'm fine," I said. "I mean, I don't love that your mother
thinks I did this. On purpose. That I am some fame-seeking
whore or something."

"Lydia, my mother is a full-on lunatic. She was angry with
me, baby. As was my father. She's furious that she can't control
me. But the important thing here is that *you* are all right." The
tension was clear on his face, wrinkling his brow, and he ran his
hand through his own hair as he looked slightly panicked. "I can
stay here if you want. I don't need to go to see my parents."

Why was he so worried about me? Where was this panic

coming from? And then it dawned on me—this was what had happened with Grace.

I put my hands against his bare chest. "I'm okay. Sure, I don't *like* this. I hate those pictures." I crossed my arms against my chest as I spoke. "I hate that, even if just for a minute, I was part of something that might hurt Hale Architecture and Design or make things with your family worse. I hate that apparently, at any minute, without my knowing, someone can add 'spin' to my life," I continued. "But I'm okay."

"Damsel." He rubbed his hands up and down my arms. "This shit is going to happen—I can't stop it." I could tell by the way he was saying it just how much he wished he could. "My parents have a point—I *should* have known better. I should have thought about your shirt—it should have occurred to me. I'm used to this, and I need to look out for you better."

"Dylan," I said, looking squarely into his eyes, "I'm okay." The worry was still there, etched firmly in the wrinkles of his brow, but after a moment of staring at me, obviously looking for signs of freaking out, he calmed.

The truth was that I *was* a little freaked out, but I didn't need Dylan acting any more protective or worried than he already was. As much as I knew this was a mutual fail, I couldn't help but feel like I'd let him down. I'd thought I knew what I was doing. I'd thought I had a handle on it. I hadn't really believed the paparazzi were a *thing*, not one that would affect us, anyway. So I hadn't thought twice about how I behaved in public, about how I skipped into his arms or reached for his hand. But I realized now that I was going to have to be much more careful going forward. For both our sakes.

"We were only outside the hotel for a second," I said, wondering aloud at how easily this could happen.

"A second is all it takes." He leaned forward and kissed my neck.

"The worst part is that I loved that afternoon, and now it's ruined."

He cupped my chin with his palm. "No. Don't let them taint things. Once you let them take what's perfect, what's ours, and change it, we're doomed. So no. It's still our afternoon, understand?"

I nodded, still uncertain, and he moved his palms to my thighs.

"I still licked this pretty pussy," he said as he pried my legs even farther apart, looking down appreciatively. My shirt was entirely unbuttoned and now I was spread before him, completely open.

"I still toyed with these gorgeous tits," he added, moving his thumbs to my nipples, stroking them. Suddenly, in one fluid effortless movement, he had me on all fours on the couch, and he was behind me.

"And if I recall, I still fucked this marvelous cunt from behind." He ran his finger through my opening. He loomed over me, taking control, blanketing me.

"So no, baby, that afternoon. This afternoon. It's all still ours, and you keep it that way. Understand me, sweet girl?"

I nodded, biting my lip.

He hovered, kissing my back, stroking my arm. He was trying to coax me back, but in that moment there was a wedge. My anxiety over the photos, maybe his frustration with his parents, his worry over me. He wanted to bring me back into his fold, regain control of this situation, but I couldn't quite get there.

"Baby?" he asked quietly after several minutes, and I could hear the resignation in his voice, like he knew I might need more than a minute to digest this. "At least there's one good thing about *HELLO!* printing that story."

I turned my head and looked at him, questioning.

"Now every lame fucking wanker out there who thinks he ever stood a chance with you, who might have pathetically convinced himself that we weren't real or that I didn't own every inch of your perfect ass, can shut down any pipe dream they ever had about you. You're mine, and any article that makes that even the tiniest bit clearer, is fit to print."

I smiled and flipped onto my back. I looked up at him, leaning over me. Using all of my strength and a little kick to his leg to make him lose balance, I pulled him down on top of me. I whispered into his ear as he tried to prop himself on his elbows to relieve me of having to bear his weight, "You're all mine." And for the third time that morning, he made love to me to try to make me forget, only this time it wasn't so easy.

* * *

"I'm sorry about this," Dylan said, and to be fair he really did look apologetic. "I was looking forward to today." He was pulling a shirt over his head, and it struck me as cruel to show me that toned torso only to cover it so efficiently with his worn-in T-shirt.

"It's okay," I said, slipping on some underwear and sitting cross-legged in the chair. I was disappointed—I wanted the day I had been promised. But if there was any chance that time with his dad might resolve some of the stress between them, then I was glad he was going. I still didn't know what was going on between them, and I was curious, but I also knew Dylan was private. I figured he'd tell me if it was important. Or I hoped.

"How about a late dinner at Will's tonight?" he asked. Will was Dylan's best friend from childhood and the head chef at the restaurant they owned together. Dylan looked at me expectantly as he pulled on the jeans from the bag Lloyd had brought. While I was free to spend the day in his shirt, he had to get dressed if he was going to spend the afternoon, however reluctantly, with his parents. Whenever he went to his childhood home, he always seemed to dress in preparation for a long walk. Jeans were fastened, and up next would be thick socks, followed by a crazy-sexy chunky-knit cream sweater.

"Sure. What time will you be back?" I said as, sure enough, he pulled the socks out of the bag.

"I can collect you at nine or so."

I nodded. "Who do you walk with when you go to your parents' house?" I asked.

"Humboldt Park."

"Who?" I asked.

"That's what the house is called. Humboldt Park."

"Oh."

"I'd like to take you there. If my father wasn't determined to serve me my arse and discuss the business, I'd take you today, but—"

"Um, yeah. I have a feeling today isn't the day for me to make a good impression." I had finished his thought.

"I was going to say that they don't like surprises," he said. "I do want you to see it, though." He paused for a moment, and I could see his mind drift to a more pleasant place. "There are these woods behind the house, and there's this small lake where deer often congregate…It's really quite stunning this time of year. Next weekend, perhaps?"

I smiled, imagining him there in the woods. "I don't know,

Dylan. I mean, I don't get the sense your parents are exactly over the moon that the first girl you've chosen to date publicly—"

"At all. Date at all."

"Fine, at all, is an American commoner." He looked at me sharply. "I know I'm technically British too—"

"That's not what I was going to say. I don't care if you were raised by kangaroos on Mount Kilimanjaro—"

"I don't think kangaroos live on Kilimanjaro—" I objected, but Dylan swooped in and shut me up with a kiss to my lips.

"Will you let me finish a thought for once?" he asked, half smiling, half scolding. "What I meant was that their disapproval means nothing to me, and your provenance will mean nothing to them once they get to know you."

"Okay then," I said, "you can take me to your childhood home, but only on one condition." I rose onto my knees in the chair and wrapped my body around him, basically climbing him. He caught me as I jumped and landed with my legs around his waist.

He raised his eyebrows at me, waiting.

I whispered in his ear, "Take me to your childhood bedroom and do that thing you do with your tongue."

"Which thing?" he asked, smiling.

"The one where you put your fingers in me, and then use your tongue to tease my—" He cut me off by diving towards my mouth, kissing me hard and fast, and then gently, slowly rimming my lips with his tongue so lightly that I couldn't be sure if he was actually touching me or not.

"That's the one."

He smacked my ass hard, making me jump higher into his arms, and then put me down.

"Wait, so who do you walk with?" I asked again, gesturing towards his clothes.

"No one. By myself," he began. "When I get there, I need some time before I see my parents."

When he said things like that, I didn't think he realized what he was saying—that he needed to what? Prepare? Brace himself? Before he could spend time with his own parents, the people who should love him unconditionally? Although what was I even thinking? My own mother had disappeared completely.

"Are you sure you have to go there this afternoon?" I was trying not to let it show, but I was so disappointed to lose this day with him.

"I'm afraid so, baby. He was on me about heading out there this weekend to discuss some things about Hale Shipping, and I said no. These photos gave him the excuse to insist." There was an element of disgust in his tone, and frustration.

"What did the magazine mean about there being trouble at Hale Shipping? Is the company in trouble? Does he want you to deal with it?"

"Possibly. My father fired someone who's threatened some kind of tell-all about him. It's a mess." Dylan walked around the room, picking up odds and ends, then laced up his shoes.

"Does the guy have any real dirt on him?"

"I'll tell you about it sometime, but not now," he said, rubbing his temples with his thumb and forefinger, and once again not *really* telling me what I wanted to know. "I've summoned Frank—he's parked outside. Please don't go anywhere without him." He said this with a raised-eyebrow plea, because he knew he didn't have the authority he wished he did with me.

"I'll do my best. But, you know, I'm perfectly capable of being on my own," I said, smiling.

"Oh, I know," he replied. He shook his head slightly, and as he turned around, he said, "Be good, you little minx. I'll collect you a bit before nine."

I watched him walk out of my bedroom and heard him descend the creaky stairs of the little house. That morning I'd woken up feeling impossibly close to him, like the day was ours, like we could settle into *our* world. But in the past hour, I'd been reminded, once again, of the ways in which his life was a universe away from mine.

* * *

It was ten minutes before nine that night when I got a text from Frank.

SATURDAY, 8:50 pm
Mr. Hale just texted and said he'd like me to bring you to the restaurant. I'm warming the car and am ready when you are.

That was weird. Why hadn't Dylan texted me himself? Since when did we have a go-between?

SATURDAY, 8:51 pm
Thanks, Frank. Be down in a sec.

"Frank?" Frank asked incredulously as I slid past him and into the warm interior of the Jaguar. It had been the first time since meeting him that I'd called him by his actual name. I'd been so thrown by his text, or more accurately by him texting me instead of Dylan, that I'd slipped.

"Oh, sorry, sweets. Do you need some affection?" I looked up at him, batting my eyelashes and willing myself to smile a little more as I fastened my seat belt and he closed the door.

"Not at all, Lydia, just wanted to be sure it was really you I was texting with and not your sinister evil twin," he replied happily while pulling into the Saturday night Notting Hill traffic.

"Is Dylan okay?"

"I believe so," Frank said, looking at me via the rearview mirror.

Ten minutes later, we pulled up to Will's restaurant. Dylan was there outside the door, looking earnestly at the screen of his phone. He noticed me and came over to open the door and pull me out of the car into his arms before the seat belt had fully recoiled.

"Whoa, hi there," I said, my words muffled by his jacket. Even though his arms were blanketing my whole body, holding my head close to his chest, I could hear Dylan talking to Frank.

"Abbott, thank you. We'll see you tomorrow." Dylan had addressed Frank by his last name, dismissing him. Then he held me just a little tighter. "I missed you," he whispered into my hair.

I looked up at him. "Everything okay?" He was different from this morning. As though he'd been to war and back.

"It is now. Let's eat." But he still had that cold tone he got after spending time with his parents. And before I could press for details, he pulled me into the warmth of Will's beautiful little restaurant.

Two enormous bowls of pasta later—butternut squash ravioli with sage and some kind of roasted sausage bits—and Dylan, Will, and I were at risk of polishing off our third bottle of wine. Dylan had been quiet, sipping slowly. I could feel that he had slipped into his faraway place, as though he were standing behind a black screen, lost in his thoughts, and I couldn't reach him. It was concerning—I didn't *like* seeing him all knotted up, ruminating—but it was also frustrating. He'd been at Humboldt Park all day, and now that he was back with me, he still wasn't even really here.

"So, little lady," Will said, looking at me, pulling me out of my thoughts. "I hear you may head out to the farm one of these days."

"The farm?" I asked, taking another large sip of wine.

"That's what we called Humboldt when we were in school—'the farm,'" Dylan explained halfheartedly. "There is still a working farm on it. I'll show you."

"Ahh," I said. "So would you milk the cows before or after school?" I looked at Dylan smugly, knowing full well he'd probably never even seen a cow being milked in his life. Meanwhile, Will nearly fell off his chair laughing.

"Milk the cows," Will sputtered and squeaked—the words barely discernable in his fit of laughter. I giggled with him, but Dylan just sighed heavily, resigned to being made fun of. Eventually Will wiped the tears from his eyes. "Blimey. Your girl's funny, mate."

"Should I be nervous?" I asked Will, but he looked confused. "About going to Humboldt?"

"Well, whatever you do," he said, conspiratorially leaning over the table, "don't tell the duchess that you like the Roman statue in the fountain." I looked at him quizzically. I could sense Dylan stiffen in warning to his friend, but thankfully Will was too drunk to notice or care. "About ten years back, old Geoff's lady of the hour chose to drape herself over the statue for his birthday."

"That's just odd," I said.

"Wearing nothing but an enormous red ribbon in her hair."

"Oh."

"The statue has been a bone of contention ever since."

"Understandably," I added.

"I don't even remember telling you that horrible story," Dylan said, staring with a half-glaring, half-puzzled expression at Will.

Will shrugged and continued, "Primarily, I'd be nervous about this man of yours finding the time to take you out there. If old Geoff has his way, this poor bugger"—he pointed at Dylan—"will be running Hale Shipping and taking over for the old man before sundown Sunday." He put his hand on Dylan's shoulder. "Why, he's already got our boy in on more deals than I'd ever thought possible—between HS and the architecture firm, I'm amazed you see him at all. I got an email from him at nearly three in the morning this week!"

"You've been *working* for Hale Shipping?" I sobered a little and looked to Dylan. At some point this week I'd been sleeping soundly beside him and he'd been awake, working. It felt weird not to know that. And it felt weird that Will did.

"A bit," he said, and I looked at him, worried. He'd just taken on a new design in Amsterdam and was finishing up a bid for the Olympic Stadium in Auckland, and I'd often heard him talking about a personal project he was working on for himself. Working for his father too seemed outrageous. Worry, at least, was a feeling I was familiar with—it had been my primary emotion for eight years as I cared for my father, and as much as I didn't like thinking about how stressed out Dylan clearly was, and as frustrated as I was that Dylan wasn't communicating with me about all this, for a brief moment, I actually felt relieved to be on familiar emotional ground.

I may have wanted him to open up to me about all the things that made him rub his forehead the way he was at that moment, but right then I just wanted him to snap out of it, to come back to me. After this day, I wanted to feel close to him again, and I wanted him to feel close to me. I reached over and kissed him on the cheek, and in doing so allowed his hand to slip fully between my legs, right at the top. I heard his breath hitch slightly, saw his eyes widen a bit, and a tiny lustful smirk wrinkled his brow.

I continued to fill Will in on the progress with the store and the goings-on at work, all while slightly shifting below the table. Will shared advice on managing a retail space in central London and clarified a zoning code question I'd found mind-boggling. We talked about business, design, food, fashion. I asked about Will's famous whisky-distilling family and told him about New York. All the while, I just let Dylan come down from whatever dark place that had him. And slowly I felt him inching closer, chiming in to say how proud he was of my work on the store or about how my father had owned the last standalone sheet music store in New York City. Inch by inch he came back to me.

"So, Dylan, have you asked Lydia about the CBC yet?" Will directed a mischievous look at Dylan as he said it.

"CBC?" I asked, gripping his hand tighter as it rested on my thigh.

"Conservation in Building Conference," Dylan explained, more relaxed. "It's an international conference—"

"A meeting of the architectural geniuses of the world, your boyfriend included," interrupted Will, pointing at Dylan proudly.

"Yes, well. The queen has asked my father of all people to open the conference and to have us for tea afterwards. The first time in his life when he's taken the least interest in my chosen profession, and of course it's to serve his own needs."

"Architecture? Shouldn't it be you opening it or leading it?" I protested, my hand flying upward and banging into the underside of the tabletop, which caused Will to look down at us curiously and Dylan to firmly clasp my hand and bring it straight back between my legs.

I coughed slightly and took a big gulp of wine.

"It would be improper for Her Majesty to bypass my father and only invite me," he said. "So he'll be the star, but I will be there to make him a legitimate choice." Dylan loosened his grip on my hand only to move his fingers right up against my warm center. The tables were turning. Not only had I gotten Dylan to snap out of his funk, I had awoken the monster.

I took another swig of wine, tried to keep my head in the conversation, and asked, "What did Will think you'd ask me about it?"

"If you'll go with him, of course, meet the old bat!" Will interrupted, smiling big and answering for Dylan.

"The old bat?" I asked, not fully understanding, and then I realized. "To have tea with the queen?" I looked wide-eyed at Dylan, and he nodded in affirmation. "The *queen* queen?"

Dylan chuckled and nodded again.

"Uh, yeah. Of course I'll go," I said, and I could see the corners of Dylan's mouth perk up a bit. "You'll prep me, right? I mean, I have no stinking clue what to say to the queen, for Christ's sake."

"Well, not 'for Christ's sake,' for starters, or she may tell you that yes, that is exactly for whose sake she is there." He was full-on smiling now, clearly pleased that I'd be there. He pulled my chair closer to his.

"When is this shindig anyway?"

Dylan turned more fully towards me and grabbed my face in his hands, pulling it towards his own. "Two weeks, sweet girl." And he gave me that look. His *I love you* look. And he kissed me. Softly at first, then harder. He even let just a flash of tongue in before letting me go.

"Ah, Jesus," snorted Will. "Off with you two, and don't come back. You're clearly a filthy pair." We were near giggling in our seats, and we looked back to Will, not apologetically at all.

Chapter 8

W e didn't get home that night until nearly two. I was asleep before we got home and had no memory of being brought to bed or undressed.

The next morning, whenever I'd start to stir, I'd happily roll back under my covers and into Dylan's warm body, prolonging sleep as effectively as I could. When I woke up for good, it was because Dylan was drawing circles with his fingertips on my bare chest, making ever-wider shapes, tracing invisible pathways and leaving a cool alertness in his wake. I smiled before I opened my eyes.

"There's my girl," he said, and I squinted into the bright room, taking him in. He was lying on his side, his head perched on his hand, supported by his elbow. In the mornings Dylan looked just a little less precise, a little more rugged, like his cool, polished exterior had been marched through an outdoor sports magazine. His scruff was at its longest, his hair was at its most unruly, and his smell—that refined warm earthiness that was unmistakably him—was at its most pronounced. It was possible that I loved him more first thing in the morning than I did at any other time of day.

His whole hand was across my chest, a couple of fingers lying just atop the lower curve of my breast, others wrapping around my side, tapping my soft skin there. It was a subtle drumbeat, not overtly sexual, but summoning my blood all the same.

"Morning," I said, stretching my arms up above my head, running into the headboard, and incidentally pushing my chest farther into his hand.

"Good morning," he said.

Oh.

It was subtle, but I could hear the calm control in his voice. It was *that* tone. His hand gripped a little tighter, moved a tad higher, so his thumb was right by my nipple, not quite touching it.

I reached my arms over his head, moving to wrap them around his neck, but he gently gripped my wrists in his hand and firmly placed them back above my head. He just shook his head, indicating that no, I couldn't, shouldn't move my arms again.

"How did you sleep, damsel?" he asked smoothly, again that control right at the surface.

"Well." I gulped a little, feeling the anticipation, my arousal shifting, awakening. I cleared my throat. "I slept well."

"Good." His hand steadily drifted down my torso and resumed drawing those tantalizing circles around my hip, swiftly brushing over my landing strip, then lower, but never close enough. Lazy, as though he had no intentions, as if this were totally innocent, naïve. As if.

"Not too hungover?" he asked.

I mentally ran a check over my body, and by some miracle I was foggy but not in the misery I probably deserved. I shook my head.

My hips shifted involuntarily, tilting, hoping to coax him into accidentally speeding up his process. But he lifted his hand altogether and made a quiet tsk-ing sound.

When his hand returned, it was to grasp my upper thigh under the light sheet and pull it firmly towards him, so my knee ran into his rock-hard stomach. I lay on my back, my arms arched above my body, my breasts exposed, nipples taut, my legs spread wantonly, and goose bumps rising to the surface of my skin. My breaths were shallow, and I shut my eyes, trying to revel in the purity of this feeling, this readiness.

Dylan ran the cool back of his hand up one thigh and down the other, again and again, making a circuit but only ever just touching or just missing my damp core. God, it felt good. He wanted me soaking wet, and I would be.

"I know you feel like I'm not telling you everything."

My eyes shot to his. Now? Was he going to open up to me now?

"I—" I started in a husky whisper.

"Shh, baby. I know." He moved entirely on top of me, my face framed by his forearms, his body tenting mine. I was practically shivering from physical anticipation underneath him, and now I was also out of my mind with anticipation for what he was going to say.

He was holding my wrists in his hands, stroking my palms, and he had kneed my legs apart and settled between them, hovering above me. Unbearably, our bodies were not touching anywhere except our hands and where he held my legs apart with his knees.

"Damsel. I don't talk about my business or my family. I never have—I've told you more than I've ever told anyone."

"Dylan—"

"And I know I've not been around as much as you deserve."

He let his body drop a fraction, the air between us getting warmer. "But be patient. Let me take care of you. Trust me." He kissed my lips hard, firm, conveying the seriousness of his request. "Trust me to protect you."

"No," I said firmly, surprising even myself and feeling the warmth dissipate.

He tried to silence me with a kiss, but I turned my face, only to find him confused, annoyed even. But fuck it. He wasn't going to get away with only pretending to open up to me. I wanted him to keep doing what he'd been doing—Christ, he was so freaking good at seducing me that stopping him required a willpower I hadn't known I possessed—but in my gut I knew that I couldn't just keep waiting for him to open up to me.

"Lydia?"

"Nope. You're talking to me," I said, inching up into a seated position and bringing the sheet with me to cover my breasts.

"About what?" He reached for the sheet, but I slapped his hands away.

"No, sir, not until we talk. About all of it. About your crazy need to protect me. About what's going on at work, with your father. Anything. Everything. I know you're seeing a lot of your dad, and it's upsetting to you, but I don't know why, not really. I know you're working for him—or I do now, thanks to Will—but again, I don't know why. And I know there are things you're not telling me about whoever is emailing me. There's all of that, but it's more. There is just ambient tension around you. You were in another place entirely last night."

"But last night was lovely—"

"Yes, eventually, after I roped you back in. After I *distracted* you by putting your hand between my legs. Dylan, I want you to *talk* to me."

Silence.

A sigh.

"Lydia," he started, but he didn't continue.

"Dylan," I replied, trying my best to convey that I was serious.

Dylan looked at me as though he were lost, as though no one had ever asked this of him in his life. Like I was asking him to jump into a volcano or swim with sharks. And I realized in that moment no one probably ever *had* asked him. Not only that, but it was highly likely that no one had ever really communicated with *him*. Maybe if I wanted him to open up to me I needed to do more of it myself. Maybe I wasn't communicating with *him* either.

I let the silence remain between us for another moment, giving him a chance to start speaking, and when he didn't, I took a deep breath and decided to try leading by example.

"I'll go first," I said. "I'm scared." I felt my chest tighten a little as I thought about what I was saying—this *was* hard.

He looked at me again, longer, harder, almost as though me saying something so bold, so vulnerable, was tilting his world into a different axis.

"I think about my dad every day," I continued, taking a deep breath, tightening the sheet around me, and inching closer to him. "I think about how wrong it feels that I am in love with you, and my father didn't even get to *know* you. I think about how I am living in a new city, a city he once lived in with my mother, the city where I was born, and I don't get to tell him I am finally seeing it, that I get it, that I see what is so beautiful about this place. I think about how you shut down after seeing *your* father, and it must be something so intense that is happening between you two—something so painful or stressful or scary or maybe even good sometimes—but how you won't share it with me, not really.

And how *that*, even more than not being able to talk to my father, *that* makes me feel alone. That very fact scares me."

I glanced up and Dylan's eyes were glassy, his hand smooth on my back.

"So please," I pleaded. "Talk to me."

"Lydia," he said again. "I…"

I waited, my hand on his chest, unflinching, as though if I moved I risked reminding him that he was someone who never shared anything with me.

"What you want from me…I can't…." He sounded sad as he said this. "I don't…" He sighed again, and I could feel the sadness in his chest, his shoulders. "I just need you to trust that I tell you everything I can, trust that I love you. You know more about me than anyone."

I waited a moment longer, waited for a conversation that might still happen.

"I do," I said, because I didn't doubt that.

"Your father sounds like a good man," he said after a few moments.

"He was," I said, and as I said it, he pulled me down to lie next to him and stroked my side, as though he knew the tears were forming in my eyes.

"My father isn't a good man," he said, and the way he said it I knew that it was more of a confession than it even sounded.

His grip on me grew tighter. He kissed the top of my head and then pulled me up as he slid down, bringing us face-to-face. He looked at me for a long moment.

"I'm sorry, baby. I know you want more from me. I'll try," he whispered, and he kissed my cheek, each of my eyelids, my lips. Then my neck more firmly as his hand reached for my breasts. "I'll give you everything. I will."

With each kiss he tried to tell me that even if I didn't understand all he was going through, even if he couldn't fully open up to me, that it was all there for me, waiting. It felt like a promise. And it was so close to enough.

"Move in with me," he said, as he did at least once a week, and his kisses became more forceful, deeper, begging.

"No," I replied, half-smiling at his predictable plea but half-sad as he kissed my collarbone. I couldn't give him more until he gave more to me.

He grunted in frustration, and even with the disappointment of not knowing more, of still feeling in the dark, and even though I knew I might be fooling myself, I let him promise me that there was more to come.

* * *

Later that morning we sauntered down the high street—or more accurately, I sauntered and Dylan took march-like strides, pausing to impatiently wait for me every once in a while. It was as though as soon as we were out of the house, out of our bed, his stress, his Dylan-esque need for efficiency took hold. During the week I was all for the urban power walk through city streets, but on a weekend I just wanted to relax with him, not check things off some invisible list.

Dylan got a phone call and gave me the one-minute sign with his finger as I window-shopped while I sipped my coffee. The store I stood in front of was just opening, and I ducked inside. The sign read LOCK & CO. It was a proper hat shop, and I wanted to touch those hats, try them on. Milliners were definitely not something we had in such abundance back in New York.

I browsed the men's hats, arranged and labeled by type: trilby, homburg, fedora, panama. And I had the realization that these esoteric names, these specialty hats, were oddities in my world, costumes or something a hipster Brooklyn guy would wear and talk about to sound cool. But Dylan probably knew just the occasion for a Vienna fedora versus a Town Coke; in fact, he probably owned versions of these somewhere and maybe even wore them for their intended uses. On one hand, it was so cool—my boyfriend was of this deep, traditional, storied past, and I thought it was beautiful and unique and odd, all at once. On the other hand, even a simple hat seemed to symbolize the gulf between our worlds.

I picked one up from the ladies' section, a purple disk purporting to be a hat, with a thick fan of felt feathers radiating from its side, and I stood in front of the mirror. I was holding the hat perched on my brow, experimenting, when my phone buzzed in my pocket. I looked out the shop window and Dylan was pacing in front of the store, still on his phone. I looked down at my own and saw it was a text message from Fiona.

SUNDAY, 9:45 am
Don't freak out, but also maybe don't look at the *Daily Mirror*?

Oh fuck.

I hastily put the hat down, skewed and out of place on the table, and walked out of the shop. Whatever was in the *Daily Mirror* was obviously bad. And there was no way the deep, aching pit in my stomach was going to go away before I knew exactly what it was.

I walked past Dylan, who immediately started to follow while chattering away about mahogany from Brazil, oblivious to my anxiety, and I approached the first newsagent I saw.

I didn't even have to go inside.

There. Outside the shop, on the tented sandwich board, was pinned an enlarged copy of the newspaper's front page. A huge picture of me in that gorgeous green dress at the Serpentine. Standing next to Dylan, who was charmingly engaged in conversation with his ex-fiancée. But I was looking off to the side, away from him, with an unmistakable look of displeasure on my face. The headline, bold, in white capital letters:

Trouble in Paradise for DyLy?

Those fucking shoes.

Or more accurately, my fucking inability to ignore the pain I felt because of those shoes. I hated this. I felt dirty. I felt guilty, like somehow my expression had been about Dylan, which of course it hadn't. But it was like the newspaper somehow made it true. Or that he would think it had been about him. Or his parents would. Or Caroline. Or Hannah. That anyone would believe this made me cringe. I hated this, and I hated myself in that moment. How could I have been so careless? How could I have let my guard down?

The thing in *HELLO!* magazine had been both of our faults, but this fell on me. Then again, this *wasn't* my fault. How was I supposed to know that I couldn't even flinch or a photographer would catch it? This whole thing felt like a glaring sign that I wasn't *good* at this, that I didn't know what I was doing.

I felt Dylan's quiet presence behind me as I stood there, staring at the sandwich board, willing its contents to change. I knew what my best friend, Daphne, would say if she were here and not back in New York: *This would pass.* That it felt bad now but in a few days no one would be thinking about it. That these things simply happen, and they are not the end of the world. Intellectually, I knew that was all true. But it was the sudden lack of control over how I was perceived in the world and the fact this affected more than just me that had me spinning, wishing I could turn back time. The panic was making my chest tight, making it hard to breathe. He wrapped his arms around me, holding me against his body.

"It's all right," he said quietly.

I just shook my head, horrified, and threw his arms off of me. I was both paralyzed and agitated. I wanted to be comforted and to crawl out of my own skin. I was furious, with no one but myself. How couldn't he be too? "It's not all right! What if people think it's true? Look what I've done!" I said, dejected, pointing to the sign.

"What *they've* done—" Dylan started, trying to interrupt me.

"No. I shouldn't have been so careless. I made such a rookie mistake, letting something as silly as discomfort show on my face, when I knew full well that photographers were there." A woman passing turned her head, and I immediately pulled myself together, tried to put on a blank expression, and started walking back towards my house. Game face: on.

But Dylan grabbed me by both arms, halting me, and pulled me back into his chest. We were off to the side, under the awning of a coffee shop. I felt a single tear escape from my eyes, as though simply being held firmly by him had allowed me to release some of the panic.

"Listen to me, damsel." Dylan spoke quietly and calmly into my ear from behind. "The photographers at that party had been vetted. Someone's head will roll for selling this photo—I promise you that. This *isn't* your fault. This takes practice. You were stunning that night, lovely, and this asshole got one off moment." He turned me around towards him, and wrapping his large hand around the base of my head and arching my lips to his, he kissed me. He kissed me with possession and fervor. He kissed me to reassure me that he knew what the paper said was crap, that there wasn't an ounce of trouble in DyLy land. He kissed me to calm me down and bring me back to us, to our safe bubble.

But the problem was that with every day that bubble felt smaller and smaller, and the aggressive world outside seemed to be pushing against its walls. And I didn't know how to make it stop.

Chapter 9

That afternoon Dylan had to go into the office at Hale Architecture and Design. He probably could have pushed off whatever project he was working on—he was the boss after all, and it wasn't as though he was hurting for clients. But I had a feeling it was more about him needing to go and work on what he loved, to stay connected to his craft, to design. The more often he saw his dad, the more time he spent at Humboldt Park and at Hale Shipping, the more he needed to draft and, cruelly, the less time he had to do it.

While he was doing that, I settled onto the couch and called Daphne.

"So how are things with His Royal Highness?" she asked, never missing an opportunity to make fun of Dylan for his aristocratic title and life. She'd recently addressed an email to both of us: *To my best friend and the Baron of the Bedroom*, which prompted a conversation between Dylan and I about exactly *how* much I'd shared with Daphne about our sex life. I'd told him she was part of the package and that he got exactly zero say in what I revealed to her. After that he started referring to her as the *Minister of Internal Affairs.*

"Busy," I replied quickly.

"Well, thankfully he wasn't too busy to have Thomas arrange my flight over for Thanksgiving," she said, "which was awfully accommodating of him. I'll have to think of something nice to do for that duke and his court jester."

"Which one is Dylan?" I asked, harboring a suspicion.

"The court jester. Obviously," she said. "He—Thomas, I mean—said he needed a copy of my passport and my social security number first, something about security?"

I breathed through my lips, annoyed on her behalf. "I know. It seems ridiculous, but Dylan's security people are taking things to a new level given this whole email situation. I'm sorry. Do you mind?"

"Of course not. It's not like I have anything to hide, except you know, my porn-y search history on my computer."

"Like you watch porn," I said sarcastically as I removed the sea-green nail polish from my toes with a cotton ball, but she was mysteriously silent on the other end. "Wait. Daphne. Do you? Watch porn?" Silence. "Daphne!"

"I plead the fifth." I could practically see her zipping her lips with her fingers as she spoke.

"No way! Like what? What are you into?" I'd abandoned the nail polish removing instantly. This was too good.

"No. I'm not doing this."

"You so are."

"I'm so not!"

"I told you about that night at Dylan's country house!"

"But only because someone creepy emailed you about it!" She was protesting through an audible smile, giving herself away completely.

"You're so annoying. I will so get this out of you," I said, and

I would. "Speaking of, I received another email last week."

"Oh god. Really?" she asked, and I could hear all the concern in her voice.

"Yeah."

"Are you okay? Wanna talk about it?" she asked, and I could tell she was settling in for a good long chat.

"Nah. I'm never without Dylan or Frank around, and I don't *really* think I'm in danger anyway. The worst part is just having it be this open-ended thing that's happening. Dylan's dealing with all of it. He's consulted with his security team, and they seem to be on it—out there gathering the passports of my best friends and who knows what else. But he hasn't really *told* me anything about it."

"What about the police?"

"He doesn't trust the police anymore. Not after some of them were complicit in tapping his phone a few years ago. If it gets worse, or if anything too threatening happens, he said he'd bring them in, but he'd rather handle it on his own. And by 'his own,' he means him and his security. On one hand, I appreciate that he wants to protect me from the whole thing, but on the other hand, I hate not knowing what's going on. This feels like it should be *our* thing to deal with, you know? I want to help. And it's the same thing with everything else in his life." I had abandoned my place on the couch and was now pacing a bit, making my way towards the kitchen, towards more wine. "Did I tell you that he's *working* for Hale Shipping now?"

"What? No. How is he doing that and running his own architecture firm? And why? I thought he had no interest in the shipping business."

"Thank you! Exactly! I should be able to answer these questions for you, but I can't. Because he doesn't talk about it. Not really. His dad is pressuring him, wants him to take over. But anytime I ask, he gives me some little tidbit and then distracts me. Asks me to trust him. It's like he's physically incapable of just saying 'Lydia—'" I began, saying my name in my Dylan accent, deep and English.

"Damsel," Daphne corrected me.

"Right. 'Damsel, so here's who I think is sending you threatening, terrifying emails, and by the way this is the history of why my relationship with my father is really complicated, and here is why I feel pressured about working with him, even though I have concerns about my own company, and I can't really talk about it easily because no one in my family talks about these things, and I didn't really get enough love as a child, and...'" My fake accent had fallen away, and I was silent for a moment. Now that I was saying out loud everything I wanted from him, it was bigger than I'd realized. "I guess these aren't simple things to talk about."

"They might not be simple, but talking about the tough stuff is important. Have *you* talked to *him*?" she asked, not-so-subtly reminding me that I had a tendency to do the same thing, especially recently.

"Yes!" I exclaimed defensively. "This morning! I told him a little about my dad, and I told him this whole not-talking-to-me thing was bothering me."

"Good. Lead by example," she said in her Daphne-knows-best tone. "Lyd, he might not be ready to talk about some of this stuff. You might have to be patient."

"You don't think this is a bad sign? That he won't open up to me? That he's always just saying 'Trust me' and expecting it to be enough?"

"Well, do you? Trust him, I mean?"

Why was that so hard to answer? I knew how wrong it would feel if I were to say I didn't—I couldn't even utter the words. They weren't true. I *did* trust him. "I do, but I just also feel like I'm waiting. I'm waiting for the part when I get to support him through whatever it is he's going through, when I get to feel more like part of a team and less like a…like a concubine," I said indignantly. I'd been trying to make her laugh, and it had worked, but it was also honest.

"Daphne?"

"Yeah?" she said calmly.

"Do you think I'm right for him?"

"Lydia!"

"Stop—I'm not having a self-esteem crisis here. I mean, is this a good idea? Are we some ill-fated *Romeo and Juliet* situation?"

"Are you guys going to commit joint suicide on me?" Now she was just being snarky and a know-it-all, a classic Daphne tell that she was getting impatient with something she thought was unreasonable. A lecture wasn't going to be far behind. Thank god. I probably needed one.

"You know what I mean! Don't you think his life might be easier for him if he was with someone who was as high-powered and high society as he is? Someone who knows how to navigate all of this press and media without causing trouble or creating *more* chaos? And don't you think *my* life would be easier if I wasn't trying to figure out how to adapt to being in the press, to walking through the world without showing emotions?"

"Good luck with that. You're the most transparent person I know."

"Daphne! I'm serious. I feel like not only do I have to learn how to be in a relationship, but I also have to learn how to dress for things, like *meeting the queen*—"

"Wait, *what*? Seriously?"

"Yeah, see what I mean? I come from a—"

"You're meeting the *queen*?! Like the real one?"

"Yes. But aren't you listening? It's the queen! And, I mean, who am I?"

"Lydia, stop. Holy hell. I can't. Okay. I mean. What are you going to *wear*?"

"Daphne!"

"Okay, okay, okay. But we're coming back to the whole queen thing. Lydia, you have a three-point-nine GPA from a leading university. You're kicking ass at your first real job. You bravely moved to a whole other country and totally landed on your feet. So this is your first time at the rodeo when it comes to the paparazzi, but you're a smart girl. Give yourself some credit. And cut yourself some slack. Dylan obviously doesn't feel this way."

I let out a slightly relieved laugh—I loved it when Daphne got onto one of her *Shut-up-and-listen-to-me-because-I-love-you* rants.. "You two can figure this out, *if you want*. Don't lose yourself, okay? Don't move in with him until you're ready. And if you really can't stand him not talking to you, well, only you can know your limits on that one. But remember that two months ago this guy told you you were going to have just a sex fling with no strings attached. Now he's fending off paparazzi and sending jets to pick up your friends."

I exhaled deeply, resigned to being baffled by this whole relationship thing.

"And I hear you about him talking to you about his dad and why that's frustrating. But I kind of see his point with the email stuff—he has a whole team of people who can handle this stuff. This seems to fall into his wheelhouse. Lydia, why are you so on edge about this exactly?"

"I just—" I couldn't finish the thought. I didn't know why, but I just felt icky. I hated screwing up with the paparazzi. I hated being the target of these emails. I hated not knowing what was going on with Dylan, not being able to make him feel better.

"Oh, I get it," she said before I could even get started.

"What?"

"Nothing," she said in a way that suggested she knew the key to my problems but didn't think I'd want to hear it, in a way that made me want to throttle her through the phone.

"Daphne!"

She sighed, and then, as I knew she would, she caved. "This isn't about you taking care of him. It's about letting him take care of you."

"What?"

"You've never done that before. I agree—he should open up to you more. And I understand that you want to support him—that's, like, your natural habitat. But compared to where he was a month ago, he might as well be a guest on *Oprah*. You, on the other hand—you've never let *anyone* take care of you."

I was silent. I didn't like where this was going.

"It's okay," she continued, and all of a sudden she had her Daphne-knows-best tone again, which drove me really crazy. "We don't have to talk about it."

"Has anyone ever told you you're really annoying?" My toes were curling into the blanket at my feet, and I felt...I felt uncomfortable. I didn't want to think about the idea that maybe I was resisting Dylan's comfort, his desire for me to trust him, his protectiveness, simply because I wasn't ready or it was too foreign. Because even if that was true, I was right to want more. I was right to want to be a *team*. I wanted to take care of him, and he wasn't letting me. But I guess I wasn't letting him either. All of a sudden what had just felt frustrating felt so *confusing*. Meanwhile, Daphne sighed and chuckled a little. "Daphne," I said, quieter than I'd been all night, "this is hard. Harder than I thought it would be."

"I know. But you love him, right?"

"So, so much."

Chapter 10

By Monday morning, I had to admit that I was happy to be rescued from a weekend plagued by my own personal foibles with the press and Dylan's ever-morphing stress. The moment I arrived at work I was balls-to-the-wall busy. Things were humming, buzzing. It was one phone call to the next, one email to another. I was totally in the zone. And thankfully Hannah seemed too distracted to confront me about my hotel tryst—either that or she didn't read *HELLO!* magazine. Either way I was grateful. At least at work, if not in the rest of my life, everything was going perfectly, and it felt amazing.

By noon, I had the store's location squared away—a small space on the ground floor of a large old banking building. Right on the corner, next to a mews. It was unassuming, but elegant. Small, but bright. And it situated Hannah Rogan right where she should be, within spitting distance of other great shops—agnès b., Carolina Herrera, Alexander McQueen, and others.

Now I was waiting for a call from the marketing team, who

would arrange the COMING SOON signs that would hide the construction. I was feverishly scanning through the information I'd been sent by our business advisor about stocking and projected sales for the spring line when our intern returned with lattes for Fiona and me and the largest portfolio carrier I'd ever seen. The poor girl looked like she was auditioning for the balancing act in the circus.

"What in god's name is that?" I asked her, rising to relieve her of the coffees.

"The interior designers, Holt and Carroll, sent a messenger, who was just leaving this with Josh when I came in," she said, huffing and ruddy cheeked from carrying it just from the reception desk. Holt and Carroll were the interior designers Dylan had used for his last two buildings, and he'd been adamant that I use them for the store. He hadn't taken kindly to me demanding a detailed pitch about their merits over dinner, but secretly I think he admired that I didn't just take his advice without question. He had, of course, been right—they were amazing—and Hannah had been over the moon about the choice.

"Ah, wow. I didn't expect to see anything from them until—" Just then Hannah swung our office door open.

"Lydia," she said, almost smiling, which for Hannah might as well have been doing jumping jacks of joy. Fiona, the intern, and I all looked up, at attention. "I just got off the phone with the team at Holt and Carroll, and they said they were sending over some swatches and plans. Oh—" she interrupted herself. "Those must be them?"

"I think so—" I started.

"I can't believe you secured them. I don't know how you did it. Did you know that they just did Jason Wu's Paris shop last year? People are *raving* about it." She was talking a mile a minute, something none of us had ever seen before. "Tom Ford apparently heard through Carolina Herrera, and he just called to congratulate me on the shop," she said in a way that was dangerously close to giddy gossip. Given her tone of voice, I half expected her to suggest we all sit down and paint each other's nails.

We all looked at each other in disbelief—this store was apparently turning out to be something bigger than I had imagined, and apparently bigger than even Hannah had imagined. She grabbed the heavy portfolio by the handle and looked right at me. "Come to my office after lunch, and we'll go through these together." As she left I was pretty sure she was actually humming.

"Well, that was unexpected," started Fiona, who then returned her gaze to her computer. "I guess we won't be going out for a cuppa later, then?" She looked at me, confirming that for what was definitely not the first time I would be ditching her last minute for something store related.

My meeting with Hannah turned out to be an all-out devouring of the materials the designers had sent over. She and I spent three hours on our hands and knees making decisions about fabrics, flooring, and couch options. I was in my element. One part business, one part collaboration, and one part creativity. We were in the flow of it. Even though Hannah was my boss, and I was pretty sure I'd always be just a little intimidated by her, it felt incredible to be collaborating, to be getting lost in something.

When I finally emerged from Hannah's office at nearly five, Josh was sitting at my desk, and he and Fiona were giggling about something on Josh's phone.

"Hey, guys," I said.

"Oh, hi," said Fiona, cooling visibly.

"Hi, lovey," said Josh, definitely with more warmth. He looked between me and Fiona, and it was clear that Josh also knew there was tension between us.

"How about a drink?" I asked, suddenly feeling the very real pull to get my friends on the right side of a bar with some proper cocktails in front of us. The flagship store was coming along perfectly, but these friendships were important, and I'd been neglecting them. I'd had to decline the last two times they'd asked me to go clubbing.

Fiona opened her mouth, and I have no idea what she would have said because Josh quickly put his hand over hers, gripped it, and answered for both of them: "Absolutely."

* * *

Twenty minutes later we were at the wine bar around the corner. Fiona and I had suggested the pub, but Josh had scoffed, claiming he was going gluten-free or something. So wine it was.

"So, ya wee Yank, fill us in. What is going on with you and the Greek god you share a bed with?" Josh curled his fingers around the stem of his wineglass and gave me a look that said *Tell me everything*.

"You have such a way with words, Josh," Fiona added.

I thought for a moment and realized that when it came to most aspects of my relationship with Dylan, they only knew what the media knew or what little bits of information I let slide about upcoming events or whether I'd spent the previous night at his place or mine.

"You know," I began, "it's weird. It's like the wall between his life—you know, all his aristocratic stuff, his architecture firm, most of his friends and, god, *his family*—that wall is just as thick, just as fortress-like, as it was when we were a secret." Josh's and Fiona's faces were still, like they'd expected more of the same from me, which is to say no real information. In that moment, I realized I'd been withholding from them the same way Dylan had been withholding from me. Keeping them at an arm's length with hollow phrases like "fine, thanks" or "busy but good"—the kinds of phrases that actually told them nothing. I'd been self-conscious about the attention from Hannah, about having my picture in the paper, about dating someone everyone seemed to know everything about. I realized I'd been receding, hoping that maybe, somehow, if I didn't say much, Josh and Fiona would not notice all of this was happening. I realized in that moment how idiotic that was, how absurd.

"I guess I just thought," I continued, "that when we went public, his personal life would be public to me too or something. Like he'd just open up. The book of Dylan would fall open, and I'd be let into the inner sanctum. But it's not like that. He's such a private person. There are still so many private hidden parts of his life. It's just that I'm not one of them anymore.

"And it's harder than I thought it would be, being a *public* part of his life, I mean. I keep ending up in the papers in a way that makes me look bad, or him, or I don't know." Josh put his hand on mine, which was resting on the table, but I noticed that Fiona remained calm and cool, leaning back in her chair. I gave them the details behind the "quickie" incident and the Serpentine Massacre.

"Aw, sweets, the media are just *vultures*, aren't they?" Josh said indignantly, and I could feel Fiona roll her eyes.

"They are, but I should have known that. He did try to warn me—I just never really understood I guess." I couldn't go into the email business—no one knew about that, so I'm sure my reactions seemed outsized to them, but my anxiety seemed to want to lay itself out on the table. "It's just an adjustment, that's all. I finally understand why he made such an effort to keep his life so simple, so private and uncomplicated for so long. And I just wish I could fix it, make things easier. But instead I feel like I'm prancing around London like some kind of fool demonstrating to everyone, every Amelia, every other person out there, that I'm not fit to be Dylan Hale's girlfriend." I exhaled through my lips, in a weird lip-fluttering sigh, and I looked and sounded defeated. Josh was sweetly rubbing my arm.

"Well, that's just bollocks, a heaping pile of rubbish," Josh said, defending me, and I smiled weakly at him.

"I know. It is, right? It's just hard to remember that in the moment. I mean, *I* know I'm fit to be his girlfriend, but it kills me to give that…that…"

"Hoity toity twat," Fiona finished for me, almost reluctantly.

"Exactly. To give the Amelia Reynoldses of this town, not to mention all the other women he's slept with," I added and rolled my eyes for good measure, "the satisfaction of thinking, even for a minute, that something's awry."

"Fuck the lot of them—that's what I say!" exclaimed Josh, and I laughed, so relieved for his vibrant, enthusiastic humor. Even Fiona couldn't help but laugh when Josh went into his overdramatic mode. "Blimey, Lydia, your life is so deliciously dramatic," he added.

"Oh, well, there's another thing," I said, looking at them to make sure I hadn't yet overstayed my welcome with Dylan talk. "I'm going to meet the queen," I said, covering my face with my hands for a moment and then only peeking out through my fingers to see their reactions. It just felt so surreal, so silly, so completely like someone else's life to be saying that out loud that I couldn't help but feel embarrassed.

"What?!" They both said in unison, and I nodded into my hands, as though they could save me from the huge part of that upcoming event that stressed me out.

We ended up setting up residence in that booth for another two hours. I told them about my upcoming tea with the queen, and they shared every story they'd ever heard about their friend's aunt's best friend who'd met Her Majesty at some point. We gossiped about the intern, we strategized about Josh's love life, and we commiserated about the horrible new HR person and the tongue lashings she'd given each of us on various occasions. But Fiona seldom looked at me—she was mad or hurt or maybe just tired of sharing an office with the girl who was dating Dylan and demanding so much of their boss's attention.

* * *

The tea with the queen *was* fast approaching, and I enlisted Dylan's sister's help in preparing. After a series of emails and texts, Emily and I had finally figured out that Friday was the day to meet up. I'd liked her when I'd met her at the Savoy, and we'd talked about getting together, and now we had a good excuse—she was going to help me figure out what on earth one was supposed to wear to meet a monarch.

I had taken the afternoon off, and Emily was taking a break from her studying. We'd decided to begin the excursion by fueling ourselves.

"Have you been here before?" she asked me. She settled into the banquette, perching her excruciatingly on-trend designer handbag on the seat beside her. Emily somehow pulled off the socialite look while also looking like the down-to-earth, kind, and funny person I was beginning to understand she was. It was on her face and in her body language—she was as smart as a whip and totally genuine. It really had to be her eyes that did it, because as soon as she slipped on those Chanel sunglasses, she looked just as cold, aristocratic, and socialite-y as the Amelia Reynoldses of the world. And technically Emily, as the daughter of a duke, outranked Amelia.

Today she was wearing a flirty floral dress that I was sure Urban Outfitters was knocking off; a trim, tailored jacket; and knee-high riding boots. With her long dark hair flowing down her back, she was a knockout. I was three years older than she was, but there was still some part of me—the Brooklyn, beer-drinking, pizza-eating part of me—that was intimidated by her.

"I haven't," I replied as I slipped into the other side of the curved, red banquette.

"I love it. The food is fabulous, and I like the atmosphere, but because it's stuck back here in the land of finance geeks, none of the usuals are ever here. I never have to worry about running into people I don't want to run into, except for maybe one of Dylan's business friends or one of my father's cronies, but none of my set, which is a relief." She nodded at a waiter or host behind me in a practiced way that was seamless.

The restaurant was a simple brasserie on the ground floor of a big banking building just a couple of blocks from the Thames.

"Perfect," I said, slumping a little in my seat with relief. Not that I was worried about seeing Emily's friends. It was more that I figured it also meant the paparazzi might be less likely to be lurking about, hoping to catch a picture of some socialite, or me. I accepted a menu and was grateful for the water being placed on our table.

"They've been rough on you guys, haven't they?" she asked, reading my mind.

"It's fine. It's part of the deal. I know that."

"Yeah, but it must be brutal. I've never had to deal with that really, unless I've been out with Dad or Dylan. That's the relief, I guess, of being neither the heir nor a spare."

"What do you mean? Aren't you the spare? And if you had been born first, wouldn't you be a duchess? Or a marchioness? Or wait—how does it work?"

Emily was already shaking her head before she began. "Primogeniture," she said, as though that explained everything. "The title and the estate only go down the male line. So it's Dylan or bust, I'm afraid." She took a sip of water before continuing, "I'm a lady, and the buck stops there, unless I acquire a different title when I marry."

"Does that bother you? I mean, that you couldn't ever inherit Humboldt Park or have the title or anything? Does it feel unfair?" Again Emily was shaking her head before I even finished.

"No. Of course it's sexist and archaic and all that, and I do believe the whole thing is a bit vestigial—how could you not? But honestly, it's a bit of a relief. For Dylan's whole life he's been groomed, handled differently, followed. His life is under a microscope. It's like he was a future duke before he could be anything else. I always felt a bit bad for him actually."

I nodded my head. It made me sad to think about that side of Dylan's life, and it just made it seem more like a miracle that he was the amazing person he was and not a complete ass. Although, now that I thought about it, he did have the reputation of being the most difficult architect to work with in the northern hemisphere.

"I will say that it seems pretty intense from where I sit."

She nodded but wisely and properly chose not to go further.

"So you've never really had to deal with this *HELLO!* magazine crap?" I finally asked.

"Not really. Like I said, only occasionally, at holidays and things. And I don't really date in this scene, so it never happens there."

I could actually feel my eyes light up. "Wait. Emily, are you seeing someone?" Emily was twenty-two and graduating from college soon. Of course she dated. But if you talked to Dylan, who of course was the only one in their family I spoke with, you'd never know it.

She paused. "Let's put it this way. I'm not single, and I'm not *not* single. And I don't go for guys that I want my father or brother to know about." She was half smiling while she said it, and now my curiosity was really piqued.

"Emily—"

"Sorry, Lydia. You're sharing a bed with the number two enemy of my love life. We'll have to get to know each other a lot better before I drop any more hints."

I laughed out loud, a release I needed. "Got it. Fair enough. You're a canny one, aren't you?"

She laughed at that but also gave me a wink. Something told me Emily was not to be underestimated. "So," she said, "tell me about this store of yours."

I told her all the details I could about the design and the approach, the long-term plan, and, to my surprise, she was riveted.

"You know," she said, "you might want to think of a concierge service."

"A what?" I asked, suddenly panicked that maybe there was some obvious feature I'd missed.

"Well, Hannah originally wanted a private studio, right?"

I nodded in affirmation.

"But now it's a flagship store, which in some ways is the opposite, at least in terms of the elite being able to feel elite." She was totally right. "So that doesn't completely solve Hannah's problem of the increase in orders from people like Amelia Reynolds," she added, making a gagging gesture that made me laugh out loud and kind of shocked me coming out of her posh mouth.

"You know, you're right."

"A concierge service would be like a private VIP aspect of the store, appointment only, certain designs only available that way, etcetera."

"Emily, that's kind of genius."

"Eh, I've been around."

"No, seriously, I think I should bring you on as a consultant or something."

"Not necessary. Just promise me you won't tell Dylan that there is anything to even be hinted at regarding my love life. Fair?"

"Deal. But there is one other request," I added quickly.

"Oh?"

"Come to Dylan's for Thanksgiving dinner?" I looked at her expectantly as she sipped her wine. "It's in a month, a Thursday night. I'm going to do the whole American thing—turkey, pie, maybe even some pilgrim decorations. They were, after all, your people. I've invited my friends from work as well, and Dylan's friend Will. Please come."

Emily gave me the warmest smile. "I'd love to."

"Good," I said, and I looked down to realize our plates were empty, which meant the whole purpose of this visit was about to begin.

"Okay," she said, zipping up her fancy handbag, "let's do this. Tea with Her Majesty."

"Right," I said. "Thank god you're here. This is one area where I have zero confidence in how I should dress, and I don't think anyone else at my office has any idea either. And Dylan—"

"All Dylan has to do is put on a more conservative tie. You're a totally different story." Emily dropped her bills on the table next to mine, and we headed for the door. "First stop, Harvey Nichols."

"Okay, but remember," I said, climbing into the back of the Jaguar. It was raining, and Frank held the umbrella over our heads while we ducked in. "I don't have the Hale budget. We need 'good enough for Her Majesty' on a second assistant's dime."

Settled into the car, Emily pulled out a black credit card. "Ah, but we do have the Hale budget. Dylan told me to use his credit card."

"First, do you mind if I ask why you have Dylan's credit card?"

"Oh, there was this one time I went to Chamonix over school holidays. It was my first time abroad without our parents, and he wanted me to have a backup emergency card in case I got into any trouble I wouldn't want to tell our parents about," she explained as she tucked the card back into her wallet. "He might see me as an infant half the time, but he really does take care of me."

I thought for a moment about what it must be like to have a sibling. I'd always thought Daphne was like that, and she was, to some degree. But sharing your parents was a whole other thing—the enormity of having another person who knew your family life as well as you did, of sharing that with someone, settled over me. I was so happy for Emily that she had Dylan. Happy for Dylan too.

"Okay. Well, more importantly, no. I don't allow Dylan to buy me clothes. He knows better," I said reflexively.

"He'll be furious if I let you pay. Dressing for the queen is no joke." To be fair, Emily did look a little nervous, and the truth was I wouldn't even be *seeing* the queen if it weren't for him. I thought of what Daphne had said, that I didn't let people take care of me, and I figured fuck it—if there was ever a time to let Dylan spend his money on me, this was it.

"Lydia, I really think you should let—"

"Okay," I said, taking a deep inhale and letting myself smile at the idea of this shopping trip. Emily had been looking at me, ready to argue, but she stopped herself and smiled.

"Good," she said, clearly pleased with herself. "Now let's do this."

Shopping with Emily was an entirely different experience. The girl was like a ninja, expertly eyeing, selecting, and dismissing with only a glance or sometimes a quick touch of a garment. She nixed one dress I found because it was too short. "Think about sitting with your legs to the side—that will show way too much thigh."

"Right," I said and kept digging.

She nixed another for being too bright. "This is the queen, not a rave." Another for having straps too narrow. "You want your bra straps to peek out?" No. No, I did not.

Another for being too low-cut. "Remember, you'll be bending to curtsy, and she does not need to see your cleavage." Oh, Christ. All of a sudden I had flashbacks to the ridiculous and clearly failed attempts at my curtsey with Fiona. "Don't worry, we'll cover that later." Thank god.

After three hours of scouring the racks and trying on various skirt suits and dresses with jackets, Emily shrieked from a far corner of the store. She came running towards me carrying a black-and-white garment flapping around on a hanger.

"This is it. Put those down," she said, indicating to the *maybe*s I'd been carting around.

When I emerged from the fitting room, I had to agree with her. It was one of those rare finds. A one-off, only in my size. The A-line skirt came to just above my knees, and the dress had a high neck and three-quarter sleeves. It was a warm white with black naturalistic flowers growing from the waist up the bodice and down the skirt. It felt almost Victorian in the pattern, but it was high fashion and modern. And it fit me like it'd been made for my body. I looked at the price tag and gulped when I saw it was nearly thirteen hundred pounds—the *sale* price. I didn't tell Emily, but knowing it was on sale made the whole thing easier to swallow. I may have been letting Dylan pay for that dress, but taking the thriftiness out of this Brooklyn girl was going to re-quire more than one shopping trip.

"I love it. I mean, I really love it." I looked at myself in the mirror and couldn't believe how great I looked. It was one thing to feel like this when I was standing in Hannah's studio being gussied up by professionals, but when I saw this kind of dress on me in a regular old fitting room it was almost alarming, like one of the first real signs that dating Dylan and everything that meant for my personal life was real. I was really going to meet the queen. With my boyfriend. Who was a marquess. Holy shit.

Chapter 11

An hour later the garment bag was hanging off one of the chairs in my kitchen, and Emily and I were collapsed on my couch.

"Good. Now, you have black heels, right?" she asked, looking at me in a way that suggested she was trying to tell me what shoes to wear but disguising it as a question. It was kind of lovable actually.

I nodded, thinking of the Manolo Blahniks Dylan had gotten me for my birthday.

"I seriously don't know how I could have done this without you," I said, sipping from a glass of wine. A bottle of the good stuff Dylan had hidden away in my house.

"You'll do fine. She's actually really nice. Kind of like a really reserved grandma. Only, you know, with way more power and some gravity-defying hair."

I laughed, and it started out like a normal chuckle. But I was so tired, I'd had just enough wine, and I was worn out enough that it turned into one of those belly laughs I couldn't control. I heard myself uttering nonsense like "curtsy" and "cleavage" and "grandma" and just laughed. Emily thought I was nuts at first, but the thing about laughter is that it's contagious, and within minutes we were both crying.

"I really like you, Emily," I sputtered while catching my breath and wiping a laugh tear from my cheek.

"Aww, that's so American of you, telling me that! I like you too." I was pretty sure Emily and I would have been friends no matter how we met—it's just that we probably never would have met otherwise. "So are you seeing my stuffy, cranky older brother tonight?" she asked.

"Who knows?" I said. "I mean, yes. He's coming over, but lately I'm asleep when he comes home."

"He's been awfully busy lately, hasn't he? Although not nearly as hostile, which is probably due to you. Thank you for that."

"No problem."

"Father's been taking him to task. The two of them always seem to be seething at one another." Emily's eyes were closed while she talked, her head leaning against the top of the couch. We were both destroyed by our afternoon shopping. But I couldn't help wanting to know more. I wanted to probe, to get her to tell me everything, but I knew that would just put her in an awkward position.

"He's taking me to Humboldt Park tomorrow," I said and looked at her for her reaction. Her eyes opened and her eyebrows rose. "I haven't seen your parents since the party at the Savoy."

Emily leaned forward, putting her elbows on her knees. "Don't let them intimidate you, okay?" she said, but before I could press her for more information her cell phone rang. While she chatted on the phone, I brought the dress upstairs and poured some more wine.

"I've got to be off," she said, and she was smiling. I'd bet my left arm it had to do with whatever mystery guy she was dating or not dating. She came over and kissed each of my cheeks. She was already at the door when she added, "And don't fret about tomorrow. Dylan will be with you, and he'd probably murder our parents if they treat you with any less respect than you deserve. I've never seen him so protective before. Well, at least not with anyone other than me."

* * *

I realized that I hadn't checked my phone in hours, so I took it from my bag and began scrolling through the notifications. I'd missed a few calls from work, a text from Josh, and texts from Dylan.

FRIDAY, 1:15 pm
Emily just texted. Finally letting me buy you a dress, are you? Did I just cross over into an alternate universe?

FRIDAY, 3:56 pm
Home at half 7. Don't eat. I'm cooking you dinner as a reward. XX

Dylan cooking? That was a surprise. I texted him back.

FRIDAY, 5:26 pm
Well, hurry up then, Hale. I'm hungry! XX

It was only five thirty, so I had some time to recover from the day. I was beat, and all I wanted to do was collapse and watch the episodes of *The Bachelor* that Daphne had put on DVD and sent over to me. Which was exactly what I was about to do when the doorbell rang. I looked out the window, and it was pouring rain. Whoever was out there was getting soaked, so I jumped up to get to the door.

"Michael!" I said, probably sounding more surprised than was polite.

We'd spoken once or twice in recent weeks—about the package at my door, which Frank had picked up, and he'd called about what he thought might be an animal in my yard—but I had only *seen* Michael once since that evening when he'd come by only to have me rudely shut the door in his face. Dylan had forced us to retreat to his house to escape my neighbor's attentions, which I still found absurd. He was a sweet guy, and harmless, I was sure.

"Um, come in," I said after too long of a moment. He was getting completely drenched on my doorstep. I stepped aside, and sure enough, a puddle was forming beneath him. "Do you, um, want a towel? Are you locked out or do you need anything?"

Michael stood there, dripping, looking sheepish. Was it really raining that hard out? I looked past him to the window.

"Coffee? Can I get you coffee or tea?" Was he okay? I couldn't figure out why he wasn't saying anything. Another moment went by. It was getting awkward.

"I've been standing outside your door for a half hour," he finally said.

I looked at him, confused.

"Trying to get the courage to ring the bell," he continued.

I looked him over and only then saw the hard copy of *HELLO!* magazine in his hand. Even from the side and even soaked I could tell it was turned to the page with the pictures of me and Dylan from the hotel. Oh god, had he really *not* known about me and Dylan?

"Michael—"

"No—" He stopped me and looked up. "I'm sorry for being awkward. This is terribly rude. I've been rather foolish, haven't I? And I wanted to apologize."

"Oh, that's not necessary, Michael—" But he held up his hand.

"I like you, Lydia. Obviously. But had I known that you were involved with *Dylan Hale*," he said, rubbing his forehead with his hand. He suddenly looked up, slightly panicked and looking around. "Oh god, he's not here, is he?"

I shook my head.

"Well, I'd like to think I would fight to date you no matter what, but I fear I don't stand a chance against a man like that."

"Michael, that has nothing to do with it. You'd stand a chance with any girl, and any girl would be lucky to have you fighting for her." I could see his chest letting down, his sigh of defeat. "Dylan is the person I fell in love with, but it's not about power or money or anything. It's just…I'm sorry."

"You love him?"

"I do."

"Will you tell me if you break up?"

I smiled halfheartedly. "Sure. But, Michael, I think you can do better than being someone's rebound. Don't you? You're a catch."

Michael looked up through his sopping brow and smirked a little. "You think so?"

"Of course!"

He smiled and then looked back down at the magazine in his hands. "You two look good together."

"Thanks," I said, but I couldn't help feeling that those pictures didn't tell the whole story. They showed us flirty and lovey, but they didn't reflect how I felt at the moment. I was in love, but I also felt far away from Dylan, and that feeling was nowhere to be seen in the pictures.

"You sure you don't want some tea? Or a towel?" I asked as Michael started to head towards the door.

"Nah, that's all right. Thanks for letting me in."

"Of course! Hey," I said, stopping him. "You should come to our Thanksgiving dinner. It's at Dylan's in a few weeks."

"Really? You don't think that'd be awkward? Is that really a good idea?"

It would definitely be awkward, and this was probably a horrible idea. "Of course!"

Dylan would just have to get over it. Where I came from, everyone was invited to Thanksgiving. Especially soggy, sad guys on your doorstep whom you've just rejected.

* * *

"You bloody invited him to dinner?" Dylan was trying not to yell, but he was kind of yelling. Or was on the verge of it—he was using his big bad architect voice.

"Where I come from, everyone is invited to Thanksgiving," I said, going to the refrigerator for the wine.

"Wait, since when are we hosting Thanksgiving dinner anyway?" he asked, rummaging through my cupboards for clean glasses.

"I emailed you about this on Thursday. You said okay."

"I did?" He had the glasses in one hand and was rubbing his temple with the other.

I couldn't believe him. "Seriously?"

He turned around. "No, rather, I do remember that now. Sorry—it's been a hellish week."

I went up behind him and wrapped my arms around his waist, resting my cheek on his T-shirt. He'd worn dark jeans and a faded grey T-shirt under his leather jacket to work today, and I loved it when he was all relaxed. At least relaxed looking.

"It will be fine—it was the generous thing to do, invite him."

"But he said he *likes* you."

"Yeah, but I like *you*," I said, and he turned in my arms so we were hugging and kissed the top of my head. I could hear the glasses clinking behind my back. "I love you."

He pulled away to look at me. "I suppose I'll be there to defend your honor, damsel," he said with a little too much of a twinkle in his eye, like he couldn't wait to have the chance to humiliate poor Michael or hit him or something else boorish and adolescent.

He shook his head with acceptance, and then I felt him chuckle into my hair.

"Like you've left me with any honor to defend, *knighty*," I scoffed, imagining all of the ridiculously dishonorable things he'd done to my body over the past couple of months. He gave my ass a quick slap, and I jumped a little in his arms.

"Okay, dinnertime," he said while stepping back and rubbing his palms together.

"This oughtta be good."

"Oh, ye of little faith," Dylan replied, rolling up his sleeves and tying my floral apron around his waist. I flung myself onto the countertop next to the place where he was setting up his cutting board and ingredients. I gripped the edge of the counter and leaned over, examining his project. "You know, there are plenty of chairs," he added, smirking at me.

"Where's the fun in *chairs*?" I asked as I ate a small chunk of Parmesan that had found its way off the cutting board. "What are you making?"

"Gnocchi."

I raised my eyebrows. "I don't see any potatoes."

"Not that kind of gnocchi," he replied in a way that clearly conveyed that I was not supposed to ask any more questions. So I sat there, dangling my feet, wine in hand, and watched him cook. He put on some Louis Armstrong and just did his thing.

Forty minutes later I was taking my first bite of something that could best be described as a cloud. A cloud dripping with the most flavorful olive oil I'd ever tasted.

"Holy fuck, what is this?" I mumbled, and Dylan just chuckled.

"Ricotta gnocchi with sage," he said.

"How did you learn to make it?"

Dylan shrugged. "I was in Florence for a summer studying with an architect there. His mother was an amazing cook." As though that explained everything. As though it didn't open up an entirely new folder in the Dylan part of my brain now labeled *Sweet Young Man Who Learns Italian Cooking from an Old Lady*. As if that entire folder didn't make me love him just a little more.

"Well, now I feel like a prostitute, because I will definitely have as much sex with you as you'd like in exchange for this," I said.

"You'd be a terrible prostitute."

"Excuse me, but I think I'd be fabulous," I protested.

"You're far too generous a lover," he said, leaning over my plate and kissing me with his wine-flavored lips. "You'd go broke."

We ate slowly, savoring, and I was so grateful to feel calm after a week when I'd felt nervous about us, uncertain.

I told him about the day I'd had with his sister, and he smiled curiously through the whole description, as though he'd never seen her the way I did.

"What?" I finally asked. "Why are you smiling like that?"

"You two have become fast friends, haven't you?" he asked, almost surprised, curious.

"She's kind of awesome," I said. "In case you hadn't noticed."

After dinner Dylan mumbled about being coated in cheese and flour and went upstairs to take a shower. I pulled on a T-shirt and sleep shorts and crawled over the bed, ready to nestle in with a book while I waited for him. As I pushed the duvet aside, Dylan's slick leather laptop bag fell to the floor, and a small stack of papers spread out from its unzipped top. I went to pick them up and paused when I saw my own name.

It was an email. To Dylan. Just like the ones I'd received—a series of random digits as the sender. The subject line was just my name, in all capital letters: *LYDIA*. And the body had one line of text:

You won't be able to protect her forever.

Below the text was an icon indicating that an audio file had been attached.

I stood there, stock-still, staring down at the email. I looked at the date. It had arrived three days earlier.

I heard Dylan emerge from the bathroom. I could feel the steam enter the room. I could smell his body wash on him, feel the heat coming from his body, but I couldn't look at him. I just held the slim paper in my hand.

"Three days ago?"

"Lydia—"

"You got this three days ago and didn't tell me? I thought you were going to tell me if there was any new information!"

"There was no need to worry you—you're safe." Dylan was now standing right in front of me, his warm, damp hand cupping my chin, trying to coax me to look at him.

"What was in the audio file?" I demanded, shaking my face free of his hand.

"Lydia, it's not important. I've got it handled." He was withdrawing at the same rate I was.

"Dylan," I said, all the warmth from the evening gone.

He sighed, his hands dropping to his towel-clad hips.

"It was a recording of a conversation between Frank Abbott and me. Discussing your schedule. We were discussing when there might be a couple of gaps—when he couldn't be there, and neither could I."

My eyes went wide. I really hadn't thought I was in any danger, but this scared me. All of a sudden I didn't think of Frank as a lumberjack so much as a ninja, a ninja I wanted around.

He must have seen the look of fear in my eyes, because he put his warm hands around my upper arms and looked me straight in the eye as he said, "You're safe. There are no gaps in your coverage. I promise. Because I had to be somewhere, he and I solved the problem over text immediately after this recorded conversation, but the person recording us clearly wouldn't have known that."

"But—"

"Look, this asshole hasn't been able to get close enough to you to get any more intimate pictures. That scare tactic is off the table. So he went directly to me. We found the recording device. It was stuck to some flowers that were delivered to Thomas from Alex."

"Why didn't you tell me any of this? I've been wandering around thinking everything was status quo, and *now* I find out that this lunatic knows all of these things about my schedule, is looking for times when I won't have any protection?!" I was trying not to sound panicked, but I knew I was failing.

"Good."

"What? What do you mean, 'good'?"

"I mean, I didn't *want* you to worry. The whole point was for you to be able to go about your day *not* worrying."

I groaned and grunted and threw up my arms in frustration.

"Dylan," I began, "I don't want you to handle all this on your own. I want to help. I want to be involved. I want to know what's going on." Inside I was an indecipherable swirl of hurt and sadness, anger and frustration. Outwardly I was just exhausted. Mere hours ago I had been shopping for a dress to wear to tea with the queen, and now I was discussing whether or not our threatening cyberstalker was getting closer to committing actual harm.

He pulled me to his chest and held me tightly. "Damsel. Let me take care of this. I won't let anything happen to you. This is my world. You don't know how these assholes work—"

"And you do?" I asked, pushing my palms against his chest and creating distance. Since when did being a marquess involve investigating criminal activity?

"I do," he said firmly. I looked into his eyes, and he did.

"But you're not going to tell me how you know."

He stood there silently, not budging.

"I think you should go," I said. Not fully believing the words myself until they were out of my mouth.

"What?"

"I'm mad, Dylan. You promised to keep me posted. You

promised to tell me what was going on with this. This is *worse* than just having some weirdo freak emailing me."

"You want me to *leave*?" he asked, still incredulous.

"Either talk or leave." I stood there, my arms crossed. Just as mad about ruining what had been shaping up to be a perfectly lovely night at home with him as I was about him not talking to me about this in the first place.

"I can't," he said, sitting on the bed.

"Dylan!"

"No, seriously, I really can't. The people I am quite sure are behind this are dangerous, Lydia. Frank isn't around for no reason. I wouldn't hire security for you if I thought this was some prank."

"So you *do* know who it is?"

He shook his head. "Not for certain. I've not been able to confirm it, but I'm ninety-nine percent sure."

"And you won't tell me?" I was still standing, partly in shock that he was actually communicating, partly just eager for this information.

"I'll tell you at some point—" I rolled my eyes, and threw my hands in the air. "Lydia, I'll tell you when I know what the situation is. Right now I don't want to expose you to any more. It's sensitive information. It involves my father and some horrible decisions he made, and it involves some…criminal information." I opened my mouth, about to press him further, but he gave me a look that said *Please don't.*

"Baby," he continued, and he fell back onto the bed, grabbing one of my pillows and tucking it under his head. "My father…" He exhaled and rested his forearm over his eyes. I remained standing, still not quite ready to give in. "When I left secondary school, I had top marks and was already certain I wanted to be an architect. My family had taken a trip to Los Angeles when I was fifteen, and I'd seen the Getty Center. Have you been there?"

I shook my head.

"God, its stunning. Architectural perfection. I was mesmerized. When I got home, I took in everything I could. I read every book." I felt myself give a little, crawled onto the bed, rested my head on his shoulder, and placed my palm on his flat, bare stomach, somehow trying to coax more words from him. "Of course I knew that someday I'd be Duke of Abingdon, but my grandfather ran *his* own company while he was duke, and he enjoyed my newfound passion. He even took me on a trip to Paris to look at Le Corbusier's buildings. He encouraged me."

"He sounds amazing—I wish I could have met him." I felt myself soften even more.

"As do I," he said and wrapped his arm around my middle. "God, I had so much energy for it. I was feverish. I went to Cambridge and studied with a fabulous professor. By the end of the first term I had even earned a spot working with him, a kind of apprenticeship—we'd be designing council housing blocks, providing a real service and doing it well, solving problems. I'd found what I wanted to do with my life, and I was *good* at it."

"That's incredible, and you are. You're amazing at it," I said softly, letting my anger fade. He was talking. He was telling me what he *could* tell me, even if it wasn't the information I'd asked for. And I was all ears.

"Then I came home for Christmas. I felt so alive. I couldn't wait to tell my parents. I won't ever forget this conversation." He paused for a moment, and I thought I could feel him cringe or gulp, like he was bracing himself.

"I came into the library. The fire was roaring. My parents already had their drinks, of course. Emily was off watching the telly or something. It just spilled out of me—the courses, what I'd been learning, the apprenticeship, all of it. I remember my mother smiling, but it was almost a sad smile, and my father told her to leave the room. She gave me one of her patented non-hug hugs without saying a word and left. My father said it was time I grew up, that he barely recognized me as his son. That I was living some pipe dream. He wondered at how I could have missed that my job—my *only* job—was to fill his shoes. To run Hale Shipping. To be duke. Why else would he have had a son?"

"He said that to you?" I asked, flabbergasted.

"He said that I shouldn't make the mistake of thinking my life was my own. He couldn't understand why my grandfather had ever encouraged me. He eventually conceded, in as disgusted a way as possible, that I was free to do what I would while at university, as long as I understood what my real obligations were. That he hoped by the time I was done with Cambridge I would have come to my senses."

Dylan spoke in such a detached way that I understood it was too painful for him to remember. He'd told me before about his early childhood, his parents instilling him with a sense of duty, but I hadn't realized that he had held on to hope for so long, that he must have been an optimistic child and adolescent in spite of his parents. That it wasn't those early toddler moments that had crushed him, changed him, but this moment. The one he shared so vividly with me now.

"I'm so sorry, Dylan. No father should say those things to his son," I said, stroking his stomach and laying a kiss on his chest. "I don't understand—your grandfather sounds so wonderful, so open-minded, like such a vibrant person. How did your father become so cruel?"

"I honestly don't know. But it changed me. I didn't do the apprenticeship—when I thought about it, I just felt the weight of my father's words. He robbed me of the pleasure, the joy I'd found in it. That's when I started acting like the asshole you've read about online, like the aristocratic son he wanted me to be, one he identified with—someone who looked like money and treated others accordingly."

"How did you finally start designing again?"

"Well, you know about Caroline—that was me trying to please him in a way. But one day my grandfather took me to task. He'd been trying to talk to me for ages, trying to bring me back to life, but I had shut down, lowered the curtain on that part of myself. Then that night he took me to dinner, which was normal, but afterwards he had Lloyd park in front of a hotel. I asked him what we were doing there, and he told me to wait. About ten minutes later I saw my father, drunk, with his hands on the ass of his secretary."

"Your *grandfather* is the one who told you about your father's philandering?!"

"Yes. And he said—I'll never forget his words—'He is half the man you could be.' He said there was nothing he could do about the fact that Hale Shipping and the title would go to his son, but that he had been proud of me when I'd found my passion. That he still desired that I become an architect. That he knew I could do something important. No one had said anything like that to me...probably ever."

"I'm so glad he did."

"Me too. I broke up with Caroline—I told you a little about that—and I went back to work. It all came back. But I still...I don't...Lydia, I've never told anyone any of this." He whispered it, almost as though he couldn't believe he'd just told this story at all.

"Not even to Will? Or Caroline?"

"No one. No one but you. You have to understand that even though my grandfather brought me back to life, there was a part of me that died that day my father spoke to me. Since then, as a rule, I've never dared share anything I truly care about with him, really with anyone. I learned the hard way that he could kill it."

Suddenly I understood Dylan a thousand times better. How closed off he was. How he insisted on control, was pained when he had to give it up. I thought of every time I'd pressed him, defied him, insisted that he move outside his comfort zone. Each time he'd laughed, he'd played along, but I could see now that each time it had also probably been a challenge. Each time I'd been breaking a well-formed mold that had, in some ways, saved him.

"Tomorrow, at Humboldt Park, I will break that rule for that first time in eleven years," he said and squeezed my hand, linking our fingers.

"What do you mean?"

"I'll share you."

Chapter 12

That night we fell asleep after our conversation drifted to more mundane topics, like the first building he'd ever designed—an annex to an old office building that he said he'd made outrageously overcomplicated for what it had been, but he was still proud of it. And I told him about my only grandparent I'd ever met, my father's mother, who'd died when I was seven, but I could still remember the soft, leathery feel of her skin.

Now it was Saturday morning, we were decidedly awake, and I was fretting, packing for one night with his parents, which after last night made me nervous. Nervous for me—I wanted to do what I could to make it go well—and nervous for him, for all the reasons he'd shared.

"What about this one?" I asked, holding up the same printed wrap dress I'd worn on one of our first dates. It was a bit summery but also really cheerful, which I thought might be a good note to strike.

"I told you, damsel, any dress will do. You'd look stunning in a paper sack," Dylan replied unhelpfully, looking at his computer from my bed. I was pretty sure he was trying *not* to think about this visit, or certain parts of it.

I groaned in frustration. "Dylan, I've never visited anyone who 'dresses for dinner,' and the last thing I need is to get this wrong. Please—be specific. Help me." I was now holding up the wrap dress and one other—a red, tailored dress that I'd always liked.

Dylan had assured me that I had nothing to prove, but he and I both knew that was bullshit. His mother, the Duchess of Abingdon, hated me or at the very least prayed daily that Dylan would get bored of me. And I hated to admit it, but lately I was wondering myself when Dylan might get a little tired of the antics involved in dating again. I was just waiting for him to decide his original plan—hiding out in his architecture firm until he died of old age—was better than this one, which involved having paparazzi comment on whether he wore boxers or briefs (boxer briefs, naturally) and speculated about whether or not I was on birth control (taking it faithfully).

Dylan reached back into my closet and removed a tailored crepe navy-blue dress with a pleated skirt, three-quarter sleeves, and a subtle eyelet trim at the scooped neck. "This one."

"Really? Not this one?" I double-checked, holding up the red one. "I always get compliments when I wear it."

Dylan slowly caged me in, backing me against the edge of the closet door, pressing his front into my own. He held the navy dress by the hanger in his hand, high against the wall behind me. "That's because it's red and fits you like a goddamn condom. And every time you wear it, every bloke who passes within a mile sees you, sees how fit you are, and can't help imagining what it would be like to fuck you." He was whispering in a controlled, determined way, his face above mine, looking down. "And every woman who passes wants to *be* you. You should be grateful I allow you to wear it at all," he said, glancing down at the red dress still pressed into my hand.

I gulped, and Dylan knew he had me. He stroked the hair from my face and tucked a loose strand behind my ear. Whenever he did that, I felt like he was trying to uncover me, see me. Then he grabbed the wrap dress from my other hand and shoved it harshly against my bottom, pulling me even closer to him. "This one I can't look at without remembering the first time you wore it. When I tied you up, plugged this perfect ass, and fucked your mouth. If you wear this at my parents' I will be drooling at the table."

I chuckled between my increasingly shallow breaths. "We wouldn't want that," I said back, my voice barely recognizable.

"No," he said, leaning down to brush my lips with his own. "This one is perfect," he added, tossing the navy dress on the bed behind him and then running his thumb along my lips while my cheek rested in his palm. "Now. Damsel. Stop worrying. And get this sweet, perfect ass into your jeans. I want to get there in time for a jaunt around."

My heart rate, which had been elevated with anxiety only a moment before, was now elevated for entirely different reasons. I was completely seduced and gave a frustrated groan as he backed away, fully prepared to leave me all hot and bothered.

But he quickly turned on his heels and came stalking back towards me. "Fuck it," he said under his breath, and he lifted me against the closet door as I smiled and laughed into his shoulder. I guess we could be late after all.

* * *

An hour later than planned, Dylan sat behind the wheel of the Land Rover and drove us east, out of the city, towards Humboldt Park. I sat cross-legged in the front seat, flipping through my email on my phone while he switched from classical music to a mix I'd made him of indie bands from New York.

A new email arrived, and my hand stilled.

It was from Daphne and the subject line read, *As if you'd ever get Botox. Gross!* I clicked the link to some royal gossip blog and was afraid to start reading.

"What is it?" Dylan asked, interrupting my anxiety.

"Daphne sent me a link to a blog post about me."

"Oh? From where? What does it say?" Dylan's hand moved to my thigh, and I could feel him tense a little. "Read it to me."

"Okay." I gulped. "'If the American shopgirl wants to land Dylan Hale for the long haul, she'll have to learn to piss with the lords (and ladies). Well, Lydia, we're here to help. We asked, and here are the top six things our readers think you can do to be more aristocratic.'"

Dylan chuckled. "Well, this ought to be good."

I gulped again. "It's a list...and some pictures." All of a sudden I really didn't want to do this.

Dylan slid his hands between my thighs and gave my leg a squeeze. "Go on, then."

I exhaled loudly. "'One. Hold your fork properly.'" I wrinkled my nose in confusion. "There's a picture of us eating at that restaurant in Butler's Wharf." Dylan quickly looked over my shoulder at the photo. "I don't get it."

"Oh, well, we don't eat that way over here."

"What way?"

"You switch the fork from your right hand to your left to cut your food, and then you switch it back. We keep our fork in our left hand over here." He shrugged his shoulders. "It doesn't matter."

"Have you noticed that?"

"Damsel, it's meaningless. Don't you think if it really mattered I would have told you? Come on, don't be daft. What's number two?"

I already hated this game.

"'Two. Don't wear T-shirts with writing on them.' There's a picture of you and I running, and I'm wearing my Brooklyn Lager T-shirt." I looked down, and sure enough, under my sweater I had on an old concert T-shirt. "Is that really a thing?" I searched back through my memories and couldn't remember one instance of Dylan wearing a T-shirt with any kind of logo or writing on it.

"That's ridiculous," he said. "I love all your worn-in old T-shirts. They're adorable. Never stop wearing them."

"But is it true? Do you not wear T-shirts like that?"

Dylan just shrugged.

"Okay, 'Three. Go blond.' There's just a picture of a debutante ball somewhere and all the girls are that perfect shade of sunshiny blond."

Dylan looked over my shoulder to see the picture again, flicking his eyes back to the road. "Oh, that lot. Boring. Don't go blonder, please," he said, and he ran his fingers through my decidedly dirty-blond, light-brownish hair, cupping the nape of my neck.

"'Four. Get Botox.' There's no picture, thank god." I flicked down the mirror in the sun visor and started to look at my lips. But before I could get a good look, Dylan flipped it back up.

"Don't be ridiculous. You know how I know your lips are perfect?"

"How?" He opened his mouth to speak, but I stopped him. "No. Wait. You're about to say something dirty."

Dylan laughed, clearly caught. "No," he emphasized. "I was just going to say because I can't take my eyes off them."

"Yeah, right." I gave him my best exaggerated eye roll before continuing. "'Five. Attend Ascot.' Again, no picture of me, just a picture of Ascot."

"It's not till June, but I'll take you if you want."

"'Six. Learn your place.'" I stilled. In other words, *You don't belong here.* Below were photographs of the several single, beautiful, young aristocrats who would be deemed better girlfriend choices for Dylan—daughters of earls and barons, fashionable, willowy, *sunshiny* blond model types caught leaving exclusive nightclubs, dining in members-only clubs, and just walking down the street. The kind of women found in the society pages not because of who they were dating but because of who *they* were. Amelia Reynolds was number four.

Dylan peeked at my phone again, catching a glimpse. "Damsel, that's ridiculous."

Just then another email arrived from Daphne with the subject line *Ignore my last email!!!!!!* I opened it and read her begging me not to read that terrible post and how she should have finished reading it before sending. Too late.

"Damsel," Dylan said, hearing my heavy exhale for what it was: the desire for blog posts like this to disappear from the Internet. "You must develop a thicker skin. Trust me, this kind of thing has nothing to do with you and everything to do with selling adverts. And it won't stop. At least not until the next exciting thing comes along."

I nodded. In a few short months I'd come to need him, to want him, to not be able to envision my life without him, but things like this—this litany of ways in which we were different, our worlds were different—nagged at me, frayed the edges of my confidence that those differences didn't matter. He would always be the one born to be a duke, and I would always be the one born to be a normal person, someone for whom Botox would be out of the question. I could never go back to pre-Dylan, but there was a part of me that didn't know what it meant to go forward.

Dylan interrupted my ruminating—his soft fingers stroking my leg. I realized that the car had stopped. We were pulled over to the side of the road. I looked at him, wondering what was happening, and he swiftly lifted me and pulled me over the console so I was straddling his lap.

He held my face in both of his hands, forcing me to look right at him. He kissed me firmly on the lips, slow, warm, and with total conviction.

"Number seven. Nothing. Dylan Hale wants Lydia Bell in the exact package, the exact character, and the exact delightful attire in which she arrived on British soil." His hand was now playing with my shirt and creeping up under it towards my breast. "Trust *me*, damsel. Thicker skin."

I nodded and inhaled just in time before his lips met mine. His tongue pried my lips apart and coaxed me into the kiss. He refused to let my mind wander back to that blog post and instead, with every flick of his tongue, with every movement of his lips, with every stroke of my skin, insisted that I be right there with him. Only with him. If only I could stay in that kissing world forever.

Chapter 13

An hour later we approached a driveway entrance flanked by two tall stone pillars. In some ways the entrance was unassuming—the pillars were covered with ivy, no signs or gilded gates. The only reason I even knew it was the entrance to Humboldt Park was because Dylan uttered "Home sweet home" as we turned into the road. It snaked around bends with fields on either side, wooded areas in the distance. I could see farmhouses and outbuildings a ways off, and I was simply taking in the enormity of the place.

"What's that?" I asked, pointing to a square, stone, towerlike building deep in some gardens.

"It's called a pigeonnier. It gives the birds a place to nest, and we collect their eggs. We used to occasionally collect the birds as well but haven't done in some years. My father prefers shooting parties."

We continued to round the estate and came across the edge of a large pond, with a bridge over it. It reminded me of Central Park, with its winding paths crossing over water and its crisscrossing walkways. "Is this all part of it?" I asked, nearly leaning over Dylan to get a better look out the window.

"I'll show it all to you later."

When the house finally came into view, my jaw dropped, and I felt my eyes bug out of my head. This place was a palace. I'd seen pictures of it online, but it was different to have it looming over me in person, to feel so dwarfed by it.

When I was a child, my father and I went to Newport, Rhode Island, one summer to look at the mansions. The memory had been long buried, nestled somewhere under a zillion movie nights and years of cancer treatments, but it emerged fully realized now. That was the only other time I'd seen houses like this one, and we'd had to pay for tickets to get into those. People rented them for weddings, for Christ's sake. This is where Dylan had grown up? Holy fuck.

"Dylan, I…" I couldn't finish that thought. I had no idea what to say. The house was enormously tall and so grand. We rounded a corner and a stately columned façade came into view with several steps. There was a curved driveway in front, and I couldn't miss the Roman statue and fountain. I remembered Will's comment about Geoffrey's mistress.

"Come," Dylan started after a moment of silence and as the car rolled to a stop in front of a grand set of doors. He leaned over and kissed me quickly but firmly, even though I barely registered or responded. "It's just a house." Yeah, and the Grand Canyon was just a ravine.

An older woman in a crisp blue dress was waiting by the door, and a younger man in a collarless button-down shirt and a pair of pressed trousers was approaching the car.

"Hello there, Jake," said Dylan to the guy with a genuine smile. "Our bags are in the boot."

"Right, sir. Her Grace has Miss Bell in the blue room," he added, looking at Dylan as though he knew this cryptic phrase would get a response, which it did—a huff of anger.

"Of course she does. Please put Lydia's bags in *my* room as well, if you would."

"Of course, sir," the young guy replied with a barely noticeable smirk.

Dylan then looked to the warm older woman waiting for us by the door. "Mrs. Barnes," he said, giving her an all-encompassing hug. "It's lovely to see you."

"You look so well, my lord."

"It will never feel right for you to call me that."

"Fine, then," she said, pleased with herself. "Master Dylan it is."

Dylan chuckled. "You haven't called me that since I was a boy." He sighed. "Anything's better than 'lord,' especially from you." He was smiling so warmly towards her, it was almost as if this woman were his mother. You could feel the comfort radiating from her. And Dylan's respect for her. In the next moment, he turned and gestured back towards me, and I stepped forward. "Mrs. Barnes, I'd like to introduce you to Lydia Bell, my girlfriend."

Mrs. Barnes beamed and took both my hands in her own. She looked me over and took me in with the eyes of someone who loved Dylan without end. "I'm so pleased to meet you, Miss Bell." And she held my hands for just a moment longer.

"Lydia," Dylan said, turning to me, "Mrs. Barnes has been the housekeeper here for nearly forty years. The story goes that my parents attempted to hire a nanny, and Mrs. Barnes here was charged with interviewing them, but there were no good candidates, so she was left with the onerous task of looking after me herself."

"Now," said Mrs. Barnes, "I won't have you telling falsehoods while you're under this roof. The truth, Miss Bell, was that I couldn't part with young *Master* Dylan here. I'm sure any one of those nannies was perfectly qualified, but none was good enough."

"All for the best," Dylan said. "I'm sure I would have ended up hiding under your apron regardless." I'd never seen Dylan so warmly embraced, so much like a son, until this moment. It was the first time, apart from moments with his sister, that I could truly see him as part of a family.

"You? Hiding under an apron? Why do I find that hard to believe?" I asked, looking at Mrs. Barnes as I spoke, and she hollered in reply.

"Oh, you know him well, don't you?" she replied, and we both laughed as she followed us into the house.

We walked into a great hall with ceilings higher than those in any museum I'd been in, certainly any home. Looking around, I was pretty sure that some of the paintings on the wall were taller than my ceilings back in the New York apartment.

"Their Graces are in the library," Mrs. Barnes continued, "but I imagine you'll be going for a walk before joining them?'"

Dylan nodded in confirmation. "I'll show Lydia my room. Could you please have Jake round up Cider and Monty? We'll take them with us." I looked at him, confused, and he clarified, "The dogs."

As we walked through the house, away from the main staircase, we passed endless entrances to endless hallways, windows big enough for elephants to climb through, and furniture that I was pretty sure dated from before the founding of the United States. "Is it really just your parents in this place?" I asked, holding Dylan's hand for dear life, afraid that if we got separated I might never find my way back again.

"Well, my parents and six staff who live here. And

guests—they often have guests. In fact"—he slowed—"up here."
He tugged me through a doorway in the wall that didn't even
appear to be a doorway—it blended in completely with the ornate wallpaper—and dragged me up a flight of stairs. When we
arrived at the second floor, he opened the first door we passed,
and we stood in the doorway looking in at an astoundingly
ornate bedroom. "Rumor has it that a French monarch was con-
ceived in this room."

"Seriously?"

Dylan nodded. "Not in my day, obviously, or in my grandfather's for that matter, but you know, back when."

We finally arrived at a door at the end of a hallway, and Dylan
opened it to reveal a suite of rooms that felt thankfully more
modern than the rest. Sure, the bed was still a grand mahogany
four-poster that made me feel like a miniature person, and the
drapes looked heavy and silken, and the rugs looked foreign and
fancy. But there was a TV mounted on the wall, a comfortable
and worn-looking velvet couch, and bookshelves lined with trophies and evidence of a teenage boy's existence. Photographs
and concert tickets pinned to shelves, rugby jerseys draped over
hooks, paperback novels strewn about a table. Thank god. And
somehow our bags were already there.

"This is yours?" I asked, starting to poke around and finding
myself at a window looking out on a vast wilderness with the
occasional evidence of man's reining it in with box hedges and
pathways. I felt Dylan's hands on my hips and his front pressed
to my back before he actually spoke.

"You can snoop later. Let's go for a walk," he started and
turned me around to look at me, browsing my attire and landing
on my sneakers. "Can those trainers take a few rocks and twigs?
Maybe a little muck?"

I nodded.

"Good, then let's get out of here." As we began to descend the main staircase, the enormity of this place registered full force. There were coats of arms everywhere, tapestries that looked old—like, really old—hanging from the walls. What kind of life was this? All of a sudden I understood, just a little bit, what Dylan's future meant. I knew Dylan in his modern London architect world, where his being a future duke felt like a funny quirk, a *wanna-hear-something-crazy-about-my-boyfriend?* kind of thing. But being here made it real. Suddenly I understood why a world of bloggers thought I wasn't aristocratic enough.

* * *

Cider and Monty were two Irish setters, and Dylan was clearly their master. They bounded around him, swarmed him, nuzzled him, and licked him silly. I actually felt honored when Cider licked my hand and gave me the time of day.

It was three in the afternoon when we set out, and we walked for nearly two hours. The property was so different from the property at Dylan's own country house—what I called his hideaway—which was sprawling and natural, and felt untouched apart from the deliberate and minimalist landscaping around his moderately sized modern house. Humboldt Park was vast, almost like a city of landscape with different neighborhoods. There were gardens around the pond, with carefully articulated spots for fishing. There were highly structured and elegant English gardens, with different "rooms" and themes—roses or various perennials. And there were orchards, wooded areas, and a deer park.

There were pathways and trails and huge swaths of wild land, all so beautiful, and they made me feel like we could be in any time. While walking across one trail, we ran into an old gentleman in his walking cap who bowed his head and said "G'day, milord" to Dylan in a way that made me feel like we were in the late-nineteenth century.

"Who was that?" I asked.

Dylan shook his head. "I don't know him."

"But he was walking across your land," I said, confused. Surely he'd know the strange person walking through what was essentially his backyard.

"Freedom to roam," he said. "It's the law here. Anyone is free to walk across anyone's land. Not the house, of course, or any private gardens or anything, but large parks like this are open to any walkers or hikers."

"That's so cool," I replied, looking around as though I might see another Englishman or lady popping out of the woods. "I love that. My country is filled with NO TRESPASSING signs. Different mindset."

Dylan just chuckled. "Yes, well, different histories."

And the history of Humboldt Park was everywhere. It felt old, not in a costly *Lifestyles of the Rich and Famous* way, but in a calming way, as though all of the tradition, the lack of technology, the beautiful oldness of it all, actually made it humble. As though it was purposely taking a slower path to change, hanging back, being cautious, and reverent of the idea that this was part of a country's history.

"I understand why you like to walk here, I think," I said to Dylan, our hands linked, my scarf muffling my words.

"Is that right?" he asked, just as we came to the top of a small hill. He pulled me close to him, resting our linked hands at the base of my spine. I leaned into him, resting my cheek on his wooly sweater and prompting him to put his broad hand against the back of my head, stroking it. I could feel and hear the dogs circling us.

"I feel calmer. There's something about this place that feels almost centering, clearing, like I can breathe easier. It's beautiful."

"It is," he replied and took my face in his hands. "I'm so glad you like it. When I'm in that house, it's easy to feel suffocated, but out here…"

I looked back at the grand house in the distance. "So *you'll* be 'Your Grace' someday."

"Hopefully not for a long while," he said.

"I know you don't want to be like your father, but do you want to be duke?"

Dylan didn't reply for a moment. "No one has ever asked me that before."

"Really?"

"Well, it's not as though I have a choice," he said very matter-of-factly, and he took my hand, guiding us back down the hill.

"I never thought of it that way."

"Because of the way these things work, the title only goes to sons—"

"Yeah, Emily explained that bit."

He nodded. "Right, well. So if I die, the title dies."

I stopped walking, jerking him back a bit. "So if you don't have a son you'll be the last duke?"

"There's actually a third cousin, who I believe is currently twelve, who lives in a hippie commune in the Australian outback. Technically he may have a right, but there is some dispute about that, because his grandmother wasn't actually married to my father's second cousin when she gave birth to his father, who subsequently died in a some horrible business involving wild dogs."

I couldn't help but chuckle. "Not really?"

"Really."

"So you'll be the duke, then."

He nodded solemnly.

"The only way to get out of it is to commit a horrible crime, wherein the queen will take the title away, or to die. Neither of those is on my list." I remained quiet for a moment, hoping he'd continue. "And I don't know if I'd want to even if I could. I am proud of this place, of my family's place in history, in keeping this part of my culture alive." He looked to me. "There are only twenty-five dukes left in the country. I mean, dukes that aren't directly related to the royal family. There have been a few unlucky generations—lots of daughters. I mean, I'm sure they were lucky in their delightful daughters, but it was bad for the title, obviously."

"Obviously," I smiled, ribbing him. There was no way I was ever going to let him forget that at least a part of this was just crazy.

He laughed a little, but the seriousness was so near the surface for him. "But then I look at my father," he continued. We were looking over a vast green area, and I could see some deer skirting the edges of the woods. "Earlier this year he fired a footman who'd been with our family his whole life. He was born here, for fuck's sake. I mean, literally—he was born *in* the house. His father had served my grandfather. And you know why the bastard did it?"

I looked up to him, holding his hand, and I could feel the anger pulsing through it.

"His favorite Scotch had run out."

"What?"

"It wasn't even Robert's job to make sure that Scotch was in stock. Really that's my mother's job more than anyone's—she's the one who suffers the most, normally...But poor Robert went to pour it, and there wasn't a full glass left, and my father fucking fired him. I'd grown up with Robert. I may have high standards and expect the best from my employees, but I reward them handsomely, and I'm loyal, just as much as they are. No one should be treated the way Robert was, and I don't want any part of it."

"What happened to him?"

"Well, actually it worked out for the best. Will hired him at the restaurant, and he was quickly promoted and now holds a high post at the Ritz. So, well done for him—probably the best thing that ever happened to him. But I mean, bloody hell. The old man hasn't a shred of decency."

"But you'd never be like that," I urged, not even sure why I was pushing him, except that I could see the part of him that loved this place written so clearly on his skin, in his eyes. I wanted him to see himself in a way he wasn't—he was seeing his father mapped onto himself. But he was better than that.

He closed his eyes for a moment, contemplative. Then he opened them and put his palm against my cheek. I could feel that my face was a little windburned, chilled from the cool breeze. "You're cold. Let's get back, damsel."

And that was that. A part of me wanted to dive at him with a hundred more questions, but I knew, now more than ever, that when we were just about to dine with his parents was not the time. The one question I wasn't even willing to look at, but I knew was there, lurking, was: If this was his destiny, was there really any place in it for me?

* * *

We'd been at Humboldt Park for four hours before I set eyes on Dylan's parents. The sun had set, giving the house a medieval quality, lit mostly by wall sconces and table lamps. We entered the lounge, a sprawling living room that reminded me of the living room back at La Belle Reve, the Canadian mansion the Hales also owned and where I had originally met Dylan. The duke and duchess were sitting properly, elegantly, but somehow managing to also look relaxed on couches by a roaring fire. Jake now stood in full livery, waiting to pour us cocktails.

"Laphroaig for me, please, Jake," Dylan said with his arm around me. Then he looked down at me without letting go and asked quietly, "Champagne?"

"Yes, please." I was so glad I'd worn the dress he'd suggested. It felt country club-ish, which now felt appropriate. Dylan was wearing a dark grey suit with no tie. I noticed his father *was* wearing a tie.

"Dressing down tonight, Dylan?" He actually huffed with disapproval.

Dylan ignored him and bent down to kiss his mother on the cheek. "Good evening, Mum. You remember Lydia." She was wearing an elegant knee-length teal dress with lace sleeves.

Charlotte politely looked up at me from her seat and said, "Of course. Welcome to Humboldt, my dear," without a trace of emotion.

"Thank you, Your Grace," I said to her, shaking her hand, which all of a sudden felt like a very American thing to do, and I looked across to the other couch and addressed the duke. "And you, Your Grace. It's lovely to see you both. Thank you for having me. Dylan took me around the property today, and it's just stunning."

Neither of them said anything, and I gratefully took my glass of Champagne from Jake, who gave me a wink.

Dylan clasped my hand and moved us to stand by the fire.

Everyone seemed so quiet, and it was driving me crazy.

"Ma'am," I said, deciding to just go for it and addressing Dylan's mother according to the rules I'd memorized and rehearsed with Fiona that week at work, "Dylan showed me the gardens earlier, and I noticed the beautiful stone animals towards the far end. They add so much spirit to the garden. Have they always been there?"

She hiccupped a little, maybe surprised that I was making the first move so willingly. But of course I was. I loved her son, and I wanted to know her, even if I hadn't heard the best of things. "No, actually I commissioned those when I first arrived from a London stone smith."

"They almost reminded me of the Beatrix Potter books I read as a child," I continued, and she almost—not actually, mind you, but almost—smiled.

"Mmm, yes, I've thought the frog by the tea roses did have a Jeremy Fisher quality to him. I'm glad you enjoyed them, of course." I think I saw, maybe just for a moment, this woman's guard drop, a slight slump in her perfect posture. It felt somehow as though with two sentences I'd cracked something.

"And have you seen Amelia recently, my dear?" She looked at Dylan pointedly as she asked the question.

Or maybe not.

"Mother," Dylan said sternly. "Behave."

Oh boy.

"Dinner is served," Jake chimed in from the doorway. Thank fucking god.

Dylan's parents rose, and Dylan held my elbow, pulling me

back. He leaned down and whispered into my ear. "You're beautiful, you know that?"

I smiled and squeezed his hand.

We sat at the far end of a long table that looked like it could seat at least twenty people, and the entirety of dinner was a dance between cold apathy and elegant passive aggression between Dylan and his parents. There were some *Please pass the salt cellar* and *The carrots came in nicely this year* interspersed with complaints from his father and social inquiries from his mother. Charlotte also asked a lot of seemingly casual questions about Emily, which revealed just how little she knew of her children's lives. At one point she asked if Emily was enjoying her psychology studies, and without thinking I piped up and said, "Emily's studying art history."

Dylan stilled as he was bringing water to his lips. I think stunned that I had just corrected his mother about his sister, but I could see the edges of his mouth curl up.

"Of course," Charlotte replied, and she quickly turned the conversation to something about horses.

After dinner we retreated to the library for cards and what I feared would be another hour of polite non-conversation. We drank some more, and I fielded questions about where I'd travelled and what my father had done for a living. Even though I stayed firmly in polite meet-the-aristocratic-parents mode—my ankles crossed, my hands in my lap, my back straight—I told stories of my life before the way I would to any boyfriend's parents. I was determined to be myself.

Dylan sat near me on the pink silk sofa and occasionally elaborated on a story I was telling, always demonstrating his pride in me. And every time he spoke I recalled his words from the previous night, about how much was at stake for him, sharing things with his parents. After everything I'd heard about Geoffrey, I half expected him to just usher me to the door or come out with something cruel, but in the end he never moved from his post by the fireplace and demonstrated only the minimum interest in our conversation. And his mother barely said a word as she sat primly on the chair across from us. As the night wore on, I realized this kind of indifference was almost worse.

I was looking at my own hands in my lap, thinking about how sad this all was, when Dylan's hand landed on top of my own. Just the touching of our skin brought me back to life, sending a jolt of energy flying across my skin. I shivered slightly, and my eyes snapped to his.

He rose, urging me to stand with him, and looked me in the eye as he said, "Mum, Dad, we'll see you in the morning."

I cleared my throat and forced myself to look at his parents. "Thank you so much for dinner. It's quite incredible to be in a place like this, and I really appreciate you having me."

How I got those words out, I'll never know. In that moment, Dylan's fingers threading with my own, him pulling me towards the door, I remembered all at once why I was even there. Dylan. And as he came back into focus, after hours of tense conversation, I wanted nothing more than to dive into him. As we left the room, I let myself sink into the feeling of just being together, into the anticipation of being alone in his room, and I was relieved to let him lead me there.

Chapter 14

Dylan urged me through the door to his bedroom, his palm spread widely across my lower back. "In you go," he said firmly.

I stepped into the dark room, lit only by the light coming from the bathroom door.

Dylan moved behind me, to the side, and stood me in front of a leather club chair. I waited as he poured himself a glass of water and placed it on the table next to the chair after taking a long swig.

"What? No more Scotch?" I asked, following his eyes as he circled me, coming to stand behind me.

"I want my senses about me for this. You were bloody gorgeous tonight," he said into my ear, his fingertips stroking my arms. "So perfectly yourself. You didn't let them get to you, and it was fucking thrilling. I want to reward you. I want to sink into you. I want to goddamn consume you," he said slowly, taking his time, and I gulped in anticipation. "And no more talking," he said softly, finally settling into the chair before me and gazing up at me. "Undress."

I giggled a little. "So it's going to be that kind of night."

He tsk-ed at me, wagging his finger as he sat down. "Shh, damsel. This will be better if you follow instructions."

My skin was singing—it felt like there were a million little weather systems moving in the air around me, all electric, all feverish. My breathing was picking up.

I walked up to him, put my hands on the armrests of the chair where he sat, leaned over, and kissed him slowly on the lips. No tongue, just firm, warm lips.

"Can you unzip me at least?" I whispered, our faces centimeters apart, the air between us warming. Our eyes met, and my little challenge added heat to this game. He was getting ready to devour me.

I stood and turned, so my back was to him, and I felt him rise behind me. He dragged the zipper slowly down my back and slid his hands into the dress. They were so warm and felt so big, like he could grab me fully around my middle. His thumbs stroked my underarms, and the subtle movements caused a ripple, a shiver of anticipation.

The dress, now loose, slumped off my shoulders, making room for his hands. He unclasped my bra, and it fell into the dress. Then he pushed the whole thing off my arms and down my body, so it hung in front of me, and my bra spilled to the floor. "I think you can handle the rest yourself."

I shimmied out of my dress, kicked off my heels, and turned to see Dylan shrugging off his jacket and rolling up his shirtsleeves. "On the bed, damsel." He smacked my ass—hard. I smiled, eager, scurried to his majestic four-poster canopy bed, and perched myself on its edge. I bit my lip between my nervous teeth and sat on my hands. My hair, grown in the last couple of months, drifted around my shoulders. The pit in my stomach and the round ache between my legs were getting sharper, firmer, more demanding. I wanted his hands on me, all over me. He was taking this too slowly, like he was stalking his prey.

Dylan reached into his bag, parked by the base of the bed, and lifted out a long coil of velvety-looking fabric, wider than rope, softer looking. "You game for this, sweetness?" I nodded hungrily, shamelessly. "Good. Then up at the headboard. Now."

I crawled on all fours and turned back to look at Dylan stalking me. "Thought this through, did you?"

Smack.

Another crisp slap to my ass.

Right, no talking. But if that was my punishment, I might have to keep rebelling. I couldn't stop the eager smile forming on my face, and Dylan shook his head. "Incorrigible."

I got to the top of the large mattress, and Dylan removed all but one pillow from the headboard. He lifted me and placed me square against it, so my ass was on the fluffy pillow, raised, and my back was flush with the upholstered headboard.

"Arm out." Dylan spoke with precision and pointed to my left arm. I couldn't help but just stare into his face, taking it in. The late-in-the-day stubble, the flustered bits of hair haphazardly arranged on his forehead, the sharp definition of his shoulder muscles and biceps, not to mention his pecs and abs, the bare light of the room highlighting every delicious shadow on his torso. I drank him in.

I had remained still, arms at my sides, wanting to prolong whatever devilish plan Dylan had brewing but also simply because I was already lost to this feeling, this closeness, this electric air in which we were floating. One of his free hands landed on my pussy, and his mouth hovered by my ear. "You need a reminder of who gives instructions around here and who follows, baby?" He inserted a finger into me and crooked it, hitching right into that spot, my ignition. I threw my head back and mewed. "Arm. Out," he instructed again.

I flung my arm out to my side. Dylan swiftly tied one end of the long piece of fabric to my wrist, testing it to make sure there was enough slack for comfort, then looped it around the post of the bed behind me, tugged it but didn't tie it down anywhere. What was he doing? He quickly arranged my right arm the same way, so my breasts were projected out, my upper back was cushioned against the headboard behind me, and my legs were stretched out on the bed before me.

Then I felt a tug on my left arm. Dylan lifted my left leg by the knee and wrapped the soft fabric around my thigh, just above my knee. He tied a similar knot, leaving some slack but getting my knee at just the right height, just the right angle away from my body.

Oh god.

Thirty more seconds and he had me just the way he wanted: arms splayed and thighs spread, my feet resting on the mattress, my pussy on full display. Suddenly that soft bathroom light felt like too much. I'd never been this restrained before. Or this exposed without any hope of hiding.

"I can't imagine this is typical Humboldt Park behavior." I smirked at him. "Aren't the ghosts shocked right now?" I heaved out. My breath felt short, like my vulnerability was registering in each tiny corner of my lungs.

Dylan smiled and shrugged. "It's an old house. I'm sure the ghosts have seen plenty."

A sheen of sweat, purely from anticipation, and the tiniest hint of fear—the good kind—coated my forehead.

"Dylan," I started breathily.

"Shh, baby." He trailed one finger down between my breasts,

landing it right in my slick slit. "So wet for me. I love this little pussy, you know that?" I gasped and threw my head back only to be stopped by the high headboard. "Watch—I want you to watch everything."

Fuck, I was so primed. Just by virtue of being tied up this way, exposed to him, the very fact of my inability to do anything to curb my arousal fueled it. I looked down to see his finger sliding in and out of me, spreading my wetness, and I had to close my eyes. I was raw, on the brink.

Dylan was still fully dressed and I was trussed up like some kind of trophy on his wall. He removed his finger and leaned back over the bed to retrieve something else and returned with a small pink vibrator.

"Dylan, I can't handle—"

"You can," he said matter-of-factly. He switched on the toy—I could hear its subtle hum—and he slid it into me. I wanted to writhe; I wanted to squirm. But I couldn't even lift my ass. I clenched my stomach muscles, trying to do anything to cope with the sudden sensations, but nothing worked. I had no purchase, no control. Dylan placed his broad palm between my breasts. "Shh, baby." He was cooing, calming me like I was a spooked horse. "Just take it."

The vibrations weren't enough to get me where I needed to be. Instead the vibrator sharpened everything, urged me to the edge of the cliff while also holding me back. There was nothing tender about this, nothing sweet. It was brutal and passionate and the hottest thing that had probably ever happened to me.

"Dylan!" I begged, but in response to my begging, he retreated, got off the bed. "What the—?" I objected. "Where—?" I moaned.

"Shh."

"Dylan! Stop fucking shushing me and start fucking fucking me!"

He slapped my thigh, making me jolt. Then the man had the nerve to say "Tsk, tsk," shake his head, and actually leave me there, wanting. He went into the bathroom and closed the door! I was about to kill him. I felt sweat run between my breasts and wished like hell I had the use of my arms, not just to relieve the tickle of sweat rivulets on my body but also to be able to touch myself.

Dylan emerged from the bathroom only in his trousers, and I thanked all that was holy that he was back. But then he lifted the club chair and placed it at the foot of the bed. He retrieved his water and sat down, legs crossed, and looked like he was settling in for a goddamn movie or something.

"You have to be kidding me," I breathed. "Please."

"What's the rush, baby?" He leaned forward, elbows on his knees. "You're fucking beautiful like this. I could watch you all night."

"No," I groaned. "Dylan!"

My pleasure was pulsing through me, none of it enough, all of it delicious. Thankfully he had no intention of torturing me indefinitely, which was good, because I was a hair away from charging him with the crime of orgasm denial, which had to be a real thing.

"Okay, okay, baby, I got you." Done teasing me, he said the words softly while crawling onto the bed and approaching me on all fours. He kissed his way up my leg and landed at the crux of my leg and my sex. I was breathing so hard. I needed him inside me. A hundred desperate snarky protests rolled through my mind, but they all remained just out of reach. I couldn't focus enough to speak. All attention was on us, on the feverish anticipation coursing through me.

He withdrew the vibrator, inciting as much relief as yearning, and replaced it with his tongue. "God, baby, you're drenched. You taste so fucking sweet."

Dylan proceeded to do *that thing* with his tongue, and in a flash I was thrown into oblivion. Had I been able to move I surely would have knocked him out with my pelvis. The pinpricks, the starbursts, the goddamn supernovas that were dancing over my body took me over. I crested, but the craving was still there. The orgasm was no match for the need he'd created—no orgasm would have been. It was so good, but it wasn't enough.

"More!" I cried.

"Oh, you're getting more," Dylan said sternly, playfully, and before I knew what was happening he dragged his finger through my wetness and plunged it into my rear. I groaned—it felt fucking amazing. I felt so possessed. He fucked me there with his finger and went back to work on me with his tongue.

"No, I want *you*," I begged. "Not fingers. Not your mouth."

In a second, Dylan untied the fabric around my thighs, freeing me. He hurried out of his trousers and deposited me firmly on top of his hard, waiting cock. Moving like some kind of gymnast, he had me riding him in the blink of an eye. My wrists dragging lengths of velvet rope, my hands gripping his shoulders, and his hands on my hips, I leaned back and took him as deeply into me as I could.

I know I started to scream, because Dylan pulled me down to him, covering my mouth with his own. "Shh, baby. I love your screams, but they're only for me." I kissed him to stop myself from making noise.

Dylan pushed me onto my back and quickly flung my legs over his shoulders. The moment he thrust into me, that one perfect moment when he hit me square-on, the deep need I'd been a slave to broke into a thousand pieces. I have no idea how long it went on or when Dylan came. It was satiation embodied, and I was lost to it completely.

When the world finally came back into focus, I had collapsed into his firm muscular side, my head on his chest, most of my body draped over his, and he was gingerly untying the fabric from the easily accessible wrist on his chest. When he was done, he rubbed it tenderly and kissed it.

Then he lifted me effortlessly and repositioned me on his other side, giving him access to the other wrist. When I was completely disentangled, he moved me so I was draped entirely on top of him, my legs between his own, my front pressed into his, my cheek resting on his firm chest. I was dreamy, barely lucid, and relishing our contact. My hands were tucked under his back, and he was drawing slow, lazy circles on my back.

"You all right, damsel?"

"Mmm-hmm."

"You handled tonight beautifully, baby."

"Which part?" I asked, and I could feel his chuckle vibrating in his chest.

"All of it, you cheeky thing. I know my parents aren't the easiest people to be around. You even got my mum to laugh—I haven't seen that in a long time."

"I did?" I hadn't noticed her laughing, which was probably a testament to how odd and foreign and formal the whole evening had felt to me.

"You did. When you were telling them about your trip to Peru in college, that story about the salt in the tea. You were brilliant."

"I don't know about that, and I am still pretty sure your parents don't like me."

"You let me worry about my parents. You're right where you belong, Lydia."

"What? Naked and pressed up against your male member?"

"Precisely," he said, and I scoffed.

* * *

"I can feel your eyelashes on my skin."

Dylan's words startled me—I had been sure he was still asleep. I was just waking up. The sun only just slipping between the heavy drapes in his ornate childhood bedroom, a column of brightness in an otherwise dark room of red-and-gold brocade. Dylan's whole body was cleaved to my own, as though we'd tried to maximize contact in our sleep. His breathing was steady, and his heavy, broad hand heated the expanse of my back.

"And now I can feel your smile," he continued and moved his hand into my hair as his other hand went to rest on my ass.

"Shh," I said, wanting to fall back into sleep. "I don't know what you're talking about. I'm sleeping."

"Babe, it's already eight, and it would be wise for us to get downstairs," he started and rolled to hover over me. "I don't want to stay here all day—I want you back in London, where I can coax that pretty little cunt of yours into submission. Again."

"Funny," I said and closed my eyes again, not wanting to move from my current position.

"Come on, damsel. Let's clean you up."

"You know," I said, remembering the night before, "I can exact my own torture."

"I'm counting on it," he replied, then he stepped back, taking a deep breath as though to calm himself down. "Let's dress, damsel. It's time for breakfast."

Chapter 15

By the time we were both dressed, I had remembered where we were, that outside his bedroom door were his parents and the castle that was his birthright. I found myself grabbing his hand as we left his suite of rooms and entered the hallway, concerned that I might actually get lost in the place. When I attempted to turn to the right, towards the grand central staircase, Dylan pulled my hand to the left. "This way—we have to go down a rear staircase over here."

"Why?"

"Second Sunday of every month the main house is open to the public."

"Like a museum?"

"Indeed."

"But not the whole house?"

"Certainly not," he explained as we wound down the narrow back staircase. "All the big estates began doing it during the Second World War. Now it's a public service, so people can get a bit of history, some proper English heritage. The visitors book

weeks in advance. They come to see my grandfather's collection of cars—some are from before the turn of the century.
They can see the central part of the house and the east wing." I
must have looked in want of a compass, because Dylan clarified
and pointed. "That's west, where we came from and where my
parents, Emily, and I have personal apartments. That way"—he
pointed in the opposite direction—"is east, where there are
more guest apartments, a ballroom, billiards, a second larger library with a map room, among other rooms."

"Otherwise, does Hale Shipping support your family and the
house?" I asked, and he nodded.

"Income from HS, other assets that my grandfather accrued,
and income from the remaining tenants. We own parts of the
village as well. Thankfully there are customs about not raising
rents and such. Otherwise I'm sure my father would bleed the
lovely people dry."

"You own parts of the village? Like the shops?"

Dylan nodded again. "It's not uncommon. My grandfather
sold some land, but for the most part the tenancy is still intact.
Some families have been with us for six generations or more."
God, six generations? I had no idea what my family had been up
to six generations ago. It seemed impossible in this day and age
that anyone did.

"But I thought you said being the Duke of Abingdon was just
a title, that it didn't involve much work?" I recalled our first conversation in London, the night Dylan and I had embarked on
our relationship. He'd made it sound as though being a duke was
no more than pomp and circumstance.

"We have an estate manager who takes care of it all, and with
the right staff, the right organization, the place basically runs itself, or should. Ideally my father would know when to chime

in and when to leave it be, but that's not really his strong suit. In fact, Mrs. Barnes has told me some details about how my father seems to be running things that give me concern. We employ over two hundred people at various times of the year, nearly sixty year-round—there are a lot of people's livelihoods at stake, and it's an expensive enterprise."

"Two hundred?!" I asked, imagining the music shop my father had run with a friend when I was young, which had employed a mere four people. I suddenly realized why it was such an enormous responsibility being the duke, and why Dylan must find it so offensive if it was being done poorly.

We landed in a vast warm green kitchen with a lovely large wooden table and huge windows looking out onto a small garden. Mrs. Barnes was at the stove, hovering over a pot of water. Dylan came up behind her and touched her shoulder.

"Good morning, Mrs. Barnes. What can I do to help?"

"Oh," she started and smiled. "Good morning. You're such a dear. Rosemary?" She was practically singing, and Dylan nodded and ducked out the back door. I looked puzzled for a moment—shouldn't he be going to a cabinet or a refrigerator? But he quickly returned with a sprig of rosemary and handed it to Mrs. Barnes, who thanked him distractedly while she removed perfectly poached eggs from the pot. Dylan pointed to the door he'd just come through and simply said "Cook's garden" by way of explanation. Because of course—why wouldn't there be an entire perfectly located garden devoted to the cook's needs?

Dylan poured us coffees, and we sat at the big table and began munching on freshly baked bread with butter and jam. He leaned in to kiss my cheek, which I thought was sweet until I realized it was just a ploy to land a dollop of raspberry jam on my nose.

"Dylan!" I scolded while giggling, wiping the jam from my nose and then promptly licking it off my finger. I stuck my tongue out at him, and just as he was laughing back at me, his father entered the room. Dylan stiffened, any trace of playfulness and humor disappearing.

"Good morning, Father."

Mrs. Barnes put plates of poached eggs and rosemary potatoes in front of us, but before he could pick up his fork, Geoffrey said, "Thank you, Mrs. Barnes, but Dylan will be joining me in my office. He'll breakfast later. Lydia, my dear," he said looking at me now, "why don't you eat and wait for him in the small library when you're through?"

I began to nod, but Dylan stopped me. "Baby, go wherever you'd like. I'll find you, and I won't be long." There was a concrete-like hardness in his voice. The tension between father and son was so hot and so hard. And I was right smack in the middle of it.

As soon as Dylan left the room, the whole place felt bigger. Without him, I felt like a tourist myself, in the walls of a giant forbidding museum. With him, it felt like it could be a home.

I ate my delicious eggs, drank my coffee, and contemplated the total oddity of walking around a castle that had tourists milling about but where I'd had crazy kinky sex the night before. In London we had just found that sacred personal bubble where we could be us, and it had become so important so quickly, our defense against the flashbulbs and blog posts. But being at Humboldt expanded my understanding of that bubble, stretched its parameters. I could see more fully now who Dylan was, could get a hint of what he was contending with. This place was part of him, and he'd wanted me to see it, for better or worse. The *worse* was that it was harder to get a handle on where I fit in this sphere, with its archaic rules and estate managers. And there was the possibility that Dylan's life here in this grand mansion was more real than the world we'd built back in London.

I was grateful when Mrs. Barnes called me out of my thoughts. "Miss Bell, my dear," she started.

"Please, please call me Lydia, Mrs. Barnes." She smiled at that. "I can tell how much Dylan loves you." As soon as I said that, I realized Dylan had probably never said any such thing to her, that the level of impropriety of such a thing was probably vast, but oh well. Date an American, and you're going to some frank talk about love and emotions.

Mrs. Barnes stilled for a moment, and if I wasn't mistaken, her eyes were even a bit misty. "Excuse me if I made you uncomfortable." I tried to put her at ease. "But it would feel strange to me for someone so close to Dylan not to call me by my first name. But then again, I've been working on Lloyd for months, and he still insists on 'Miss Bell,' so I'll understand if you must."

"Nah," she said, her northern accent rich and earthy. "Let's have it be 'Lydia' and 'Christine' between us women, shall we?"

"Christine," I affirmed, smiling. "So you've been with this family for a long time."

She looked at me like she knew exactly where I was headed. "I've known Master Dylan his whole life, my dear."

I looked into my coffee and wished I could know what this woman knew about him.

"I've never seen him this happy," she said, and I looked up to her face, eyes wide. "Are you close with your family, Lydia?"

"I don't really have any," I said. "I never knew my mother, and my father died earlier this year." Suddenly grief filled my chest. Falling in love with Dylan and moving out of New York had dulled the ache of loss, but when it returned, it was like a flash flood. I gulped and tried to regain a little control. "But I was very close with my father. He was my best friend, really."

Mrs. Barnes put her hand over my own and prompted me to look into her warm maternal gaze. "I'm sorry you lost him—that is cruel, isn't it, love? But it is wonderful that you had each other."

I nodded, and she looked contemplative, hesitant, before she continued. "Dylan is blessed that his parents are still alive, for many reasons, but they've led a different kind of family life." I nodded again, trying to convey that I understood, that she didn't have to say more if she didn't want to. "Dylan will make an excellent duke someday, but I know it's not all he could do with his life. That's his cross to bear. Be gentle with him, dear. It's not all it's cracked up to be," she said, gesturing towards the high ceilings and towards the door that led to the rest of the grand estate.

"He's a marvelous architect," I said, "and he loves it so much."

"He is, and he does," she agreed. "I wish he could see that his life doesn't have to be either-or. His lordship expects Dylan to take over Hale Shipping, as I'm sure you know, but—" She stopped short. "I'm sure you know the gardens are open to the public today."

I was wondering what the hell her sudden shift in topic was about when I heard movement behind me. I turned and saw that Charlotte had entered the room. Coiffed perfectly, not a hair out of place, in a wrinkleless cashmere turtleneck sweater and a knee-length wool skirt. She looked elegant country through and through, like something off the pages of *Horse and Hound*. Sure enough the dogs came bounding in after her, running up to Christine, who scolded them for begging before giving them each a scrap of meat from a bowl on the counter.

"You spoil them," said Charlotte coolly.

"Good morning, Your Grace," I said. Each time I spoke that title I felt like I was playing make-believe at some weird Jane Austen theme park, but I also hoped like hell she'd say something along the lines of *Oh, please, we're practically family! Call me Charlotte!*

"Good morning, Lydia. You slept well, I hope." No such luck.

"I did, thank you." All of a sudden I was cringing at the possibility that she'd heard us the night before.

"Do you happen to know where I might find my son?"

"Um, Dylan and your husband went to his office."

"Yes, well," Charlotte said, looking at me, "do enjoy your morning, my dear, but I advise you to steer clear of the gardens. They're swamped with busybodies this morning," she said with slight disgust. "It's a necessary evil, I'm afraid, but such a nuisance. Which reminds me. Mrs. Barnes," she said with irritation, "do remember to tell Bexley to clean up the lawns tomorrow—after these horrid days, there are always rose petals about and divots in the paths. You'd think they could show a little respect since we're letting them into our home. Honestly."

And with that she turned and left, with the dogs in tow.

* * *

Christine left shortly after Charlotte, and I found myself wandering the massive house alone. I knew I wanted to steer clear of the tourists—every once in a while I saw groups of heads bobbing outside a window I passed. I walked down long hallways lined with enormous oil paintings in frames as thick as my legs. I thought I was headed towards the main hallway, but after another twenty minutes, I had to concede that I was definitely lost.

My new goal was to find Dylan's room again, maybe find my sneakers and explore some part of the outside not populated by a group of strangers. But after turning down yet another unfamiliar hallway, I heard voices emerge from an open door. I knew those voices, and I slowed.

"Tristan says you haven't returned his calls. Or taken his meetings." Geoffrey's voice was stern and cold.

"Is your little lackey feeling ignored, Father? Whatever he needs from me, I'm sure it can wait."

"You know very well that Tristan needs you to sign off on the deals."

"You've never required this of me before. Why must you drag me into it now? *You* know very well I don't have time. As it stands I've already put off the Olympic committee twice in the name of coming to your rescue at Hale Shipping. Even I can't put them off a third time," said Dylan.

"I must say I'm rather surprised and disappointed that after ten years we are still having this discussion. I'd rather hoped you would have worked that out of your system by now. Let me remind you, Son, you have real obligations. This company is your legacy. I won't have you betraying everything your grandfather worked for." His father's voice was so tense, so rigid, he almost sounded panicked.

Dylan snorted disdainfully. "Grandfather would be thrilled, I'm sure, to learn that you summon his 'hard work' so effortlessly in the name of your own schemes when you showed nothing but blatant disinterest and contempt right up until his death."

"Careful, Son," Geoffrey said menacingly, and Dylan was silent. "I've been patient with your dalliance with architecture for quite a while, but being a Hale means something. It's time to get on board."

"Well, that little *dalliance* wasn't so horrible when it got you your first invitation from Her Majesty since Grandfather died, your first invitation as duke. The only reason I'm working with you and Hale Shipping at all is *because* of Grandfather and my promises to him. For him, I'll do this. But would it have killed you to take more than a criminal interest in the company your father built from the ground up?"

I heard some rustling and movement and then a searing Geoffrey. "Look at yourself, so smug about what happened two years ago, but you have *no idea* what's at stake. Maybe I should just…" It was as though I could *hear* Geoffrey's face turning red, steam coming out of his ears. "Get your act together, Son. Look around you. You think your little architecture firm is going to support this place? You'd throw your family's history away that easily? Think of your beloved Mrs. Barnes, Son."

It almost sounded like Geoffrey was threatening Christine, and Dylan was silent. I knew I shouldn't be listening, but I couldn't pull myself away, and at this point I was more terrified that if I moved they'd hear me.

"Father, don't you—" Dylan started, and I could hear the groan of frustration in his words. "If you're ready to leave Hale Shipping, then leave. I'll stay on the board, but I don't need to run the place, for Christ's sake."

A long moment of silence passed, and then Geoffrey continued. "This isn't a joke, Son. Do you understand that? It goes beyond you. You'll sit as president of the company whether you like it or not. If you care about this place at all, you'll fulfill *all* your expectations. And since we're on the topic of our legacy—"

"No. I'm not talking about this," said Dylan firmly, cutting his father off.

"And not with that *American*—"

"She's not…No, you know what? I'm not getting into this with you. I said no. You won't be dictating my personal life. I won't become an instrument of torture and repression to an innocent child."

"You'd see another ducal line—" Geoffrey's voice was hot, angry, and my shoulders stiffened with tension.

"Haven't there been enough sacrificial lambs?" Dylan was truly yelling. They both were. I wasn't sure I'd ever heard a real all-out fight between anyone before. Not one that wasn't at a bar, anyway. And I found myself shaking slightly. It was so unnerving. Dylan finally broke the silence. "Fine. I'll call Tristan tonight and give him whatever he needs. I'm taking Lydia home now, *sir*."

"This conversation isn't over," said Geoffrey, and I could hear Dylan humph loudly, his voice much closer to the door. "And don't forget about our meeting with the board Wednesday."

I heard more movement, and I quickly ducked behind a statue by the door. I stood there for a moment, holding my breath, eyes closed, trying to process everything I'd just heard. I couldn't imagine fighting with my father the way Dylan had just fought with his, with the threats, the accusations, the complete absence of love. No wonder Dylan was so ambivalent about this place. On one hand, he clearly loved this house, clearly felt so connected to it and to what his grandfather had done to keep it; on the other hand, when he talked to his father, he sounded adamant that he wouldn't have children, that he was happy to let the whole thing end. I was so still, could hear my own breathing, and I tried not to feel sad for him, for everything he was willing to sacrifice just to contain this part of this life.

"Lydia, my dear." My eyes flashed open and I was looking straight into the eyes of Geoffrey, who was wiping sweat away from his forehead with a cloth handkerchief.

"Sir, I was—" I began, terrified for a moment, but he put up his hand to stop me from speaking.

"Don't fret. Why don't you come into my office."

I gulped. Surely this was a terrible idea. I tentatively followed him, wondering what the hell I'd just gotten myself into. My palms were sweaty in an instant.

"Perhaps you overheard my discussion with my son?" he began, sitting at his desk, looking not at me but at the papers covering it.

Oh fuck.

"No, I was just passing by." But Geoffrey shook his head.

"It's good that you heard, my dear, because perhaps you understand the situation a bit better now?"

"Excuse me?" I hoped my voice didn't sound as harsh out loud as it did in my head.

"My son has obligations, Miss Bell, obligations that require his attention, but more importantly require the assistance and participation of a woman who understands her role in this life." I started to speak, but he raised his hand to stop me again, and he continued. "Come now, I think we both know that you've served your purpose. My wife and I are grateful that you've gotten our son to emerge from his selfish hole, but my son is in his thirties, and he needs to think of his place now."

"With all due respect, *Your Grace*, I would think that how he lives his life and who is in it is entirely up to him." I could feel the fury building in my chest.

Geoffrey just chuckled, which turned my fury into fire.

"I admire your passion, my dear, but it's very revealing. Do you know how my wife spent her day this past Thursday?" What? I looked at him, confused. "Of course you don't. She fulfilled one of her many duties as the lady of his household and stood in for the queen during rehearsals for next month's Christmas festivities. And subsequently she met with the wife of France's prime minister and entertained her and her children for the evening. Are you prepared for those kinds of duties? Do you know the first thing about the protocols involved in participating in international social affairs?"

I looked at him, stunned. He wasn't being fair. He knew, if not by instinct then by the look on my face, that I had no idea how to handle any of that. And I didn't even know if that's where Dylan and I were headed. He and I hadn't talked about forever, and his father was already warning me off.

"I hardly think that—" I began, but Geoffrey stood up, getting impatient with me.

He shook his head and said, "I thought not." My blood was boiling. I had that dangerous mix of brain-muddling anxiety and self-righteous certainty that meant I was about to lose it.

"You see, Lydia, Dylan is part of a great British tradition. And he must play his part. He will realize that soon enough. He'll remember who he is, and it's probably best for you to allow him to do that. You've been in London how long, Miss Bell?"

"A couple of months," I said coldly, telling my politeness instinct to buzz off so I could tell this asshole what I thought of him.

"Is there a sum that might make it easier for you to get your feet on the ground and establish yourself a bit more? To cope with the loss of Dylan's attentions?"

Holy shit. He was trying to pay me off. And it put me firmly over the edge.

"Excuse me, Your Grace, but you've seriously misjudged me if you think for one minute I love Dylan because of his money. You've misjudged me even more if you think I would ever take yours. And you've seriously misjudged your own son if you truly believe he would ever fall for anyone trying to use him. With all due respect, sir, and frankly I suspect you're due very little, I am going to be with your son. One of these days I am going to agree to *live* with your son. And who knows where we'll end up. But *if* we ever break up, I can assure you it will *never* be because of money—money he has, money he doesn't have, and certainly not any money you give me."

For a moment he was taken aback, nervous even, but then that steely demeanor returned. "Well done, my dear." Ugh, he was happy I wasn't taking the money. Fire. Pure fire in my belly.

I felt the words coming before I could stop them. "One day you're going to wake up and realize what an incredible man your son is, and for your sake I hope it's not too late. In the meantime, you can take your money and, as we *Americans* like to say, shove it up your ass. It seems to mean more to you than it ever would to me."

I gulped, not believing I'd just said that. "And Geoffrey? *This* conversation," I said, waving my hand between us, "*is* over."

Chapter 16

When Dylan found me, I was sitting on a bench next to the cook's garden, twisting a long piece of lavender between my thumb and forefinger, replaying everything that had just happened in my head. All of the warm love Dylan had ignited in me that morning was gone, and I was feeling more alone than I had in weeks. I hated Dylan's father for offering money, but I hated him even more for instilling doubt. Was I naïve to think this would ever go anywhere? *Was* I actually an obstacle, obstructing some future Dylan needed or wanted? In my heart I knew that wasn't the case, but apart from Dylan's weekly request that I move in with him, which had become so predictable and jokey, we hadn't really talked about it.

I was sitting on this grand estate, one that would belong to Dylan when Geoffrey died. I knew Dylan detested his father and talked about being a duke as though it were a fate worse than death. But I also knew how much he'd respected his grandfather. I recalled one of our first fights when he'd spouted off about *six centuries of tradition*. He *respected* this life. Assuming he did figure out a way to balance his passion for architecture with Hale Shipping and Humboldt Park, would I be holding him back from participating fully in something that was his right?

Geoffrey had just turned up the dial on our pressure cooker, and now more than ever I needed to give Dylan the space to figure everything out, but at the same time I also needed *him*. It seemed like an impossible task. That was where my mind was, heading into that unanswerable abyss, when I felt Dylan sit next to me on the carved stone bench.

"There you are," he said. I could feel his warmth, his tall, lean body leaning into mine, but I was still lost in my thoughts.

"Lydia?" he asked, and it was immediately clear that he knew something was wrong. I couldn't hide anything from this man. "Baby, what's wrong?" He wrapped an arm around me, held me tightly, and I pressed my lips to his neck and lingered there, with a long, slow, simple kiss to his skin.

I still didn't say anything. I didn't know where to begin, and sitting right outside the open door to the kitchen didn't seem like the place to have the conversation we needed to have.

"This place can be daunting, can't it?" He wrapped his long fingers across the back of my head and stroked. It calmed me instantly. The single tear that had escaped disappeared into the soft fabric of his sweater. He pulled back and cupped my chin in his hand, bringing my gaze to his. "Lydia, damsel, what's going on?"

I leaned up and kissed him. "Can we go home?"

He didn't look entirely satisfied, as though he wanted to know what was in my mind immediately. Well, he of all people should be able to summon some patience in that department.

He nodded, stood, and held my hand tightly, urging me up. "The bags are in the car. We can go right now."

"But I didn't say goodbye to your mother. Or Christine," I said, concerned. Only after I spoke did I realize I'd left out his father. I wondered if he'd even noticed.

"It's okay, baby. They had to go into town. You'll see them again."

I wondered if that was true. Now there was zero doubt about the degree to which Dylan's father, at least, and probably his mother, wanted me out of the picture.

The first ten minutes in the car were a blur. I couldn't tell you what music was playing, what the scenery looked like, or what he even said to me. I had said something along the lines of "I just need a minute," but eventually Dylan took my hand, squeezed it, and kissed the back.

"Please, baby. You look like you've seen a ghost. You seemed fine at breakfast with Mrs. Barnes. Then I went looking for you after my horrid chat with my father—you wouldn't believe the things he said to me—"

"I know," I said, staring into my lap at first. This was just going to pour out, it seemed. "I heard your conversation."

"You—" I heard the confusion in his voice.

"I didn't mean to eavesdrop. I got lost. I was exploring the house, and then I heard your voices, and I didn't want to call any attention to myself, and, well…I'm sorry for intruding, but I heard what he said."

Dylan was quiet. I wasn't sure for a moment if he was mad or concerned or neither. He just looked at the road. I took comfort in the fact that he still held my hand snugly in his own.

"I was hoping I could spare you his temper and cruelty until we'd been together, oh, I don't know, more than a few months, but…" he started and sighed deeply, and then he looked at me, worried. He was worried about me. "I guess that explains the look on your face."

"There's more, Dylan," I started. "He knew I'd heard you. He'd known I was there." I looked at Dylan and his lips were parted. I had no idea what he was thinking, so I just continued. "He invited me into his office."

Dylan's eyes turned sharply to mine. "Did he speak to you?"

"He did."

"What did the bastard say?" Dylan was seething. He'd removed his hand from mine and gripped the steering wheel, his strain and anger evident in his flexed arms and white knuckles.

"Dylan." I gulped. I didn't want to tell him this. I had some bizarre instinct to protect him from this information, but the reality was he'd probably had far worse done to him by his father over the years. "Dylan, he offered me money to break up with you."

"What did you say to him?" he asked. He was all eyes, all ears.

"Oh god. I can't believe what I said." Dylan was looking at me, so curious. "Dylan, I was totally unleashed. I told him off and said that was never going to happen and that the conversation was over. I totally lost it. I told him to shove his money up his ass." I cringed as I spoke the words, covering my face with my hands.

Then Dylan did something I never could have predicted. He was silent for a moment, then he laughed. He actually *laughed*.

"Dylan?" This wasn't exactly the reaction I'd been expecting. "What are you...?" I said and found myself laughing a little too, but more because the situation seemed surreal.

"You're my hero."

"Are you kidding?"

"No. I love you." He pulled the car over to the side of the road. We were near the highway but hadn't yet left the village. "I'm so sorry for laughing—it's just that, it's...it's almost a *relief*.

You can't imagine how often I've wanted to say that to him, for others to say that to him, but you actually *did*." He was silent for a moment, taking it in. "Lord knows he deserved it. You're bloody amazing."

I laughed a little, relieved myself.

"But, baby, I'm also sorry he did that. That's horrible. No one should have to deal with someone being so cruel, so insanely rude. And don't mistake my laughter for not taking this seriously—I want to *kill* him for saying that to you." And the anger that flashed through his eyes as he said these words left zero doubt in my mind about their veracity. "But, baby." He paused, trying to find the right words. "You just showed my father, better than I ever could, what something *real* looks like. What it means to actually love someone. I could tell him until I was blue in the face that you are not with me because of my money or title, and he wouldn't believe me for a second. Not believing me, not listening to me, is his standard perspective. But in one conversation you *showed* him."

The more I learned about Dylan's relationship with his father, the sadder I was for him. I could see the prison Dylan lived in more and more clearly, the bars coming into focus.

"I hated telling you that," I said.

"You didn't tell me anything new, not really. There's nothing you could tell me that would make think differently of him at this point. I'm only sorry you were exposed to his particular brand of malice so early. I had hopes I could spare you, at least until we move in together?" he said, raising his eyebrows hopefully, looking at me.

I smiled, relieved to hear the question. "It's too soon, Dylan. I just feel overwhelmed—not by you or us, but by the press and life and the store. I need a little more time. It just feels like too big of a change after so many changes." His smile faltered a little. "But keep asking, okay?"

He nodded, then took my hand in his again and brought it to his lips.

I hadn't known exactly how I'd felt about moving in with him until saying the words—I'd been saying no, and it had become a game, but what I'd said was true. I knew he wanted me in his house, and given that we'd only been together a couple of months, his wanting it seemed like enough. But if I listened to the voice buried beneath relationship conventions and anxieties about our current circumstances—if I dared listen to that voice—I knew what it would say. That a future without Dylan simply wasn't an option.

Chapter 17

By the time we got back to his house that night, his reaction to his father's bribe had settled more into anger and frustration. Now that the dust had settled, he was squarely back in the vortex of pressures—his work, his father, and the emails.

We sat in the lounge off his bedroom, and we were polishing off glasses of wine. He ran his fingers through his hair as he began preparing me for the week ahead, another long week in which we'd likely see very little of each other. "The Olympic committee is about to have my head, I'm afraid. If I don't submit the revised designs for the stadium by Friday, I won't be surprised if they look elsewhere." He'd been rubbing is forehead while he spoke from the chair where he was seated. He looked so stressed, torn. I stood up from my seat on the couch and walked towards him.

"I know you'll get it done," I said, stepping closer, standing between his legs.

"Of course I'll bloody get it done," he said sternly. "I've never been late on a design in my life, and I'm not going to start now."

"Don't talk to me like I'm Thomas," I said, equally sternly, and Dylan removed his hands from his face and wrapped them around the backs of my legs, pulling me closer and looking up at me. I threaded my fingers through his hair.

"I'm sorry, baby. I'm not mad at you. I'm still furious with my father. What he said to you…And then he dares to be relentless, holding my grandfather's name and company over my head—" Just then his phone chimed with a text. He picked it up and scowled at it in a way that made me very glad not to be his phone. "Tristan fucking Bailey," he mumbled under his breath, and he tossed the phone back onto the table.

"Everything okay?" I asked.

Dylan nodded. "Like I said, my father's relentless." He reached his firm muscular arms around me and pulled me down onto his lap and against his chest. "Until I figure this out, I'll be busier, I'm afraid. This week in particular."

I pulled back so I could look him in the eye, and I gave him a raised eyebrow. "Oh yeah, knighty? Well, I'm busy and important too, you know," I began. "The store opens in less than two months, and there's mountains to do. So, you know, I'm just not going to be able to cater to your whims and—"

"Cheeky thing." He chuckled and pulled me against him again. His hands ran up and down my back, stroking, soothing, apologizing for his outburst. He kissed the top of my head and pulled me closer. "I wish I could protect you from all of this."

"What do you mean?"

"You deserve a simpler relationship, one that doesn't involve a man being pulled in a thousand different directions by despicable parents, duty, and career."

"You mean one without the man I actually want? The man who has a complicated rich life but handles it with grace? That relationship? No, thanks. I'll stick with you."

"I don't deserve you."

"Well, true," I said, smiling into his chest. "But I'm obviously extremely witty and genius-like, and you can't seem to stay away, so we'll just have to cope, won't we?"

"Indeed," he said softly into my ear. He was thinking—I could practically hear his mental wheels turning. "You know what?" he asked.

"What?"

"I'm going to take a page from your book."

"What do you mean?" I asked again, this time for clarification.

"I'm going to tell my father where he can shove it. He and Hale Shipping can wait," he said with total determination. "I need to get back to my own work. I'll spend some time with the security team of course—we still have to identify whoever is sending you emails. I won't let up on that. But otherwise—"

"Otherwise, you'll be at Hale Architecture and Design, doing your thing. I think this is the best idea you've had in a while."

Dylan kissed my hair in response, and while I couldn't see his face, I could feel his satisfied smile against my skin.

"I mean, it's even better than that whole velvet-rope idea you had—"

Dylan slapped my outer thigh, making me jolt in his arms and laugh. I look up into his calmer, happier eyes.

"To bed with you, wench," he said and carried me towards the low luxurious bed behind me.

* * *

The week that followed was flying by, and I couldn't quite believe when I looked up from my desk in the middle of the day to realize it was already Wednesday. I had moved into the office at the back of the storefront, which in itself had taken all of Monday and most of Tuesday. The upside was that I now could be where I needed to be with deliveries being made, construction happening, designers stopping by. The store was also closer to Dylan's house, making the whole walking-to-work thing easier. The downsides were that there were no windows, I was mostly alone back there—apart from the deliveries, construction crews, and designers—and I missed Fiona and Josh.

That was why, after two ten-hour days in the shop and a morning of phone calls and emails with suppliers, I had decided to finish out the rest of Wednesday from the main office. Having just said goodbye to Frank outside the building, I was still in the elevator when I started to hear the excited giggles coming from reception. When I walked into the space, I saw Josh practically hyperventilating, the intern squealing, and Fiona rolling her eyes.

"This lot," she said, pointing to Josh jumping up and down, "is going mental. All because a couple of posh dunces are swooning and in love." She huffed.

"What?" I asked, confused.

Josh struggled to speak through his excitement but managed to get out two important words: *royal* and *wedding*.

"There's going to be a royal wedding?" I asked. "Who's getting married?"

"Oh, like you don't know!" Josh screamed. "Oh good god, you're going to get to actually *go*, you tramp!"

"Wait, no, seriously, who's getting married?" I asked, still confused. I put down my bag, which was heavy with binders of information to go over with Hannah and was hurting my shoulder.

Josh was back to breathing heavily and was now feverishly searching the Internet at his desk for more details about this engagement.

"Prince Richard and Lady Jemma Kirk," Fiona explained dryly.

"Oh—" I began but was interrupted by my phone buzzing in my pocket. A text from Dylan:

WEDNESDAY, 1:47 pm
If you haven't heard, Richard is engaged to whatshername.

WEDNESDAY, 1:47 pm
Just heard. Josh is going into excitement-related cardiac arrest over here.

WEDNESDAY, 1:48 pm
Well, you'd better not tell him you're going to the engagement do.

I looked over at Josh, who was now reading aloud a post about guesses at who would design the wedding gown. Hannah was apparently on the list, which was making the intern jump up and down again, and Fiona was headed back to our office, where I could hear phones ringing. I turned back to my phone.

WEDNESDAY, 1:49 pm
I am?

WEDNESDAY, 1:50 pm
You are. Two weeks Friday?
Also, I wish you hadn't been asleep when I got home last night—I was very ready to do very naughty things to you.

WEDNESDAY, 1:50 pm

Oh, were you?

WEDNESDAY, 1:50 pm
I was rather. Nearly woke you but decided to let you sleep
through it instead.

WEDNESDAY, 1:51 pm
Very funny.

WEDNESDAY, 1:51 pm
You love me for my wicked wit. And my massive . . .

WEDNESDAY, 1:52 pm
Ego.
Gotta run, knighty. Wake me up tonight. It will be worth it.

WEDNESDAY, 1:53 pm
You say that as though you have any say in what will hap-
pen. Do as you're told, and be ready for me. And by ready,
I mean naked.
Home around 10, damsel.

WEDNESDAY, 2:02 pm
Oh, and damsel? I love you.

I didn't even see that last text message until after six when I
was headed down in the elevator. It was a cold, rainy night and
dark already, so I slumped into the backseat of the Jag and let
Frank drive me home. I'm not sure who was happier about that,
me or him.

When I checked my personal email for the first time since
lunch, I also found that there were already three royal-wedding-
related events Dylan and I were set to attend over the next
month—the upcoming engagement party, a tea of some sort

for friends and family, and some kind of aristocratic traditional thing in which Dylan's father would be nominally involved.

That last one, it turned out, I wouldn't be able to go to, being neither an aristocrat myself nor married or engaged to one. I had a twinge of discomfort at the reminder of these social mores that kept me separate from Dylan, but ultimately my relief won out. As it was I would be talking to Hannah about borrowing at least two dresses for these events. Luckily it was a situation that, at least so far, benefitted us both. I got the high-end glamorous clothes I needed for these parties, and she got low-friction publicity.

Dylan did wake me up that night, well after ten, and he did deliver on his promise. A flicker of optimism had dampened the distance between us over the past week, and even seeing so little of each other, I could feel that wedge between us narrowing. Or at least I hoped it was.

Chapter 18

The next morning I sweet-talked Dylan into walking with me to the shop, not wanting to let him go. We hadn't had a non-text, non-sex conversation in three days. As we walked past Lennox Gardens, I noticed that for the first time in weeks Dylan was holding my hand while we walked, and he was…Was he actually sauntering? He seemed so much lighter than normal.

"What's with you this morning?" I asked, gripping his hand a little tighter.

"What do you mean?" he asked while raising our linked hands to his mouth and kissing our joined knuckles. Something was definitely up.

I gave him my best *oh please* look. He *was* lighter.

He guided me around some dog poop as he answered, "I haven't a clue what you're talking about."

I looked closely at him and could see his mind wandering a little, but wandering happily. Then it dawned on me. "I know what it is. You're *working*. It's architecture—you're designing. Did you finish the Olympic plans?"

"I did, and they're splendid," he said in a very satisfied Dylan kind of way while pulling me against him so his arm was wrapped fully around my waist as we walked. "And I just heard they've wrapped up work on the Amsterdam project, so that business with Piers Reynolds is finally off my plate."

"Dylan, that's great," I said. I couldn't believe how stark the difference was. Dylan was an architect through and through—this was the man I'd met and fallen for. He'd been determined to focus on his own work, and within four days he'd returned to himself. It had never been so clear to me that no matter what happened, Dylan had to keep designing.

We'd arrived at the door to the shop front, and I was now leaning against the plywood wall covering the windows, hoping my back wouldn't be covered in dust when I rose from it. Dylan was hovering over me, stroking my cheek.

"I can get behind this walking thing," he said, smirking. "If for no other reason than to see these cheeks all flushed." His earthy refined smell filled the air around me, and it comforted me and seduced me in one breath.

He reached into my coat and slid his cool fingers around my waist, pulling me against him so he could kiss me, but I rolled my eyes at him before his lips met mine.

"I would take that eye roll as disapproval, but we both know you're just as randy as I am."

"Sure, sure, knighty. Whatever. You're all talk these days," I replied, to which Dylan just raised an eyebrow. Then a lightbulb went off—I could see it in his eyes.

"Do you think Hannah will mind if you're gone for a bit next week?"

"What?"

"I want to take you away."

"Um," I said, not hiding my smile. "I mean, I haven't taken a day since I started, and everything's going well here. I can't do much else until the furniture is in. It would probably be fine. Why? What are you thinking?"

"It's a surprise. Ask Hannah, and tell me as soon as you know. We'd leave Wednesday evening, and I'd have you back for work Tuesday. No. Fuck it. Wednesday. It will be a celebration of sorts. Jobs well done. You need a break. *I* need a break. Let's get out of this mad city."

"I like the sound of that," I said, all of sudden deeply in the dream of six long days with Dylan, no interruptions, indulging in this new, freer version of my boyfriend. It would be a huge departure from the chaos of London, his family, my work, his work, the watchful eye of the press—it sounded perfect. Maybe we'd shaken something loose. Maybe we were past whatever stressful weather system had been chasing us.

* * *

Two hours later I finally found a moment to talk to Hannah in her office.

"Fiona tells me you're having an audience with Her Majesty this weekend?" She was looking up at me from her desk chair, but somehow she always managed to keep me on my toes. I had come in to ask her about the time off but had been greeted with this question instead.

"I am. This weekend. I think it will be brief, and I don't ex-pect—"

"What are you wearing?" Man, she was putting the bossy in *boss* this morning.

"Um, an Alexander McQueen that I found at Harvey Nichols."

Hannah scowled. "I gather you didn't want to wear one of mine," she said while reading papers on her desk. *Oh crap. Seriously?*

"Hannah, you've been so generous already, and I didn't want to inconvenience you. We don't have any formal agreement about this, and I didn't want to assume. I was actually going to—"

"I gather you'll be attending some wedding-related festivities with your boyfriend?" she asked coolly.

"Yes—"

"Good, then let's make it formal. I want to dress you for future events."

"Oh, Hannah, that would actually be—"

"The deal is that you give me control over the styling, and if it's appropriate, you'll agree to be photographed in the dresses and you'll credit me when asked about the clothes."

"Actually—" Her head snapped up and she looked at me, clearly as surprised as I was that I'd just interrupted *her*. I cleared my throat. "Actually, while I'd be honored to wear any Hannah Rogan gown to one of these events, this will only work if I get approval rights over the gowns. And while I'm happy to work with Stephen or others on styling, again, I'll veto and give my input as appropriate."

She paused for a moment and then nodded. "Fine, then it's settled." She smiled and finally looked at me for the first time during this conversation. She actually looked a little relieved. Me wearing her clothes to these events would help her, probably more than it would if Amelia Reynolds were wearing them.

"Great. And thank you, Hannah. I think this arrangement

will work well for both of us," I added. "And speaking of the shop, I was wondering if we might discuss a title change that was better fitting to my new role?"

She eyed me, taken aback by my having found my voice so suddenly, but also, I thought, with respect. "What were you thinking?"

"How about director of sales?"

"And I imagine this title change would be accompanied by a salary increase?"

"If you thought it was appropriate," I said.

"I do. How would you feel about a fifteen percent increase?" I could tell my bringing this up had earned me a different variety of Hannah's appreciation.

"That seems fair," I said. "Fifteen percent, and if it's not inconvenient, I'd also like to take a few personal days next week—I'd be out Thursday, returning the following Wednesday." I figured I'd better get that in there sooner rather than later. I was on a roll.

She nodded, smiled slightly, and returned her eyes to the papers on her desk. "If that will be all?" she asked as though she were dismissing me, but I knew this interaction had gone well. I nodded, stood tall, and turned towards the door.

Which was open.

And Fiona was standing just beyond it, staring into Hannah's office. She'd clearly heard the conversation, which wasn't exactly private, but gauging by Fiona's reaction, there were probably better ways to convey to her that I'd just gotten a promotion. And while I wasn't sure exactly what was at the root of the tension between me and Fiona, I knew instinctively that our friendship couldn't bear the pressure of too many more big Lydia events.

"Fee," I started, determined to get to the bottom of this.

"Whatever." She turned to walk away. "Tell Josh I'm going to the studio," she said without looking back.

Shit.

When I got to my office, Josh was there.

"Where's Fee?" he asked.

"I think she's furious with me," I started. "She just overheard a conversation between me and Hannah. Hannah's going to give me clothes for these events I'm going to. And I also I asked her for a promotion. Because of the store. And I got it."

"And she stomped out?" he asked, looking at me sympathetically.

I nodded.

"She has a lot going on," Josh said, leaning back in Fiona's chair.

"She feels like I've marched in here and taken over," I said, defeated. "I didn't mean for any of this to happen."

"I know, love. She'll come around."

I sat at my own desk and put my head in my hands, sighing deeply.

"So what will madame be dressing you for? Didn't you already get a dress for the thing with the queen this weekend?"

I nodded and gulped. "Dylan and I are invited to the engagement party for Prince Richard," I said, bracing myself.

Josh's eyes got huge. "No! Oh my god, really? That's amazing. Oh, Lydia, this is going to be so much fun. I can't wait to see what you wear. What *Dylan* wears. What *Richard* wears. And have you *seen* his friend? You know, that scamp who's always at the clubs with him? The bloody gorgeous one? I'm pretty sure he bats for my team—you must find out. Ooh, Lydia," he said, clapping his hands. "This is the best news I've heard all day!"

I couldn't believe Josh's generous nature. There wasn't a mean bone in this guy's slim body, and there wasn't a conversation we'd had that didn't result in me smiling and feeling just a little bit more like he was going to be a lifelong friend.

"Really? You're not annoyed with me too?"

"Are you completely mad? I *know* someone who will be at the engagement party of the century! My stock just went up a hundred percent. This is going on Facebook *immediately*."

I laughed, so relieved things with Josh, at least, were uncomplicated.

* * *

Saturday morning had consisted of me getting dressed at Emily's London flat so she could play Barbie on my hair and makeup and supervise the assembling of my outfit. We both knew I'd be fine on my own, but this was way more fun. Frank then delivered me to the palace at noon—I hadn't been invited to the CBC festivities beforehand, apparently something reserved only for the actual architects and elites involved.

Now I sat patiently, stiffly, hands in my lap, legs crossed at the ankles, in a gilded chair in a hallway in some non-room room in Buckingham Palace. A man in a suit stood on the far side of the room and looked at me only occasionally with complete disinterest. Dylan had said noon. It was now 12:15, and I worried if too much time went by, I'd either sweat through my fabulous new dress, fall out of my heels, or begin to wonder if this whole thing, these glorious past few months, had been nothing but the fantastical ramblings of an insane person—me—who had turned up at the palace to make claims about some nonexistent marquess she was in love with. So, yeah, I guess I was a little nervous.

Just as I was about to bolt and check myself into a mental institution, Dylan climbed the stairs and entered the room. Right behind his parents.

His father gave me a quick look of shock, followed immediately by disdain and then a quick glare at Dylan and another at his wife, who was right beside him. Why did I get the sense that Charlotte and Geoffrey hadn't had any idea I would be there? And why hadn't I anticipated how awkward it would be to see Dylan's father for the first time after our altercation at Humboldt Park?

I rose, and Dylan quickly swept to my side, kissed me on the cheek, and tucked my arm into his. It was clear his newfound disregard for his father's opinion was still running strong.

When we stepped into the golden room, the feeling that I might be in a weird dream continued. The ceilings were endless and arched, and every inch was decorated in gilded moldings. The walls were similarly adorned, and enormous mirrors shared space with oversized sconces and oil paintings and shelves of presumably priceless antiques.

I was in freaking *Buckingham Palace.*

It took a minute to register the petite, stately woman standing by the table in a blue suit, and I found myself speechless—something nobody in their right mind would ever call me. I remember curtsying, which I may have done backwards if that's possible, and saying the words *Your Majesty,* which I'm pretty sure I hadn't done since I was six and playing a make-believe princess game with a neighbor. I remember accidentally using the sugar spoon to stir my tea and then surreptitiously trying to sneak it back into the sugar bowl. I remember thinking the queen was the nicest old lady I'd met in a long time, but also having a ticker tape going through my mind that said,

Oh my god, this is the queen. I remember Dylan squeezing my hand, especially hard when his father was speaking.

But the rest of that hour was a fuzzy, pleasant blur, one of those moments that was so bizarre and extraordinary that I should try to take in every detail but also that it would be a futile effort.

When I first realized how formal the visit would be and that I wouldn't be attending the rest of the afternoon's festivities with Dylan, I wondered what the point was of my even being there. But over the course of the hour I understood. Dylan held my hand throughout, and I listened to the way he found subtle moments to tell the queen a little bit of my story, how I'd just arrived in London for the first time since I was an infant, how I'd returned to start my career, how much I loved the city. I realized he was proud of me. He wasn't showing me off or making a point to his father. He'd wanted me to meet her because he knew I would love the experience but also—and this was the part that stunned me, made me feel humbled the moment I understood it—he'd wanted *her* to meet *me*.

There weren't many moments when my stiff-upper-lip aristocratic boyfriend made his feelings clear to me—his non-bedroom feelings, anyway—but this was a moment I knew I'd remember for the rest of my life, no matter what happened. A moment when I felt truly loved.

Chapter 19

It was nearly eight in the evening, and I'd already indulged in a bowl of pasta and a solid pour of wine when I finally heard from Dylan. I'd come home after the palace, but he'd had to continue on to the actual event. It was so quiet that the buzzing phone startled me off my barstool in the kitchen, where I'd been reading a magazine.

"Hi," I said, eager to hear his voice for the first time since our audience with the queen that afternoon.

"Damsel," he said with a thick sigh in his voice.

I gulped—maybe the afternoon had not gone as well as I'd thought.

I must have been quiet for a little too long, because he finally asked, "Lydia?"

"Do you think tea went badly?" I asked, a little nervous.

"Oh, damsel, no. Tea was perfect. You were lovely, as I knew you'd be. As far as those things go, it was the most enjoyable I've had in ages. She's got more spark than one would expect, doesn't she? She was really pleased with you too, I think."

"She was probably just reassured that you're not gay or something."

Dylan chuckled. "Somehow I don't think she'd give a frog's arse if I were," he said, laughing again. "I know all that fuss is foreign to you, but you'd never know it. You were seamless. No one would ever know that you don't dine with Her Majesty on the regular."

"Maybe I do. You don't know where I have lunch every day," I said. Dylan was quiet for a minute. "You so know where I have lunch every day, don't you?"

I could practically hear him shrugging on the other end of the phone. "What do you think I pay Frank for?"

"Not to spy on me!"

"I'm not spying, damsel. And, no, I don't actually know where you have lunch, but I mean, I could know. And I think Frank would tell me if it were at Buckingham Palace. And if he didn't, *HELLO!* magazine probably would."

"How boring. I mean, how's a girl supposed to keep any secrets?"

"And what secrets do you want to keep from me, damsel?"

"Well, *knighty*, don't you know that it's all part of being a woman? Maintaining an aura of mystery?"

Dylan just laughed. Then laughed some more. Fine, so I wasn't exactly one of those untouchable mysterious girls, but he didn't have to point it out to me! "Okay, okay, you've had your fun. When are you coming home?"

Another long pause and an even deeper sigh. "Lydia, I'm sorry, but I have to travel for a few days. I need to be in Moscow until Tuesday, possibly Wednesday."

"Moscow? What do you have going on in Moscow?" I'd never heard him mention anything happening in Russia.

"It's for Hale Shipping and related to the emails, actually. I just haven't been able to access what I need from here, so I need to go there in person and see if I can make some headway."

I groaned a little.

"I'm sorry. After today I just want to climb into bed and watch you practice that curtsy a few more times."

"I'd never done it before!" But I sighed in resignation. "Fine. If going to Moscow means figuring out this whole email thing and letting poor Frank start protecting someone more exciting, then I'm glad you're going. I'm just going to miss you."

"I know. I'll miss you too. Hale Shipping is just having some upheaval. This won't last much longer. And I'm hoping this will be the end of all this email business as well." Dylan paused on the other end. "Get some sleep, baby. I'll see you when I get back. And stay at mine if you'd like. I know Molly will be sad if you're not there to debate terribly important cooking matters."

"You don't need to boil the water first to cook pasta!" I said, recalling the playful confrontation Molly and I had engaged in the previous week.

"I'm staying out of it," he said defensively, and I could actually picture him putting his palms up in surrender to my ferocious opinions.

* * *

Monday morning was one of those perfect fall days. Crisp and cool, but not frigid. Perfect weather for boots and a jacket and carrying a hot coffee while walking to work. I knew Frank was following not far behind, but I didn't care. I wanted to walk, and he was giving me the space.

I was only a block from the office, where I was stopping before heading to the shop, when I was faced with my picture at a newsstand. My body was now conditioned to react with a delightful combination of terror and anxiety, immediately assuming the worst. I'd probably scowled at the queen or called her by her first name or had a nip slip or something similarly embarrassing. The headline would be something along the lines of *"When will this embarrassing American girl just go away?"*

But that's not what it said. I was on Dylan's arm, emerging from the palace. The dress looked perfect—I looked demure but stylish. Dylan was typically perfect looking—like the duke he was in a five-thousand-dollar suit. The headline of the *Guardian* was simply:

Lydia Lunches with Her Majesty

The brief article quoted the royal press release, which had said, *Saturday morning, the 16th Duke of Abingdon opened the Conservation in Building Conference held by the Green Building Initiative. Subsequently the Duke and Duchess of Abingdon, the Marquess of Abingdon, and guest Lydia Bell were received by the queen at Buckingham Palace.* The article went on to say that I had been recently promoted to director of sales for Hannah Rogan, and it was accompanied by an official-looking photo of all of us standing in front of a fireplace.

Clean. Simple. Accurate. No fuss. For the first time, the press wasn't sending me out for the slaughter. It felt great. I felt like I'd done something right, like there was no way Geoffrey or Charlotte Hale could get on Dylan's back about this, that there was no way it could make Hale Shipping or Humboldt Park or the Hale family look bad. It put a literal swing in my step.

I had just walked into the office and was about to try to have a gossip session with Fiona when Hannah barged in behind me. "Well done, Lydia. Well done. You're oozing grace in that photo.

It's exactly the kind of press you want, and you two look divine together. And next time you'll be wearing Hannah Rogan. Between this and the store, you're certainly earning your keep around here."

Fuck. Sure, that was a good professional moment, but one look at Fiona's depressed expression, and it was abundantly clear that I had some in-house diplomacy I needed to attend to. Screw that, I had a friendship to save.

"Fee," I started as soon as Hannah had slipped back into the hallway.

"Mmm?" she asked, not taking her eyes from her computer screen.

"Let's talk."

"What about?" She still wouldn't look at me.

"About the fact that you can't stand me right now. That I'm an annoying upstart busybody who marched in as a second assistant and all of a sudden is doing this whole other thing. About the fact that if I were you, I'd be pissy as hell about it. And also maybe about the fact that you've barely mentioned Ben in over three weeks, and obviously there's something going on there. You know, about everything. Because we're friends. Or were friends. I feel like the further down the rabbit hole of this store I go and the longer I'm with Dylan, the further and further apart we get."

"Bloody hell. You Yanks really do like to have it out, don't you?" she said, now not only looking at me but staring at me the way only a Brit who's being asked to chat about her feelings can—with shock and just a little bit of horror.

I shrugged. She sighed.

"I don't hate you or anything," she started.

"Well, that's a relief."

"I'm not an idiot. I'm good at my job. I mean, for fuck's sake, I graduated from Edinburgh with a first."

"I know. You're brilliant."

"I'm just…Here's the thing, Lydia. You know what you want. You just go after it. It's not exactly your most British quality—being all outspoken and proposing grand ideas after being here for two months. But it's right fabulous, and the truth is that I wish I had your guts."

"Well, when you put it that way I'm kind of mortified. Do you think I was overeager about this whole flagship store thing?"

"Who cares? It worked!" she said, throwing her arms up in the air, both mystified by me and frustrated at her own situation, which I still didn't quite understand. I laughed, because she was right, and also because this was the most animated I'd seen her in weeks. "I mean, let's be clear: I think you're a nutter to be taking this on with no real experience starting a business, but I also think it's going to be great."

"You know, I never really knew exactly what I wanted to do within the fashion business. I just knew I wanted to be a part of it. And when all of those orders started coming in after Fashion Week, and you and I were running back and forth between here and her studio, organizing fittings and running ourselves ragged, I found myself longing for the days when I worked at this little boutique in New York. I actually thought, 'Man, I wish there was a way to help Hannah with all of these sales in a more organized way and from one place that wouldn't interfere with everything else.' I mean, isn't that ridiculous? It was like I had to reinvent the idea of a store before I even realized that's what I was thinking about." I tapped my head with my knuckles, as if to see if anything was in there at all. "I think anyone would agree this is all a bit insane. Hannah had plans for it, of course, but was thinking two years out. I was just lucky she was willing to let me go after it."

"Well, you're obviously bloody brilliant at it."

"Let's be honest—the timing was also right. Had I tried this pre-'DyLy'"—I threw air quotes around the ridiculous nickname, and sure enough, Fiona gasped and laughed simultaneously, probably relieved that I was willing to make fun of myself—"I probably wouldn't have gotten further than Hannah's threshold. I know I'm lucky. I don't even want to think about it too much, or I'll probably just realize none of it would've happened at all without Dylan, and what does that say about me?"

"Eh, fuck it," Fiona said in her perfectly vulgar and yet reassuring way. "We all have our advantages and handicaps. Best to just use 'em and accept 'em as wisely as we can."

"Wow—that was actually kind of wise... So what do you want to do? I can't imagine your end goal is being Hannah's assistant."

Fiona was quiet. Really quiet. I had a feeling she actually did know the answer to this one.

"Fiona?"

"Promise you won't make fun?"

"Cross my heart."

She was quiet for a while longer, rubbing her knuckles.

"Jewelry," she finally said in a near whisper.

"What? Really? Designing it or wearing it?" I said, looking at the long dangly earrings brushing her shoulders, and she gave me an exasperated eye roll.

"Designing it, you nag!"

She pulled out a thick binder from the side of her desk and handed it to me. I started to flip through, and there were pages and pages of sketches. They were elegant but understated. Cool, fashion forward, and totally original. "Have you made any of these?"

She shook her head, and when I looked at her, she was biting her thumbnail. "Fiona, they're gorgeous."

"Really? You really think so?"

"I know so. Would you make them yourself?"

"No, no. That's not my skill. I've gone so far as to meet with a metalsmith who could do some mock-ups for me, but I've never had the capital to get it going."

"You have to. You have to do this. These are fabulous. Have you shown Hannah?"

"Are you *completely* mad?" she asked, looking at me like I had just spoken Mandarin.

"You should!"

"No way."

"This is me—the brazen American—telling you to go for it. Or you know what? Let's think on it. I want to do this with you, help you, even just moral support, but practically if you want it."

"Lydia, do you mean it?"

"Absolutely."

We talked right through lunch, planning, scheming, and poring over her sketches. When the intern came back, I sent her all the way to Hampstead for paint swatches.

Eventually Fiona opened up to me about Ben too. They'd "had a row," but she didn't think it was over. Apparently he'd called her "daft" and accused her of not going after what she wanted, to which she'd replied that he was "a sexist wanker" and didn't appreciate his male privilege. I had a feeling they'd get past this one.

And I really did love those jewelry sketches. I didn't tell Fiona at the time—I didn't want to get her hopes up—but I was convinced some of them would be the perfect complements to the ideas Hannah was playing with for next year's spring line. She'd get there. All I knew was that I was so happy to have my friend back.

Chapter 20

I was walking on air after my reconciliation with Fiona. It felt like everything was looking up. We'd dragged Josh into our plan for an indulgent girls' night in, complete with takeout and face masks. I was in such a good mood that I didn't even mind when I received a bad news text from Dylan:

MONDAY, 4:43 pm
Damsel. Having trouble getting what I need here. Back Wednesday night. Sorry, baby.

MONDAY, 4:43 pm
It's OK. Miss you!

MONDAY, 4:44 pm
I'm still taking you away. Don't go getting all rebellious on me. I'll want you nice and pliant, ready to forgive your dreadful boyfriend for depriving you.

MONDAY, 4:44 pm
Who says I'm deprived?

MONDAY, 4:45 pm
You're in a cheeky mood, aren't you, little one? Careful.
Don't forget—you're mine.

MONDAY, 4:45 pm
Always. Hurry home. XO

It was after eleven before I'd successfully convinced Fiona and Josh to call a taxi and head home. We'd eaten our way through half the menu at the local Thai takeout place and every dessert we could put our hands on, convincing ourselves we were burning at least that many calories laughing. I felt like I had my friends back.

And it turned out to be just in time. We were waiting for their car to arrive and I was searching YouTube for a Beyoncé music video they'd never seen when my computer dinged with an incoming email.

Somehow I just knew.

It was one of those moments when you forget the immediate surroundings, forget that there might be other people present, forget that maybe it's not a good idea to act, and instead succumb to the inevitability of the whole thing.

The sender was the same, a random series of letters and numbers. But this time there was no text, just a video embedded in the email. I clicked PLAY before thinking, and immediately Dylan's voice filled the room.

"Shh, baby."

I gulped and then gulped again, starting to shake.

"So wet for me. I love this little pussy, you know that?"

Dylan's voice again, haunting me. The image was clear, and you could see everything. Me. Spread out on Dylan's bed at Humboldt Park. His hands on me.

"Watch—I want you to watch everything."

"What the fuck is *that*?" said Fiona from across the room, clearly hearing the video. I immediately slammed the laptop closed and started to cry. This couldn't be happening. It was too much. Too personal. I had no idea how long the video was, how far it had gone, but I did see that the little indicator was far to the left, suggesting several minutes of video would follow. The image had been crystal clear, as though the person taking the video had been right there in the room with us. How was that even possible?

I was mortified. Horrified. I felt dirty. I felt invaded. And for the first time really scared. There was no way Dylan knew about this. No way.

"Lovey," Josh whispered, rubbing my back. "What's going on?"

I heard him indicate to Fiona to cancel the car.

They sweetly moved me to the couch, and I told them everything. About every last email. About not going to the police. About not knowing who or why or what. About Frank. I had told Dylan this would be a secret, but the truth was I needed *him* in that moment. But he wasn't there—my friends were, and I needed them too.

They reminded me to send the information to Dylan immediately so he could act on it, and I did. I did do that. He called me within minutes, and Fiona and Josh watched as I spoke into the phone.

"I'm fine," I said, but I could hear how dead my voice was.

"No, you're not," he said sternly.

"I am. Dylan, it's fine. I'm going to bed, I promise. Just please, please make them stop."

"I'm working on it, baby. I'm working on it right now."

I was pretty sure he could hear the shakiness in my breath.

"Trust me," he said, as he had so many times before. But this time it somehow made things worse. There were only so many *trust me*s a girl could handle.

I pulled it together and glanced at Fiona and Josh, sitting on the couch. "I'll see you Wednesday, knighty," I said, but it was forced. The nickname didn't have the same lightness it normally did.

* * *

Thankfully Fiona and Josh left shortly after that. I'd been so glad they were there so I could talk to them, but then talking about it made it impossible to forget. So I was also glad when they left, ready to sink into my bed and lull myself into an oblivion where none of this was happening.

I was in a restless sleep when I felt the sheets rustle beside me. My eyes flew open in a panic—a new fear had settled over me.

But Dylan's hand stroked my bangs, and he leaned down to kiss my face, gentle pecks over my cheeks and lips.

"Don't be scared, baby. It's me."

I curled my body into his and let him wrap his arms around me.

"How are you back? Why? I thought you weren't going to be able to be back until tomorrow night," I said, breathing him in, calmed by just the scent of him.

"Shh," he continued. "I called the pilot as soon as I got off the phone with you. I needed to be here with you. I won't let him hurt you or get that close to you ever again. I promise."

It had to be near morning—the blue light of dawn was already creeping in my windows—but I fell back to sleep in his arms.

When I woke again, I saw the clock on my wall read ten in the morning, and I shot up, panicked. And then it all came flooding back to me—the night before, the video, Dylan in my bed.

"You came home," I said at the same time that Dylan's hands landed on my arms from behind.

"Of course I came home," he said.

"I have to go to work," I said and started to climb out of bed, but Dylan grabbed my hand, holding firm.

"Fiona texted me and said to say that she told Hannah you'd be in late today because of a dentist's appointment."

"She texted you?"

"Yes—I'm glad you told her what was going on. I'm glad she was here. She's a good friend."

"She is," I said, falling back against his chest, relieved not to have to rush.

"Baby," he started to say as he wrapped his strong arm around my chest, "we got the guy."

I flung my head around and looked into his eyes. "Really?" I said, so hopeful. "Dylan, you really got him?"

Dylan nodded and smiled. "I got a call this morning, and they found enough evidence on this guy's hard drive to make it pretty clear. He is denying it, of course, but it would be too co-incidental, given the evidence."

"Who is it?" I asked, scooching myself to sitting up next to him, still not believing this was behind us. Especially so quickly on the heels of that last email.

"It was just as I thought," Dylan started and pulled me against him. "He works for an old Russian family we used to do business with, the Bresnovs. Back in my grandfather's day we were partners with them—they were actually extremely helpful to my grandfather in getting Hale Shipping off the ground. But the last sixty years haven't been good to them—they're not the family they used to be," he said, sighing.

"But *why*?" I asked, still not understanding. "Why would someone do this to me? To you?"

"Spineless pricks. I had my suspicions, but *Christ*, the assholes were hard to pin down. A few years back a deal we had went south, and it really left them high and dry. Honestly it left them without options—they were desperate and trying to send me a message. Plain and simple. But it's over now, baby."

"But what does this have to do with *you*? Hale Shipping is your father's domain. I don't get it." I was now perched on my knees, my T-shirt collecting at my hips, my eyes searching his for understanding. Somehow it just didn't feel real that it was over. I'd gone to sleep feeling so utterly creeped out.

"My father made the deal. I broke it."

I searched him for more.

"I've never been very involved with the company, not until recently, but as a member of the board I do an annual check-in with the accounting group, to make sure everything's on the up and up. When I learned about this deal... The Bresnovs stood to gain a great deal at Hale Shipping's expense. I couldn't let that stand, and I've kept a closer eye on things since then. This stunt was them trying to send me a message that the conversation isn't over." His muscular arms came for me, his hands wrapping around my middle, his strength pulling me to sit across his lap and against his bare torso. "But I assure you, baby. The conversation *is* over. I won't let them harass you again."

"Thank god," I said, sighing into his chest. I could feel the stress leaving my body. "I still don't understand how they did it.

How did they get that video?" The longer I sat against him, the safer I felt, but remaining unanswered questions began popping up in my mind.

"My team is investigating. They found a camera in one of the rowing statues in my bedroom. They must have paid one of the staff or a visitor to sneak into my room and plant it. We'll figure it out." He kissed the top of my head.

I simply reached up and kissed him in reply before he continued. "I still couldn't tell you why it took two months to figure this out—why this evidence was so hard to come by—but it's done with. Now we'll really have something to celebrate on our trip."

I was still in a state of disbelief and extreme relief. This haunting nightmare, one I now realized I'd been minimizing, was finally over. I let my weight sink just a little deeper into Dylan's chest.

"So where are we going?" I asked sleepily, knowing that soon I would have to get up and go to work, but it would feel like a brand-new world when I did.

"Nope," he said, shaking his head and giving me a look that said he was up to no good. "It's a surprise."

Chapter 21

Thirty hours later and I was stepping into Dylan's silver Mercedes no wiser about where he was taking me. *Both* of us had skips in our steps. Weights had been lifted in the last couple of weeks, and I imagined this was what a real vacation was supposed to feel like—an expanse of time that had *freedom* and *new beginning* written all over it.

"So where are we going?" I asked, sidling up next to him.

"Nope."

"But somewhere where I need a passport?" I asked—he'd told me to leave it for him that morning.

"Maybe."

"This is ridiculous. I'm just supposed to wear this our entire trip?" I asked, gesturing down to the wool pleated skirt and silk camisole I had worn to work that morning. I had tights and ankle boots and a jacket but otherwise just the odds and ends that filled my tote bag. There might have been a spare pair of underwear in there if I was lucky, although fat lot of good they'd do me with Dylan around.

"I've got you covered. Literally," he said with a cheeky smile, wrapping his arms around me.

"Uh-huh." I smirked back at him. "That's probably Dylan-speak for the fact that I'll be naked the entire time we're there. Wherever it is we're going... Come on, Dylan. Where are we going?"

"Right now, to the airport," he started, and I rolled my eyes, annoyed at his stubbornness. "Then somewhere beautiful and quiet. We'll stop for provisions on the way."

"Fine. Have it your way. But know that I'll be furious if I have to ski in tights and a skirt."

"No skiing," he said, turning in his seat to look at me as he draped one arm over the top of the wide bench seat and twisted my ponytail in his fingers. I wasn't sure I'd ever seen him so relaxed. "So everything is good with the shop?"

"Hannah couldn't care less that I am leaving for a few days. She is so thrilled that Thomas Pink has agreed to produce a line of neckties with the print she is using for the next season—"

"A deal you put together."

"Well, not quite." He looked at me disapprovingly. "I mean, yes, I made the connection, but the whole collaboration was her idea."

"As long as she knows it wouldn't be happening without you," he said protectively. I loved that he was my backer, like an angel investor in my life. In his eyes I would never be given the credit I deserved, and I loved him for that. For years my dad had wanted to be able to do that for me, and he had in his own way—his leaning on me the way he had spoke of his confidence in my ability to handle it all. But this was different. Dylan didn't need me to take care of him. He just believed in me.

"I think she does. Oh, and Holt and Carroll are fabulous.

They are possibly the most professional people I've ever worked with—they're delivering early on everything."

"As it should be." Dylan was never surprised by people bending over backwards for him.

"I think the merchandise will arrive in the next couple of weeks, and we should be able to open in time for the Christmas rush. And that gives me time to figure out the concierge service that Emily suggested."

"Christ, that's fast. Baby, you're a force." He really did look stunned as he praised me.

"Well, let's be honest. I'm sure your name is part of why this all moved so quickly. I get the sense no one wants to mess with me these days. Everyone wants to impress me. No. Actually everyone wants to impress you. I'm just benefitting."

"That's not true."

I gave him an *oh please* look. "Just don't break up with me until the store's open. Okay?"

Dylan hauled me onto his lap and pulled me against him. "Never joke about that, baby. Not going to happen." He kissed me on my head, but his lips quickly moved to my cheek and neck. Suddenly I felt a little nip at my jawbone, and my breathing spiked in response. His hands were wandering, his fingers caressing and sliding beneath my camisole, searching. I could feel the lightness between us, the eagerness, the shared understanding that we were about to have six *days* together instead of six hours. I grabbed his face in my hands and brought his lips to my own, taking the kiss I really wanted, sliding my tongue between his lips, gently taking his upper lip between my teeth.

"This is going to be fun," I said, putting every delicious desire for the next few days into the word *fun*.

* * *

We only had another minute to indulge before we pulled onto the private airstrip. There was a smallish private jet waiting, with an attendant at the top of the stairs. I saw Lloyd bring Dylan's leather duffel to a second attendant. I had to wonder what I was going to do about clothing on this little adventure. Dylan had told me to leave out only my toiletry bag and passport for him to pack and said he'd take care of everything else.

The young woman ushered us aboard and showed us to our seats. There was a couch lining one wall and a few captain's chairs that swiveled. Plush, leather, and wood, the cabin screamed luxurious comfort. I wondered at what point spending time with Dylan wouldn't necessarily involve some crazy thing that landed so firmly on my I-can't-believe-this-is-happening list.

"We'll depart in about five minutes, sir," said the attendant. "And we should arrive in Athens around eleven p.m. local time."

"Thank you—" Dylan started.

"Athens!" I said simultaneously. "We're going to Athens?" Dylan politely nodded to the attendant with a huge smile on his face.

"For one night," he clarified, still looking mischievous.

"And then?"

Dylan sighed. "You've heard me talk about the personal project I've been working on?" I nodded. "When I was in Athens over the summer for the remodel of that hotel, I took a few days to explore the islands. I fell in love with Ikaria. It's less inhabited, less popular. Quiet. Private. It's not easy to get to—Thank you." Dylan interrupted himself to accept glasses of Champagne from the attendant, one of which he handed to me. "I gave myself a day there and just walked. I found this fabulous village, and I just sat and drank and chatted with the locals, who clearly love their island. The Mediterranean was right there; the temperature was perfect. The whole place smelled like olives and eucalyptus and the sea. It was absolute heaven. There was the occasional off-the-beaten-path traveller with a rucksack, but more of the people were just living their lives there."

I could see the tiny thread of longing running through his words, imagining a life that could just be lived. But he also looked so calm, at ease, like he was there again by telling me this. It was a side of him I'd never seen.

"That afternoon I saw this older man sitting in a chair outside this run-down stone wall that gated the most beautiful little house. It was white in the traditional style, with a blue door I can never forget. Flowering plants crawling all over the trellis marking its entrance. It was perched on a hill, looking down over the water, no other houses immediately visible. But it was less than a mile from the little town. I asked him about it, and he showed me around. The place was a lot bigger than it looked, but it was also falling apart. He'd been born there, as had his father and his father's father. Now his wife was gone, and his three daughters had moved to Athens. We ended up talking over ouzo while he cooked an amazing meal for me. I was there for hours, and he told me his whole story. He used to be a fishing captain, amazing stuff. He was lonely. He wanted to be with his children, but he couldn't afford to move. He couldn't afford not to—the man has grandchildren he doesn't see."

I was staring at him, I knew. "How is there this side to you?"

"What do you mean?" he asked, sipping his drink.

"At home, you're a badass. Everyone's afraid of you. You have hard lines and hard limits. You're all efficient, no rounded corners. You don't take bullshit from anyone. You're curt, sometimes even rude. You're Lord Dylan Hale, who doesn't bend for anyone. You can be terrifying, actually," I said, remembering all the times I'd heard Dylan barking orders at Thomas in that efficient way he had.

"And?"

"And then you're this other guy. The guy you are with me. And apparently old Greek men. Generous, patient, and warm."

Dylan shrugged his shoulders. "Anyway, I offered to buy the place right there."

"What? You just bought it?"

"When you see it, you'll understand why. I told Zeus—"

"His name is *not* Zeus," I said, mouth agape.

He nodded in confirmation while smiling widely, and I shook my head, laughing. "Anyhow, Zeus is welcome back anytime. Standing invitation for him and family. I even gave him a set of the new keys."

When we were safely in the air, I unbuckled my seat belt and crawled onto his lap, straddling him, kissing him. "I love you," I said, looking straight into his eyes. "I really, really love you."

* * *

We spent that night at a hotel in Athens: the Grande Bretagne—it was gilded old-world elegance, and it felt *fancy*. Not hip, modern, urban fancy, but enormous-portraits-in-gold-frames, someone-playing-the-piano, and all-the-staff-in-morning-suits fancy. The place harkened back to days of empires and gods; it made me feel perfectly away from London, from our busy lives there.

I groggily emerged from sleep at nine the next morning and pulled the pale blue sheet around my body. But within a second Dylan was on the bed, stalking me, crawling towards me. "Uh-uh," he said. "No covers for you, damsel. We are in vacation mode."

"Mmm," I groaned, wrapping my arms around his neck and pulling him down on top of me. "And what exactly does 'vacation mode' mean?"

"No covers. That's what it means."

I giggled into his shoulder.

"You need me, damsel?"

I nodded and reveled in the tingling of my warm breasts meeting his cool chest. I wanted every inch of us touching. I kicked away the sheet that separated us and wrapped my legs around his waist.

"Well then," he said, and I could hear the smile in his words, even if I couldn't see it as he kissed my neck. His large hands ran the course of my body, leaving goose bumps in their wake. My skin felt soft under his touch, warm, replete. I lived for the way his broad palms could cover the expanses of my thighs, as they were doing right now. "Let's take care of you, shall we?"

He was exuberant, energetic, and I could feel his enthusiasm, his eagerness. I needed it. He reached over the side of the bed and grabbed the hotel bathrobe from the floor. He quickly pulled the belt from its loops and with one word—"Wrists"—I presented my joined palms to him. He wrapped them quickly, but instead of stopping at my wrists, he carefully wrapped the belt all the way down my forearms, tying it off at my elbows.

"Dylan?" I asked, curious but also just the tiniest bit nervous. My movement was so restricted this way.

"Trust me, baby," he said and with one movement grabbed me by the waist and flipped me onto my knees. He'd said those words so many times over the past weeks, and each time there had been a part of me that resisted, that didn't want to trust. That didn't want to let go. But this time I caught myself before pulling away, and instead of tensing, I relaxed. I rested my weight on my forearms, my forehead on the soft mattress, and just closed my eyes.

In this position my ass was high in the air, my chest low to the bed. He was above me, behind me, and his scent and warmth were alerting my senses, so much more acutely because there wasn't a part of me that was aware of his stress or waiting for some shoe to drop. And that very vulnerability jump-started my arousal, put my hormones into hyperdrive. I could feel my heart racing, my hot breaths against the sheets, and that familiar electric tingle spreading from my limbs to the base of my spine.

He leaned down, over me, and rested his forearms alongside mine, grabbed my bound wrists, dragging them just a little further forward, which incidentally gave him better access to my boobs. "Don't hide these," he added as he moved them with his palms. "God, it feels so good just to touch you. I've missed you." I knew what he meant—somehow our minds had been elsewhere lately, but right then we were nowhere else. He took my nipples in between his thumbs and forefingers and kneaded them, rolled them. All the while his naked cock was nestled against my ass, getting harder by the second.

Dylan played with my breasts forever, stroking them, molding them, and the longer he did the longer every other inch of my skin raged against them with envy. My bare back wanted his touch. My sides—the ticklish ribbons of skin above my hips and across my lower back. My ass, presented so nakedly before him. My neck. My goddamn earlobes wanted their turn.

My sigh turned into a moan, a sound of yearning that escaped unbidden.

"Shh, darling. I've got you." He stroked my back, warming it with his palms, and settled his hands over my ass. He was being patient, steady, taking his time, slow in a way that made me notice every movement. He sank a finger into my wet slit, then another. "Christ, you're perfect. So ready for me."

My hips involuntarily bucked into his palm, but he held me steady, held me down, reminding me of his complete control. Instead of lingering there, where I wanted him most, he slid his wet fingers north to my other tiny entrance and inserted a finger, rocking into me in small thrusts. Then he added the other, turning them both, stretching me.

I gasped again, and Dylan shushed me. "I've got you. I want you here."

"I…*I* want you there. I think I'm ready for that."

"Not yet. Soon. I just want to play with this pretty ass." My breathing was so loud it was its own heartbeat in the room. It was tinged with my desperation for him.

"In fact," he said and left me for a moment, retrieving something from his bag before returning to me. "Let's get you more ready for that, shall we?" What did he mean? Then I felt a cool object being dragged through my pussy.

"We haven't played this way in a while," he said.

"Dylan—" I arched my ass into his touch, into the blunt edge of the object, letting him know in no uncertain terms I was with him.

"That's right, my good girl, show me." He plunged the plug into my pussy first, coating it in my wetness, and then dragged it up to my ass. I exhaled slowly and leaned back into it, taking it fully. Holy shit that was intense. It felt so wrong, as it had the other times we'd done this, but also so good, so full.

"Perfect." Dylan sighed and caressed my ass admiringly. I felt so coveted in that moment, so completely owned. "I can't believe this ass belongs to me," he added and started to stroke my pussy. "And this."

"All yours," I said, laying my cheek against the soft sheet, trying to absorb the intense sensation, waiting for him to cultivate this anticipation, mold these feelings into the orgasms I knew were coming.

And then he started. He entered me at an agonizingly slow pace, filling me centimeter by centimeter. I heard him whisper a swear through his breath. He cursed my tightness. He dug his nails into my hips, and the tiny sting was the perfect accent to my pleasure.

I have no idea if I made a sound or if I was silent the entire time. I have no idea where his hands were or weren't. I was all sensation. Every inch of my skin was one inch. Each touch was all touches. All I could see, touch, taste, and feel was the pressure building and the stars brightening. We'd started out laughing and ready to indulge in a romp, but that's not where we'd ended up. Instead we were just quietly, slowly, intensely finding each other.

"Come, Lydia. Come with me, baby." Dylan breathed right into my ear.

And I did. Brilliantly, all around him.

He was still in me, still moving, when he said, "Again, baby."

"I can't," I said, because I truly believed I couldn't.

"You can. Come for me." He grazed my clit, igniting that hunt in me. He knew exactly how to coerce my body, make it chase, remind me what it was capable of, and in a moment I was capsizing into a second impossibly powerful orgasm at his command.

He slid out of me, and I could feel his own breathing harsh

against my shoulder as I collapsed under him and he fell at my side. He kissed my lips, rolled to his back, and closed his eyes. I could see the sweat glistening on his chest and brow, and I loved looking at him, so calm, so sated, so stress-free.

"Um, Dylan?" I asked, and he turned to look at me with that sleepy smile on his face. I glanced up to my arms.

"Oh, sorry, damsel." He quickly unbound my arms, allowing me to finally collapse fully onto the sheets. "You okay?" he asked, sitting up now, taking each arm in its turn, massaging it, bringing it back to life.

"And the, um," I said, glancing back at my ass and then at him questioningly.

"That stays."

"You can't be serious," I said, raising my eyebrows at him.

"Deadly," he replied and pulled me against him, us both on our sides, our fronts melting together, and he placed his palm over my ass. "Just for a while, baby. I love seeing it there."

I blushed at his insistence. This was us. This was what we did—Dylan steered this boat, our bedroom antics, and I let him because we both needed it.

* * *

An hour later we'd showered and had breakfast. I was stretched out on the bed, still naked, loving the cool, soft sheets on my stomach and chest and warring with the sensation of the plug between my ass cheeks. It was there, but not there. Just present enough to keep me on edge, but not so aggressive that I couldn't relax. I sank even further into the bed, so content, pleased with all of the time spread out before us.

Dylan was in his jeans only and was stalking around the room. I followed him with my eyes, having one of those moments of not believing he was mine—those trim muscles, the way the jeans rested perfectly on his hips, and that ass. Before him, I'd had no idea I was an ass girl. I was definitely an ass girl. He pulled my favorite pair of jeans and a T-shirt from his bag—no underwear; no surprise there—and placed them at the foot of the bed. "Is that what I will be wearing for the next five days?"

"No, but I don't suppose you can go shopping in yesterday's clothes," he said, smiling a naughty smile. "Or naked," he added with a swift slap to my thigh.

"Shopping?" I asked, raising my head to look at him suspiciously.

"Shopping. I told you I'd figure out a way to make you let me spoil you." He lay down next to me on the bed, pushing my bangs from my eyes, looking into my face.

"Dylan," I said in a tone that I hoped conveyed something along the lines of *you cheated*.

"Damsel," he said, trying to mock my tone, but he sidled even closer to me, pleading, putting his hand across my back. "I am a very wealthy man, and I want to indulge my girlfriend. You work so hard, and you're very self-sufficient, which I adore. Tremendously. But I long to spoil you."

"Okay," I said, sighing but also shyly smiling at him. I was never shy with him, but giving in to him, giving him something he'd been wanting, made me feel shy. Happy.

His eyes lit up, and then he rose to kneeling and dragged me to the edge of the bed, so my feet were on the floor and my stomach still lay on the soft sheets. "And let's take this out, shall we?" He said, tapping the end of the plug. The sensation of the object pulling lose was surprisingly arousing and sent a jolt of electricity between my legs. He caressed my cheeks, trailing a finger to where the plug had just been, and I felt my breath hitch. His fingers settled between my legs and found me shamelessly wet.

"Good to know," he added, and I could actually hear him smiling in satisfaction.

I flipped over and quickly landed my own smack on his ass, although it lost some of the effect since he was already in his jeans. Then he had the nerve to start walking away.

"Oh no you don't," I said, shaking my head. "If I'm gonna wear a butt plug for an hour, you'd better believe you're gonna deliver." I grabbed his belt loops and pulled him towards me until he lost his balance.

His laugh reverberated through the room, and without much difficulty I convinced him shopping could wait.

Chapter 22

W hen we eventually left the hotel, we spent three hours wandering around Voukourestiou Street, ducking in and out of luxury shops. I protested when things were just too extreme—no, I wasn't going to let him spend twelve hundred dollars on a bikini. But basically I indulged him indulging me. He bought me my own pair of aviator sunglasses that matched his, a handful of cotton blouses to wear with my jeans, a few gauzy dresses, a couple of bikinis, some sandals and heels, light jackets for the cool evenings, and some loungewear for lounging around his new Greek hideaway.

We were on our way back to the hotel, holding hands, meandering past the last of the shops, when Dylan stopped in front of Alexander McQueen. In the window, a mannequin donned a black cashmere trench coat—warm, elegant enough for swank parties, but cool enough to wear to work. It belted at the waist but had the tiniest hint of flare in the skirt. It was stunning.

"No," I said instinctively, but even I was staring at the coat. It was beautiful.

I could feel Dylan looking at me, smiling, victorious. "Yes," he said and pulled me into the store.

And just like that, Dylan bought me a coat. An astoundingly beautiful, totally sophisticated, ludicrously expensive coat. Apparently I was letting go outside the bedroom too, and instead of it feeling *wrong*, it felt somehow like I'd let him in.

* * *

It was just after three p.m. when I found myself staring at our mode of transportation to the island of Ikaria.

"A helicopter!?" I squeaked.

"The airport on Ikaria is only open during the summer, and it's an eleven-hour ferry ride," Dylan explained. "So this is it."

I couldn't take my eyes off the window the entire trip. I was mesmerized by the blue Mediterranean below, islands marked with blue roofs, sprawling vineyards, farms, and fishing towns. It was truly glorious. It was unseasonably warm, over eighty degrees when the average high was ten degrees less than that, and the sun was dancing off the water below. Dylan kept my hand in his, resting on my lap. Occasionally he'd stroke my thigh or lean over to kiss me. Once I caught him simply staring. I smiled at him, and he smirked at having been caught, but then just squeezed my hand.

Normally my father's absence loomed large during moments like this—when I was seeing something I knew he would have loved, experiencing something so beautiful for the first time—but at that moment I was also so acutely aware that my life was fuller than it had been in a long time. There was presence here too, not just absence. Something gained, not just something lost.

As we started our descent I was sure we'd land in the water—the small patch of cleared flat earth we were headed for was situated right against cliffs that dropped into the turquoise water below and a sloping hill that disappeared into trees and brush. Not ten minutes later, we'd walked up a short winding road and come to a shoulder-height stone wall—earthy brown stones and white sandy mortar holding it together, and at its opening a black iron fence that looked recently repainted. The warm air was so fragrant, smelling of olives and herbs, and I could still hear the ocean crashing against the cliffs in the background. Dylan gestured to the road behind the gate.

"This is us," he said, smiling an eager smile.

I held the bars and looked down the path: sunny and warm down the middle but lined with trees and wild yard on either side. He waved his phone in front of the old gate, and I heard a click. "I've had the security updated and things retrofitted with the newest technology."

"I'm sure we'll be safe here," I said, rolling my eyes. "I mean, the only way in is by helicopter—it would be hard for some nefarious paparazzi to catch up with you here."

"With us."

With us, I thought, and I could feel the smile spreading across my face.

As we walked down the dirt drive, I caught glimpses of yellow above me and realized there were lemon trees lining the way to the little house at the end. All of a sudden the idea of fresh lemonade and salads with lemon dressings made my cheeks tingle, anticipating the tartness. When we reached the front doors, which were beautiful in their own right—a deep faded blue that Dylan clearly hadn't touched—he pulled me around to the side of the house facing the water and to a set of steps. It was then that I realized we were entering from the top of the house. This place was *not* tiny.

I followed him down the outside of the house, trying to take everything in—the crystal-blue water in the distance, the breeze on my skin. I was so distracted that it wasn't until we landed at the lowest level, a few flights down, that I saw the pool. It glistened a brilliant blue in the sun, and its edge was the edge of the cliff, as though it disappeared into the horizon beyond it. The place was minimalist, but somehow everything felt perfect, natural, as though the earth itself had decided on that pool, the sun had painted the shutters that brilliant blue and then faded them accordingly. This place was a Mediterranean dream—a quiet, private Mediterranean dream—and I could only imagine how much time and thought he'd put into it.

"You like hiding away, don't you?" I asked, smiling at Dylan, gripping his hand in my own. He pulled me against him, so I had to look up to see his eyes.

"I like *getting* away."

"I love this place. You can really breathe here."

He leaned down and kissed me softly on the lips, and it felt so new. The sun beating down on us, the sound of the ocean, and the feel of the stones under our shoes—they all made a kiss we'd had a hundred times before feel new. And that was just a kiss. This place was gonna be good.

He gave me the full tour, and we finally landed in the master bedroom on the top of floor. I almost lost my breath. The room was floor-to-ceiling glass doors on three sides. The panels were on rails, so they could slide to the side, almost making the room an outdoor space. The vast low bed spread across the back wall. Low bookshelves were on either side. Perhaps most surprising was a large oval bathtub on a pedestal, sitting diagonally in the corner between two of the enormous open windows. My eyes bulged as I imagined sitting in that bathtub with him later.

He opened our luggage, grabbed our swimsuits, and said "Let's go for a swim" with a twinkle in his eye. I hastily put on the tiny teal bikini, and I could feel Dylan's eyes on me as I slipped a white eyelet cover-up on over my head.

My face was still concealed by the sheer white fabric when I said, "Doing okay over there, Hale?" I finished pulling the garment over my head to reveal a cheeky smile.

He slapped my nearly bare butt, and I screeched. I went to tackle him, but he was already darting out of the room. When I caught up to him at the top of the stairs, he grabbed my hand, turned around, and kissed me. "I love you, baby."

Whoa. Where had that come from? It seemed that Greece Dylan was full of surprises.

We walked to the edge of the pool, but Dylan kept going, pulling me along. "Where are we—"

"Trust me. Come on," he said as he grabbed two towels from a chest by the pool.

I sighed in resignation and followed him to a wooden set of stairs built into the side of the cliff. They seemed to go on forever, the sound of the ocean getting louder as we descended. When we landed at the bottom, I couldn't believe what I was seeing. Emerging from the trees, there were high cliffs in an arc surrounding what could only be described as paradise. The water was richer than Caribbean blue: bluer, deeper, but still crystal clear. The sand was white and soft, and the beach was tiny, tucked into these cliffs, protected from the wind that pushed the sailboats I could see in the distance.

"Shall we?" Dylan asked, smiling at me.

I nodded as he lifted the cover-up over my head. He let the

garment fall to the sand, then pulled me close against him. My arms wrapped around him, and I ran my fingers up and down his warm back. Then I felt the strings of my bikini top falling away from my back.

"Dylan," I said, slightly panicked, hugging my chest closer to him for coverage and looking around for photographers or people with cell phones. But he took my chin in one of his hands and brought me back to him.

"No one's here but us, damsel." He untied the strings around my neck and let the top fall into the space between us. "I want to look at you out here." And he brought my arms to my sides. His hand was at my shoulder, and he slowly dragged it down my body, between my breasts, his fingers lingering there for a moment. "Christ, you have gorgeous tits."

I laughed. Loudly. Looking down at my chest, I replied, "Not bad, right? Hmm, let's see what you've got," I said, suddenly forgetting I was topless and diving for his trunks, just as he turned and ran. I jumped on his back, and he wrapped my legs around his waist, holding them tightly against him, and ran towards the water.

We spent the next hour swimming. Playing. Touching. Talking. We took each other in in a way we never had before.

"You're different here," he said at one point, as we stood in the water.

"I know. So are you. Do you think it's just because we're away from everything?"

"I don't know," he replied. "But don't stop."

The sun was setting when we finally made our way back up to the house. We luxuriated in the open shower in the master bathroom, lazed around in the lounge that looked out over the water, and eventually meandered into the kitchen. Dylan opened a bottle of wine, and I rummaged through the cupboards.

"We can go out," he said.

"Nah. I wanna stay here. I can drum something up. Trust me?" I asked, throwing his own words back at him. Dylan chuckled and sat back down at the kitchen island.

"Implicitly."

"Good." I lazily worked my way through the kitchen. I made pasta with lemons and herbs from the garden, which we ate sitting on lounge chairs by the pool, soaking up the last of the sunset.

At one point after a long moment of silence, Dylan nudged my toe with his, and I looked over at him. "Yes?" I said, my eyes gazing at the sky full of stars above us.

"Move in with me," he said. Only instead of jokey and pleading, this time he sounded serious, sincere, hopeful.

"I want to," I said, smiling, feeling how easy it was to say that. I did *want* to.

"Good. I want you to too," he replied.

I turned to look at him and was about to launch into all my reservations, but Dylan read my mind.

"I know," he started. "I know you don't feel ready. But baby. I want this with you. You know that, right?" He looked at me and then out at the ocean, as though he was saying he wanted the world with me.

A warm calm was settling over me, and I smiled. I moved over in my lounger, making space for him, and he crawled over, wrapping me in his arms so my head rested on his shoulder.

"I want that with you too," I said. "I just want to know what 'this' is for you."

"You mean, is it forever?" I didn't say anything, not quite sure that I even wanted it to be, or maybe just not quite ready to say it. "I haven't thought about forever with anything, anyone—not architecture and certainly not another person. I've trained my-self very carefully to stick to today—the future isn't something that's held much interest for me," he said, and I could imagine the thoughts of his future as a duke running through his head. "But, Lydia, I never want to be without you. Whether here, in London, anywhere. I just want you with me. Is that the same thing?"

"I think so," I said. "I feel the same way. I love you," I whispered into his neck.

"I love you too. So even if not tomorrow, you'll move in with me?"

"Yes. Not tomorrow. But yes." Because that was true. It felt inevitable. And I wanted it. I wanted it more than anything. And so did he.

Chapter 23

We lay like that, curled into each other, our dirty dishes off to the side, for several more minutes, before the chill settled over our skin and we moved inside. After his declaration, after mine, I never didn't want to be touching him. I felt like we'd just crested some hill, and we were absorbing each other in the delicious aftershock.

I leaned against the kitchen island and drank my wine as Dylan dealt with the dishes—I had that post-beach loose feeling in my limbs. My jeans felt good on my sunned legs, and my new blousy cotton camisole felt like air on my shoulders, which had gotten a little burnt. The edge of the butcher block dug into my hips, and I suddenly felt Dylan's hands slide down my arms and land on top of my own hands, one wrapped around my wineglass, the other resting on the warm wood. My breathing deepened, and as it had since the first time I'd laid eyes on Dylan, the world got fuzzy. The only things in focus were him and me.

He lifted my wineglass and brought it to my lips, feeding it to me. I drank obediently, and he ran his lips along my neck and shoulder. We were in some kind of dance—I relaxed my body into his and took another swallow.

"Good girl," he said as he put my wineglass down.

Then his hands were around my waist, under my top, the backs of his knuckles caressing, exploring, eventually grazing the undersides of my breasts. "No bra. Very good girl."

"Mmm," I said partially as a question—what had he said?—and partially as a moan, a plea to just keep touching me.

"Your skin is so warm from the sun."

"Mmm."

"Are you incoherent?"

"Mmm."

Dylan chuckled and kissed my other shoulder. "I love you like this," he added, settling his hands on my hips, the very tips of his fingers inside the waistband of my jeans. "Agreeing to move in with me has made you so pliant, soft, ready."

"I said soon."

"You said yes," he whispered as he held out his hand, and I took it.

I followed him up the stairs and into the master bedroom, already feeling submissive to his desires, trusting him to know mine. I stood in the doorway, leaning, as Dylan shut the large windows, protecting us from the cool breeze. I walked to him, to the center of the room, and put my arms around him, going in for the kiss. But Dylan pulled my arms down and shook his head. He gave me a quick conciliatory peck on the nose before stepping back to sit on the bench at the end of the bed.

I stood there just a few feet from him, the windows at my back, the moonlight reflecting off the ocean below and illuminating his face in the dark room.

"Take off your shirt, Lydia." My pulse quickened at his commanding tone, and my skin became tight, ready, sensitive even to the particles in the air.

I slid the shirt over my head and smiled at Dylan's approving gaze.

"Your jeans."

I shimmied out of the pants and kicked them aside. I hadn't been wearing shoes or panties, so that was it. There I was, backlit, goose bumps rising to the surface, breaths getting shallower. I reached back and twisted my hair, letting it fall over one shoulder. It was just getting long enough to do that.

Dylan crooked his finger, summoning me towards him. I stepped up to him, loving the feel of the soft rug between my toes. When I got to him, he remained seated and placed his hands on my hips, wrapping them around me, drumming his thumb on my hip bone.

"Lie down, baby," he said. I looked at him, curious. Where? He patted his lap, and I understood.

I climbed onto the bench on my knees and slowly lowered myself over his lap, he shifted me so my ass was front and center, and I lay my cheek on the soft linen of the bench. He stroked my back, running his right hand over my ass while his left rested between my shoulder blades.

He leaned over and kissed me sweetly on the lips then reached between my legs with his fingers, first finding my pussy and then dragging the wetness back up between my cheeks. "You're ready for this?" he asked.

I shuddered a little but managed a nervous smile. "I trust you." Because I did.

Dylan reached behind him and I heard the pop of a bottle top. Then he dragged well-lubricated fingers down, settling on the tender opening. He eased his finger in and out, fucking me tenderly. Then there were two fingers, working me open and massaging me. My chest was working itself up and off the bench with each deep breath. His fingers were so different from a plug, softer, moving. More than anything, they were *him*. I squirmed and tensed, suddenly nervous.

"Shh," he soothed, clearly sensing my heart rate rising, my breaths accelerating. He rubbed my back. "Let me in." I took a deeper breath and tried to open up to his fingers. He worked me for a few more minutes. "Okay, come here, baby."

He lifted me and moved me onto the bed behind him—I lay stretched out on my belly, ripe with anticipation. He quickly shed his jeans and came up behind me. I stared in disbelief as he stroked his long hardness with a lubricated hand. "Baby, we're going to go slow. I don't want to hurt you."

He gripped my hips and pulled back. I was resting on my elbows, my forehead on the duvet. Dylan was stroking my back, positioning himself, and I was shivering with anticipation.

"Lean back into it, baby. Take me at your own pace. I want you to do this," he instructed. Nervously, I did as I was told, anticipating the intrusion, and he guided his tip along the opening and began to feed himself into me. It was so tight and so intense. "You have to relax, baby. Breathe." I closed my eyes and exhaled, opening myself to him. "Perfect."

I pushed back against him, slowly meeting his own pressure and taking him in shallow thrusts.

"Oh god, Dylan. It's so full." I stilled and acclimated before leaning back into him, resuming.

"That's right, baby, take your time." His hands held my hips, supporting me effortlessly.

"You feel so deep." The pressure was so concentrated and

intense but also delicious. I slowly eased back against his enormous hardness until I felt his balls against me.

"Fuck, this is tight," he said. "God, look at you. This is so fucking *hot*." And it was, he was right. I'd never felt so possessed, so coveted. He reached between my legs and began toying with my clit and then pushed his fingers inside me. I could feel my own tightness, and I began to quiver. I could feel so much, every movement; every twitch inside me was a thousand times more intense. I could feel every clench, every movement in both places, and both were funneling me towards an orgasm at an alarming rate.

"Oh god, Lydia," Dylan moaned. "I can feel you getting close."

I involuntarily clenched around his fingers and his cock, and he groaned again—I couldn't believe how much this was turning us both on. I never would have imagined the intensity of this feeling, the completeness of it, the submersion. He slowly coaxed me in a way that only he could, evoking the riotous feelings, the intense craving for the coming orgasm. The pleasure undulated through my body, intensified by having no outlet, nowhere to go. I felt both like I was trying to claw my way out of the maelstrom of sensation, to escape, and like I wanted to sink into it, praying that it would last forever. And it did. The orgasm raised me and dropped me, made colors change and my skin flash with electricity. I could actually hear how our bodies were responding to one another, dancing with one another in a way that was summoned from somewhere beyond intention, and I could barely breath.

Finally, I could feel him start to come as he arched slightly deeper into me and then retreated subtly, engaging in a gentle, shallow thrusting. Each movement was an accent of my own orgasm. After a moment, he withdrew, and I collapsed onto the mattress below me, not believing we'd just done that.

"My god, I love the way you look right now, Lydia, with my cum coming out of you." His dirty words registered and fueled my dying orgasm, making me clench again to savor the remaining threads. Then he silently raised me up into his arms and carried me into the bathroom. I stood on weak legs as he dampened a washcloth with warm water. He returned, kneeling on the cool hard tile floor before me, and carefully cleaned me, planting sweet kisses and caresses on my flesh.

"Are you okay?" He looked up into my sated face.

"Am I okay?" I asked, raising a sleepy, skeptical eye at him. "Did you somehow miss that orgasm I had?"

"It was kind of hard to miss." He smiled. "That one might have influenced the tides." I braced my hands on his shoulders as he lifted my knee, exposing me further, running the warm cloth up my inner thigh. "But you liked it?" He looked up at me, a little apprehensive.

"The tides, remember?" I leaned over and gave him a reassuring kiss, and within seconds I was back in his arms and being deposited on the bed.

* * *

The days that followed were just like that, the tides. We ebbed in and out. From the bedroom to the little private beach. From the kitchen to the pool. From the balconies to the hot tub. And when we came up for air, we'd walk down the long lemony driveway and the mile into town. We'd have olive oil and bread, fresh grilled fish, and yogurt. We'd stop and admire the crumbling white buildings with their bright blue doors, the ornate Greek Orthodox church with its gilded icons, and all of the accompanying smells and sounds and foreign faces. We took it all in, especially each other.

Not once did we discuss how Dylan's new approach of essentially ignoring his father's pressures was going to play out over the long term. Not once did we think about the paparazzi or worry about unwanted media attention. Not once did we analyze the hows or whys of the emails, happy to tuck that into the past. Instead, he dreamed up new buildings and took me on tours of them in our imagination. He showed me where his mind went when he was designing, the far-flung landscape where he made things beautiful. And I told him about the shop and my vision for it. I told him about my father. About the memories of my childhood with him, listening to him play music, having adventures along the New England coastline, being taken care of by him before he became ill. And I told him about taking care of *him* when the cancer came, about the stories we told each other, about how we kept our small, painful world beautiful for each other.

During those days we drank each other in. And I felt free, possibly for the first time in my life. Daphne's words had been running through my mind: *This is about letting him take care of you.* Something about Greece made me feel safe to do that, even just a little, to let go, let him in. And even though every once in a while it sent a shock of panic up my spine, I felt like maybe it was part of the reason he appeared to be letting his guard down too. I kind of hated it when Daphne was right.

We would leave the next morning, a Tuesday, and so Monday we lay in bed and made our plans for a perfect last day in paradise. We stayed tangled and daydreaming, planning our meals, planning our swims and our walks, and knowing full well that we probably wouldn't make it past the pool, we were so hungry for each other.

After Dylan threw my newly purchased bikinis over the balcony in disgust, proclaiming that he preferred me swimming in the nude, and I fake protested, which resulted in us ravishing each other shamelessly right there on the balcony chairs, I decided on a shower.

When I emerged, I was disappointed to find him gone. I slipped on a pale blue linen sundress that tied around my neck, grabbed a big straw hat, and went in search of the man I was now so firmly in love with.

He wasn't in the house or by the pool. He wasn't in the gardens. But I finally heard his voice as I walked barefoot down the drive towards the gate.

There he stood, looking stern even if he was shirtless and wearing only a pair of trim blue shorts, and he was talking heatedly into the phone, in what sounded like Russian. He sounded angry, disbelieving, challenging. It was only a moment before he hung up and then immediately dialed another number and put the phone to his ear.

I turned before I could eavesdrop any more. I was curious, but I didn't want to spy or intrude. I wanted Dylan to tell me whatever needed to be told. So I retreated back to the house and began packing our bags for the return trip home the next day.

That night, as we ate our calamari and fresh tomatoes, our salty feta and herbs, I casually tried to open the conversation.

"I heard you on the phone earlier," I said, looking at him.

"Did you?" he asked, and I nodded.

"I didn't know you spoke Russian—is that what that was?"
Dylan nodded.

"Were you talking to someone from that family?" I asked, all of a sudden slightly nervous about this conversation.

"The Bresnovs. Yes. They deny they had anything to do with it, but it's the only thing that makes sense. I called my father about it," he started, taking a swig of wine, "and you can imagine how that went. He wants to meet when we get back, but he'll have to wait until I'm done with the project I'm working on. I'm not going to let him tear me away again."

"I'm sorry, babe," I said, frowning in sympathy. We'd had such a nice break from all of this.

"Let's not worry about it," he said. "Let's enjoy this privacy, shall we?" he added, kissing my olive-oil-coated lips. "Which is all I want with you."

He wasn't going to tell me the details. He was back in his mode of protecting me from information. Protecting this paradise we'd been living in. I could hear him already—he'd say *trust me* or *you needn't worry*, and I'd be left wondering. Wondering how my whole relationship with him was about escaping secrets, then finding new ones. Tearing down walls between us, only to find others right behind them.

Chapter 24

The trip, in spite of that nagging phone call at its end, could never truly lose its luster for me—I had experienced some of the most beautiful, authentic, simple, yet outrageously stunning moments of my life over those days with Dylan. I had blissfully forgotten about Geoffrey's bribe and the cruel Internet articles about my needing Botox. I was determined that we could hold on to it, that we could continue that bliss in the face of all the pressures and stressors that were still an inevitable part of our London lives.

But I didn't get the chance to find out—busy life resumed almost immediately. A mere two days later would be Prince Richard and Jemma's engagement party.

In the time between our return from Greece and Friday's party, Dylan delved into his work, and I made final tweaks on the upholstery for the furniture in the shop and ordered the garment bags and shopping bags. We tabled the moving-in conversation until the engagement party and Dylan's current project were over.

On Friday, after a morning of fitting and pinning and hemming, Hannah had me at her studio for a series of post-lunch final decisions about my look for the big royal event. You'd think it was my wedding day based on the hubbub. Fiona was there, running day-to-day business from a makeshift desk by the window so Hannah could oversee her as well as me. I was currently trying on a coat, and Stephen, who would return later to do my hair and makeup, was stopping by to consult with Hannah on jewelry and the overall styling. It all seemed a little excessive.

"Who is responsible for these vile coats?" Hannah said with visible disgust and irritation. "I said 'elegant Prohibition era' not 'a Kardashian twenties-themed bachelorette party.' Is it that difficult?" Hannah looked between me and Fiona, holding us equally responsible for this coat disaster. I had suggested my new fabulous black coat, but Hannah seemed to have something very specific in mind, and since I'd already vetoed two other dresses, I figured it was time to compromise.

"It's what Harvey Nichols sent over. They did send eight, I think," I said.

"Shall I ring them and have them send more options?" asked Fiona.

Hannah replied with a look that said *Do you expect me to answer that question?* and Fiona immediately picked up the phone.

"Hannah, what if we did something like this?" Stephen was doing something with the hair on the top of my head, twisting it and looking to Hannah for her opinion. Hannah meanwhile was tying the belt on a coat around my waist. I felt like a doll. "And darker?" Stephen prodded, asking Hannah for clarification.

Hannah pursed her lips, looking at my hair and then at me, almost pleading. "Lydia, how attached are you to your hair color?"

"Fine." I sighed, understanding perfectly well that what she was really asking is how much of a fight I would put up about dying my light brown locks. "As long as you're not thinking about making it purple or something."

She smiled, pleased, and began writing an address down on a piece of paper. "Good. Head over to this address and ask for Mike. Stephen will call ahead." I couldn't help but roll my eyes. I knew this was a big deal—Hannah was insane over the gown I'd be wearing—but this really did feel over the top. Then again, I guess it *was* a royal engagement party. I'm sure I wasn't the only guest out there primping.

An hour and half later, I sat in the salon chair chatting with Mike, who, according to Stephen, was a genius with hair color. This was round two of the hair dye, and the whole thing was taking forever. Mike was telling me about coloring Madonna's hair before her last tour when my phone beeped. I hoped to god it wasn't Hannah having changed her mind about something, and my smile stretched across my face when I saw it was from Dylan.

FRIDAY, 3:31 pm
Do I need to call Hannah and tell her about the underwear rule?

FRIDAY, 3:31 pm
I think underwear rule is suspended at any event where actual royalty will be making an appearance.

FRIDAY, 3:32 pm
I'm afraid I'm the only one who can make that call, baby. NKR in full effect.

FRIDAY, 3:32 pm
NKR?

FRIDAY, 3:32 pm
No knickers rule.

FRIDAY, 3:33 pm
Thank god we have a shorthand for these things.
I can count on you for efficiency, knighty.
As for NKR, we'll see.

FRIDAY, 3:33 pm
If you know what's good for you, you'll do as I say.

FRIDAY, 3:33 pm
So bossy.

FRIDAY, 3:34 pm
Always.

FRIDAY, 3:34 pm
Where are you, anyway?

FRIDAY, 3:34 pm
At Humboldt, about to meet with my father.
Don't worry, baby. I'll be in town to pick you up.
Where will you be? Apart from sitting high on my cock, I
mean.

FRIDAY, 3:34 pm
At the studio.
As for your cock: doubtful in the dress I'll be wearing.

FRIDAY, 3:35 pm
Shame.
Where are you now?

I quickly took a picture of the mirror in front of me.
What Dylan would see was me, in a black salon robe, with

approximately one zillion squares of foil sticking out of my head.

FRIDAY, 3:35 pm
My girlfriend the alien.

FRIDAY, 3:36 pm
Blame Hannah.

FRIDAY, 3:37 pm
Must run, damsel.
See you in a few hours. Can't wait to get my hands on you.

FRIDAY, 3:37 pm
XO

After Mike came Rebecca, the stylist, and I held my breath as she held the scissors in front of my face.

"Have you ever had real fringe?" I looked at her questioningly as she pointed at my long bangs with her threatening scissors.

"Um, well, my bangs have always been like this, swept to the side." She was now combing the hair in front of my face, and the hair was tickling the bridge of my nose.

There was a painfully long period of snipping and trimming. I couldn't see what she was doing or what she'd done before. After an eternity with the hair dryer and brush, she finally moved away, so I could see my reflection. I was frozen for a moment.

My hair was now a rich shade of brown with subtle caramel highlights. The layers looked somehow more natural. And my face was defined by real bangs—not ones I could twist into my long hair on the side or brush out of the way—ones that rested at my eyebrows. The effect was admittedly striking.

I was still staring when Rebecca started pulling my hair back, away from my face into a high ballerina-like bun, only somehow less severe. It was an Audrey Hepburn–ish thing, and I barely recognized this glammed-up version of myself.

Before I had a minute to truly appreciate the geniuses' handiwork, my phone rang and Hannah was telling me to hightail it back to the studio. Dylan would be picking me up in just over an hour.

* * *

I was ready ten minutes before Dylan was meant to arrive, and our little team stood in front of the three-way mirror, admiring our handiwork.

The dress was midnight blue with a tulle skirt to the floor. The belted waist was adorned with silvery crystals and beading, and the bodice consisted of two gathered bunches of the tulle arising from the belt and meeting with the silk back of the dress at two delicate points at my shoulders. While my whole back was covered in transparent navy silk, and the skirt was long and impenetrable, the V in the front of the dress was deep. It didn't actually show much skin, but it hinted at what couldn't be seen. It was classy but undeniably sexy. The shoes, not that you could see them, were silver, strappy, and insanely comfortable. Fiona and I had spent approximately four hours shopping for them earlier that week, and I'd insisted on walking around Selfridges in each pair for a half hour before committing. These shoes, while they cost me what would have been a month's rent back in New York, were not going to betray me.

Stephen slipped my lipstick into my clutch, and we were

laughing at the nonsensical name of the color, *Basking Berries in Bali*, when my phone buzzed and indicated Dylan was downstairs.

"You look perfect," said Fiona. "I mean it—you're going to be the most beautiful woman there!"

"We did well, I think," said Hannah, who I felt was congratulating herself and Stephen more than complimenting me. I looked at Fiona as I fastened my pearl stud earrings, and we jointly rolled our eyes.

I slipped on the cream-colored coat, which I thought was fabulous but Hannah had merely accepted as the least of all evils, and headed down to the car. When I emerged from the studio door, Dylan was leaning against the Mercedes, and his eyes went wide. The man looked nothing short of exquisite in his tuxedo, and it moved with him in a way that only bespoke suits can. He approached me like he was in a trance. I wasn't sure I'd seen this look on his face since that day back at the jewelry store weeks earlier, like he was stunned, shaken by what he saw.

"What is it?" I asked, worried that something was wrong.

"You," he began softly and gently brushed my new short bangs and put my face in his hands, "are far too gorgeous to go anywhere."

"Oh, really?" I asked, smiling now. "Well, that would be a shame, given all the work that went into pulling this together. And you haven't even seen the dress yet. And kiss me, for fuck's sake. I feel like this day's gone on forever!"

He pulled me against him and kissed me hard on the lips. Not one of his *I'm-going-to-eat-you-alive* kisses—this one was long, slow, and almost reverent, or even melancholy.

I pulled away to look at his face, see if everything was okay. I knew this look, a look I hadn't seen in a few weeks, a look he was fighting off—the cold concern of having been with his father. Only it was something else too.

"Are you okay? Everything okay at Humboldt Park?" I asked.

He looked thoughtful for a moment and then determined, like he was shoving something aside. "Fine," he said, taking my hand. "Come, I want to show you off." He smiled, but I could tell it was forced. Something was on his mind, and I would have to press him on it later. I was done being patient for him to open up to me about things.

Lloyd came around to open our door, and as I was stepping in he said quietly, "You look lovely, Miss Bell."

"Thank you, Lloyd," I replied and gave him an excited kiss on the cheek. I hadn't seen him in a week, and even though we barely spoke, my affection for the old man had grown. Frank, whom Dylan had yet to dispatch, was off for the night—he'd been less present since it seemed like we'd taken care of the cyberstalker on our hands, but Dylan still hadn't figured out how the Bresnovs had gotten that video footage, so my sidekick wasn't gone entirely. Maybe that was what was bugging him?

We settled into the car, and Dylan pulled me against him, but I chastised him to watch out for the skirt. "Hannah will kill me if I tear this thing before we even get there."

"Shame," he said while smiling. He reached into his pocket and pulled out a small box with a bow. "I brought you something. For tonight," he said, and he handed me the square box. He seemed happy to be back with me, but I couldn't shake the feeling that something was wrong.

I removed the purple satin ribbon and opened the lid to find a delicate display of diamonds sparkling back at me. It was a bracelet, a cuff about two inches wide, decorated with a wavy grid of diamonds.

"I had it designed especially for your miniature wrist," Dylan said, holding my wrist in his warm hand while I remained dumbstruck, turning it in my hand. "May I?"

"Dylan, I—" I didn't even know what to say. It wasn't that I needed jewelry or expensive gifts, but this spoke volumes of how much he had been thinking about me, and it felt like, well, probably like a present should. Really good. Not to mention stunning.

"Baby," he said softly, sensing the emotions taking me over. He gently picked up my wrist, kissed it, and slid the cuff into place. I looked at my adorned wrist, and the piece was regal, magnificent. I'd never have been able to even imagine something like it.

"I love it," I said, wiping a stray tear away. "It's gorgeous."

He wiped a second tear from my other cheek and kissed me gently on the hand. "As I said, I had to explain to the jeweler how my girlfriend has these tiny wrists, and it mustn't overwhelm her, but it had to be original. I had a vision, and it came out exactly as I'd hoped."

The car was slowing, lining up at the entrance to Buckingham Palace. The last time I'd been there, I'd been too nervous to say more than a few words.

"Damsel, I'm afraid I won't be great company tonight." Dylan's tone had reverted to the resigned, distracted coolness I'd caught a glimpse of earlier. I tried to get a clear look at his eyes as our car crept up in the line to the entrance.

"What? Why?" I'd been hearing for days about how big a deal this party was, how many important people were going to be there. This felt like a big night, and now not only did something seem to be bothering him, but he was also going to leave me alone?

"I don't like it either, baby," he said, rubbing his forehead. "But my father can't be here. He's not feeling well," he said, rolling his eyes. "So I'm on official duty."

"Official marquess duty?" He nodded in reply. "Like what?"

He sighed again, highlighting the return of something darker, something I desperately didn't want to believe was returning. "I'm representing my family, which comes with baggage, I'm afraid. It won't take long, then I'll rejoin you."

"Can't I stay with you?"

"I'm afraid not, damsel," he said, holding my hand in his own. He had a pained look on his face. Torn. He felt torn. And guilty. "Baby, I'm sorry. Will should be here," he added as Lloyd opened the door. "And Emily will be flitting about. It won't be for long. Don't fret, baby."

I wasn't ready to get out of this car. I wanted to hit PAUSE. Time out. I wanted to go back to Greece, to a moment when Dylan didn't seem stressed or distracted, when I felt like I had a handle on things.

After getting out of the car to the usual fanfare, he kissed my hand but then dropped it before we climbed the stairs. Someone took my coat and gave Dylan a tag for it, which he pocketed. He glanced at my dress and smiled, but we didn't even have time to exchange another word before we had to pause for photographs inside the palace doors.

A second later, Dylan was whisked away by some kind of butler in a morning suit. I saw him duck into a room at the end of the hall, followed by a waiter carrying a large tray of cocktails, and before I knew it I was standing before a wide set of open doors, looking into a buzzing ballroom in Buckingham Palace, alone.

The only saving grace was that I had somehow gotten a Champagne glass into my hand.

The room was enormous and gilded, and I felt like the whole scene was plucked from a fairy tale. It was packed with other gowns, other tuxedos and suits, and delightful, slightly buzzed chatter. Richard and Jemma's friends—the young set here to indulge and party—had collected by the bar, the girls' dresses twirling occasionally, the boys drunkenly slapping each other on the shoulder. The old important people, their parents in all likelihood—the old guard who were important enough to be here but not important enough to be wherever Dylan was—chatted more quietly at the other side of the large room.

I saw Jemma in the corner, tucked into Richard's side, the two of them beaming. It was hard to remember why I'd been so jealous in that moment weeks earlier. Standing here now, in this ballroom, I felt like there was no way she'd ever been let into Dylan's life the way I had. But in that moment I also felt this worry creeping over me that being let in might not be all it was cracked up to be.

I wandered the edges, eating the occasional canapé and pretending to admire the artwork but really trying to sort out how I'd gotten myself into this situation. Part of me was furious with Dylan. *Don't fret.* He'd said it like he was talking to a child, like my concerns about navigating this enormous event on my own were inconsequential, like he'd forgotten for a moment that I wasn't one of his boarding school mates, born into this scene, walking into a roomful of friends. But my fury was tinged with something that tasted like regret. I couldn't quite understand it.

"Lydia!" I heard a familiar voice interrupt my thoughts from behind me and turned to see Emily. She looked like she'd walked straight out of a photo spread in *Vogue*—sleek long hair with just a little wave at the bottom; a slim pale pink dress, flowing like a column to the floor. She appeared ten inches taller than she already was. "I'm so glad I found you!"

I smiled and went in for a gentle *let's-not-mess-each-other-up* hug. "Me too."

"Where's that rascal brother of mine?"

I shrugged and glanced back towards the doors at the far end of the room, doors that had formally clad staff standing guard outside.

"Oh, right—Caroline's in there too. And the other dukes and their stuffy wives. And a few of the other stodgy types. And the queen and her husband and the whole sordid lot of them. They're probably all just sipping something not alcoholic enough and congratulating each other on how proper they are. Snooze." She rolled her eyes at the whole affair.

"Yeah, well…" My words drifted. I didn't really know what to say. Emily must have seen my ambivalence, because she grabbed my elbow with one hand and flagged a waiter with another.

"Let's get you some more Champagne, shall we? And then you have to turn around so I can get a good look at this dress. And your hair! You look *incredible*, Lydia, seriously. I mean, you were gorgeous before, but golly, I feel like I'm in the presence of a Hollywood starlet or something. My brother's a moron if he stays in there one-tenth of a second longer than required."

I twirled for her halfheartedly, and we chatted for a few more minutes about how Richard was a troublemaker—*rabble-rouser* were Emily's words—and Jemma was an unfortunately pre-dictable match for him. Emily's words there were *Wouldn't it have been more fun if he'd ended up married to a barrister or a dentist or something?* followed by a heavy sigh, as though it were such a shame to be so boring. Eventually she looked up and smiled at someone behind me.

"I'm afraid I have to go mingle—one of the horrors of these

things," she said, although I doubted she really minded. She was so good at it. "I'm leaving you in capable hands."

Turning, I found Will.

"Oh, you!" I said and gave him a brief hug. "I'm glad you're here."

"You, dear Lydia, look absolutely ravishing. All of these poor buggers are surely killing themselves that Dylan found you first," he said conspiratorially, gesturing to the crowd with his glass of Scotch. "I heard on good authority that Lord Dartford nearly choked when you walked into this room moments ago, resulting in half his glass of Champagne ending up on his shirt, and his wife, Lady Elsbeth, is now giving him the cold shoulder."

"You make this stuff up. I mean, it's sweet, but you're a total liar."

"On my honor," he said, smiling, and I rolled my eyes.

"Well, you look dashing," I said eyeing him up and down. "I never thought I'd see you outside of your chef garb."

He shrugged bashfully. "So the daft wanker's abandoned you, has he?"

I shrugged. "I guess it doesn't exactly fly to introduce your mistress to one's fellow aristocrats." Will winced.

"Yes, well, he's not married, so you're not his mistress, but you're not his fiancée or wife either, and there's the rub, I'm afraid. None of that matters out there." He gestured to a window, indicating life outside the palace walls. "But in here, there are some rather old-fashioned views about these things. And after what happened with the CBC and all, I'm sure you understand. But you're here, aren't you? That's the important thing."

"Wait, what? What happened with the CBC?" I asked Will, who looked slightly pale all of a sudden, like he'd just gotten himself into trouble.

"Oh dear. I thought Dylan would have told you, and now I've made a muck of things, haven't I?"

"Will?" I said in as threatening a tone as possible.

He sighed heavily. "Knowing can only help. Apparently Her Majesty gave a disapproving glare or something to old Geoff when Dylan brought you to tea—a word, a gesture, a nod—I have no idea really. She wasn't keen that Dylan had shown up with his girlfriend, and he wouldn't give a flying fuck about that, not really, although, I mean, she is the *queen*." Will shuddered in mock fear. "Well, as you can imagine, Geoffrey ripped your boyfriend a new arsehole for that one. *No one* cares more about the queen's good graces than Geoffrey."

"I'm not totally following," I said, trying to figure out the intricacies of royal etiquette.

"You see Dylan hadn't told his father he was bringing you—he'd just rung the queen's secretary on his own." He must have noticed my look of horror, because he quickly followed it with, "Not to worry. Word has it you were stunning, and the old bat said something along the lines of you 'having spirit.' So all's well, and truthfully she adores Dylan, always has done, which is shocking given the Caroline debacle. But you see *Geoffrey* is the duke, not Dylan, and therefore it was a bit cheeky to bring you unannounced. Broke rank and all that, so liking you isn't really the issue—Her Majesty prefers things be kept in order, so to speak. Anyhow, I'm sure Dylan's just trying to play nice now."

"I had no idea," I said, thankfully feeling less embarrassed about being an uninvited guest but still frustrated with this whole mess. Would I ever understand the bizarre dos and don'ts of the royalty? What a disaster!

Will nodded. "Now let's go tackle one of these garçons and

get drunk, shall we?" Will took my arm in his, and we went looking for more drinks.

Eventually we found our way to a group of men that looked to be roughly Will's and Dylan's age. One of them I recognized as Tristan Bailey. I didn't like him, and I wasn't exactly in the mood for more snobbery.

"Will, who do we have here?" said one of the guys, patting Will on the back.

But before Will could introduce me, Tristan spoke up. "Oh, Charlie, haven't you met Lydia? This is Dylan's new lass. An American," he added, looking at the group in a way that suggested they all knew what *that* meant, presumably that I was a slut or something. "Where are you from again? Brooklyn?" The guy was drunk, and there was no hiding the derogatory tone in his words.

Will leaned in and whispered in my ear, "Ignore him, Lydia. He's an arse."

"You know, I think I'll go get some air," I said to Will, and he nodded. I just didn't have this in me. I hadn't seen Dylan since we'd arrived forty-five minutes ago, and I was pissed. I had started this night feeling so glamorous and beautiful, but now I was dejected and bored. And as much as I hated to admit it, I felt intimidated, like a lamb sent to the slaughter, like that whole room of people was ready to devour me for being "unofficial" or unsanctioned or American or un-Botoxed. The room was full of interesting people, people who probably had great stories, people I normally would have been happy to meet. I should have been enthralled, giddy, but instead I felt like I was skirting the edges, hiding. I just needed to breathe, to be somewhere quiet for a moment, so I could feel like myself. I walked to the edge of the room and stepped through a door back into the main hallway.

Chapter 25

I was only twenty feet from the door I'd come through when I felt a hand on my arm. Hopeful, I spun around, only to find Tristan, whose grip on me was getting stronger.

"Excuse me," I said firmly. "I just need to find the restroom."

"Aw, don't be like that, sweetheart," he said, and he started pulling me next to him, almost dragging me to the end of the hall into an empty room. I started to struggle, but I'd learned too many times that it was all too easy to end up being an embarrassment to Dylan. The last thing I wanted to do was make a scene with someone who worked for his father. Even if he was a dick.

The room was some kind of anteroom, like a staging area, with a couple of chairs and a desk and then a door to yet another room. But he stopped and moved me towards a wall. Suddenly I was very, very nervous.

"Tristan, what do you want?" I tried to keep my tone normal, but I was cold suddenly, and nervous. Nothing about this felt right.

He just laughed, and a disgusting bit of drunken spit collected at the corner of his mouth. Fuck, this was bad. I turned to leave—I just needed to get out of there. But before I could get very far, Tristan had grabbed my hand and pulled me back.

"Tristan. Stop. I—" But my words turned into a series of incomprehensible *no*s.

"Come on, baby," he began, and he leaned into me, pinning me against the wall with his hips. I could feel his hardness against me, and I wanted to vomit. I tried to wriggle free, but he pinned both my wrists in one of his hands and moved them above my head. His hands were clammy and too strong. His breath smelled of gin, and his face was too close, too warm. I felt disgusting. Trapped. I started to cry against all my wishes—the wet tears dropping into the bare deep V of my dress, reminding me of how exposed I was. I couldn't handle this. He had to get away from me. I couldn't do this. Even though I was essentially pinned against the wall, I put all the force I could summon into ramming my knee firmly into his crotch.

"Motherfucker!" I shouted.

He grunted in pain and swore loudly, more spit landing on my chest, but somehow he managed to keep my hands pinned to the wall.

"You bitch!" he screamed as he regained composure. "But that's how you like it, isn't it? A little rough?" He drove my legs wider, pinning them with his thighs, restricting my movement even more, and I lost my balance in my shoes. I couldn't get the leverage to try to hit him again.

"Fuck you, asshole!" I screamed, trying to keep the whimper in my voice at bay.

"Aww, sweetheart. You know you want this. You must be fantastic in the sack—why else would Dylan Hale want a gold-digging whore like you? This cunt must be pretty special." His knee was pushing the fabric of my dress between my legs. And that word, a word that Dylan made sound so sexy, felt scary coming from Tristan's mouth.

I could feel my own trembles against his chest as he pressed into me, and then his hand moved inside the front of my dress, and he roughly, sloppily grabbed my breast.

"Get off me!" I screamed, although I could hear how rough my voice was and doubted it carried.

"What? So Dylan's the only one who's allowed to tie you up and screw you, you kinky bitch? He's the only one allowed to rough you up and tuck little toys inside your pussy? Why else would a man like him tote around a nothing little whore like you?"

All of a sudden he was fiercely pulled away from me, and I sank against the wall, wrapping my arms around myself, the tears starting to come in earnest.

"Because I love her, you prick! Get the fuck off of her!" It was Dylan, and I looked up just in time to see his fist connect with Tristan's face. Suddenly Will was in the room, closing the door behind him and crouching next to me, asking if I was okay and gently rubbing my shoulder, holding me against him. I was so overwhelmed, the sensations were assaulting me, and I was trying to adjust to the scene in front of me. Will looked down and pulled my dress back into place.

Tristan was holding his nose, which was bleeding, and Dylan had him jammed up against the wall, one hand pushing into his chest, the other grabbing his chin. Dylan looked ready to spit on him. I'd never in my life seen fury unleashed, not really. This is what that looked like. It was terrifying, but there was also safety in knowing that fury was on my side.

"You?" he demanded. "Fucking *you*?" All of a sudden I realized what Dylan was responding to. Oh my god. The emails. They had to be from *him*. How else would Tristan know that Dylan had tied me up during sex?

Tristan started to laugh. "Took you long enough to figure it out, golden boy, didn't it?"

"You fucker! *How?*" Dylan wasn't screaming, but his voice had dropped two octaves, and I'd never heard a sound so threatening.

"A first in computer engineering paid off," he said, and he was actually laughing in his sense of victory. "And you and your team of imbeciles went down every false path I laid out for you." He was so pleased with himself. He was maniacal.

"*Why*, you pathetic piece of shit? Fucking why?" The veins in Dylan's neck were throbbing, his eyes could kill, and somehow he'd lost his tuxedo jacket in all of this. I'd never once, not ever, seen Dylan out of control. Not even in bed with me. Dylan was putting all his weight into Tristan, his hand now gripping his throat, and Tristan was getting redder and redder.

Tristan laughed hoarsely. "Why do you think, you precious asshole? You're a goddamn undeserving playboy. *I'm* the one who saved Hale Shipping from financial oblivion. *I'm* the one who's there for your father every day. *I'm* the one who's actually helped him run Humboldt for the past decade. Where have you been, *my lord*? Gallivanting around town with chambermaids? Star fuckers? Whoring yourself out with whatever pussy was available? And now bringing *here* some slut who has no right to be anywhere *near* the Abingdon name? Your father was right—you're shameless. It was time someone took you down a peg or two, don't you think?"

Dylan was seething. I half expected to see white foam come from his lips he was so angry.

Tristan had a bizarre look of triumph on his face as he continued. "I may have no right to Humboldt, which is a fucking mistake of birth. But I goddamn well have a right to Hale Shipping. I should be the one to run that place. Do you know how long I've been kissing your father's ass? How much I've put up with? How far I've gone to prove that Hale Shipping would be better off in my hands? And still the old man insists it's yours. How does it feel, Hale? Standing by while someone fucks with what's yours?

"And you made it easy, didn't you? You offered her up on a silver platter, fawning like an idiot, showing the world just how *in love* you were with that stunt at the Savoy. Pathetic. Your security guard made things fun, added some challenge, but I never thought you'd make it so easy to get to you, Hale. So easy, I almost thought you wanted me to watch. You two put on quite a show—"

Dylan shoved his hand into Tristan's chest in fury, jamming him against the wall. "Why? Why did you do it?"

Tristan laughed again. "Apart from the joy of watching you flail about? Of sending you on that little wild-goose chase? Easy. Now that I've had my fun—and compiled enough evidence—the press can have your little video, those pictures. Do you honestly think the board will put the company in the hands of a depraved, ruined dilettante? And who would be the best choice for your replacement? How about the man who's been at your father's side for the last decade while his real son was off not giving a shite? The best part? Where Hale Shipping goes, so does Humboldt. It will *all* be mine. Maybe not the title, but the rest of it, and I've fucking *earned* it, unlike you and your piece of ass over here."

Dylan reared back his hand punched Tristan in the face once

again, and Tristan wilted, his face in his hands, knees buckled from the pain. "Like hell you will. The first one was for Lydia, you asshole. That one was for my family. You're done." Dylan's words were like ice—fury incarnate. "Now," he said, turning to Will, "get this pathetic fuck out of here."

Will looked down at me and whispered, "You okay, Lydia?" I nodded, and he got up and dragged Tristan by the arm to the entrance of the small room. I couldn't imagine what kind of repercussions there would be for having a fistfight in Buckingham Palace.

"Baby," Dylan uttered under his breath and came rushing over to me, pulling me up and firmly against his chest, wrapping his arms clear around me. He kissed the top of my head and let his lips be planted there. He held my face in his hands and stroked my tear-stained cheeks. "Christ, Lydia, are you okay?"

But before I could answer, Will returned with the beat-up Tristan. When Dylan looked at him as if to ask *What the fuck?* Will explained that the palace had asked that we wait until the coast was clear and transportation had been arranged before removing Tristan, who was hunched over, nursing his face, and mumbling about Geoffrey and Hale Shipping.

"I'm okay," I said into Dylan's chest, but he pulled away to inspect me, to take a look for himself. I looked down and saw what he saw—the bodice of my dress wrinkled and askew, and I could only imagine what my face looked like. Mascara was probably streaming down my face.

"Oh, damsel, look what I've let happen to you," he whispered, pulling me closer, holding me against him for a long minute. I felt his head above me turn. "Will, mate—the press."

"I've taken care of it, Dylan—no one saw you come in here. Caroline will let you stay until the press are gone."

"Dylan, the video—" I said, still shaking. The only thing that could make all of this worse was if Tristan managed to follow through on his threat about sending the video to the press.

"Take the fucker's phone, Will," he said, and I could hear the movements behind me, hopefully indicating that Will was removing Tristan's ability to forward the video to anyone. "I won't let that happen, baby. We'll get anything else he has before he has a chance to do any more damage," he finished while pulling me just a little closer.

We stayed there for a moment until both of us were calm, or until I was, anyway. When my breathing had evened, when my eyes were dry. The entire time his arms were wrapped tightly around me. The warmth was returning to my skin, to my core. It was as though Dylan thought that by holding me tightly enough to him he could undo what had just happened. And I let him. I let his smell, his muscular frame, and the soothing chant of his words bring me back to him. I couldn't even tell you what he said—there were *you're okay*s on top of *I love you*s and *baby*s and *damsel*s, but it was the mere sound of his voice that did the job of relaxing me.

When I finally pulled away slightly, my hair fell around my shoulders—Dylan must have removed the pins from the bun without me even realizing it—and he gently used his thumbs to sweep the dampness from my cheeks.

"I'm sorry, damsel." He continued to hold my face in his hands. "I'm so sorry." Dylan's voice sounded resigned and sad, apologetic in a way that made no sense.

"I'm so glad you're here, that you were here, that you came." But he was shaking his head even before I had finished speaking. We were now alone—Will must have dragged the disheveled Tristan from the room. And the space was dark—the moonlight and lights from the courtyard were the only sources of brightness in the room, but they allowed me to see Dylan's expression perfectly. An expression not of calmness but of furious defeat, enraged powerlessness, had crept over him.

I was just beginning to process everything that had happened, everything that had been said. *Tristan Bailey*.

Dylan's eyes left mine and his arms dropped away. I stood up from where we'd sat on the floor against the wall, so I could see him better, so I could get a grip on the uneasy feeling seeping between us, so I could start to ask the questions I needed to ask. He rose as well and leaned away from me, against the wall behind him.

"Hey," I said, trying to get his attention, tilting my head, trying to will his eyes to meet mine.

"Baby," he said, shaking his head. I gave him a minute, hoping I'd be able to discern what was running through his mind, that the softness would return. But instead his face got harder. He somehow got further away.

"Fuuuck!" he finally said, so sternly I nearly jumped, his hands running through his hair, his foot banging against the wall behind him.

"Dylan?" I asked, reaching my hand out, but he didn't take it. I could practically see the onslaught of thoughts running at lightning speed through his mind. None of them were good. What was going on?

"Lydia," he said, and he sounded so…sad. Angry and sad, and I knew now, with certainty, that there was something else going on. This wasn't only about what had just happened with Tristan. This was about something bigger. Whatever had been bugging him in the car was bubbling up. "Bloody hell," he started again, bitter frustration and resignation tinging his words. "How could I have let this happen?"

"Dylan." I'd said his name sternly, almost shouted it—I needed him to snap out of it, to stop talking to himself, to stop working himself into an angry frenzy and start talking to me. "What is going on? This obviously isn't all about Tristan Bailey and the emails. You thought it was the Bresnovs, but it was Tristan. That leaves some details to figure out, but at least we know."

"That's the problem, though, isn't it? I was wrong. I couldn't protect you from him."

"But you did. You came in here. You ripped him off of me," I protested, marching towards him. Now *I* was frustrated. He was focusing on all the wrong things. He *had* protected me—why couldn't he see that? "Dylan, what else is going on? Talk to me." My voice was a mix of annoyance and, increasingly, desperation. I felt like he was pulling me down some spiral, to some inaccessible place.

He stroked my cheek once with his hand but then pulled back, pulled away from me. Like he didn't believe me. Like it wouldn't matter *what* I said.

"It never should have happened, Lydia. And none of this would have happened to you if you hadn't been in a public relationship with me. You would have been safe." He moved to a wingback chair and sank into it.

"Fucking stop it with the 'safe' business! Just tell me what the fuck is going on, Dylan! Why did Tristan think he could get his hands on Humboldt? What was this all about?" I was boiling over, and I had a right to be. He was descending into some dark place, shutting me out, and I needed him to stay at the surface long enough to tell me what he was going through but also to see *me*, to see *us*.

Finally, with his head in his hands, his elbows on his knees, staring at the floor, he spoke. "Lydia…" He trailed off, trying to find words.

"What?" I asked, suddenly more concerned than angry. This wasn't the Dylan I knew.

"When I went to Humboldt this afternoon, my father told me…" He paused, taking a deep breath. "Remember that deal I told you about? The one that went south?"

I nodded and thought back to that night he came back from Russia, so certain he'd figured it out.

Dylan nodded. "It wasn't just a bad deal. There's more. As I told you, two years ago I realized something was going on with Hale Shipping. I did some investigating and learned that my father had run the company so poorly since my grandfather's retirement that the place was on the verge of bankruptcy. But the year-end reports looked fine—it didn't add up. I confronted him about it."

He was staring at the ceiling and then the floor—anywhere but at me.

"He confessed that he'd gone to the Bresnovs for help, for money, and hid it from the board. As you know, the Bresnovs helped my grandfather start the company, and my father thought they'd help him keep it quiet, that a secret deal with them would buy him the time to turn the company around, and no one would ever know. He accepted a large sum from them to get the company back on track, but he was naïve about who he was getting in bed with."

He sighed and once again rubbed his forehead with his fingers.

"They essentially blackmailed him." He shook his head as he said it, almost as though he'd just made it real by saying it aloud.

"What? How?" I asked, completely blindsided by this.

Dylan sighed and took a moment. "They agreed to bail out the company on two conditions. First, he would allow them to use Hale Shipping to launder money for some of their less-*legal* operations."

"God, Dylan," I started, and I tried to approach him, but he held his hand up. He wasn't done, and he wasn't going to let me get close.

"Tristan was involved. *He* knew about the deal, helped my father hide it. I couldn't let that go, obviously. So I intervened. I dealt with the Bresnovs, and my father swore he'd build the company back up ."

"How did you deal with them?" I was still standing a few feet from him, my arms wrapped around myself, just trying to take all of this in.

"I did my own research and discovered the Bresnovs are minor players in a much bigger operation. They have connections to some of the worst criminal organizations coming out of Moscow—human traffickers, drugs, the works. So I approached British intelligence for help. I figured they'd take care of the bastards. But it turned out that the Bresnovs were already on their radar. They'd been keeping tabs on them, hoping the family would crack open their investigation into much higher-ups, bigger criminals. They weren't willing to take in the Bresnovs before they'd caught the bigger fish. In the end I struck a deal—MI6 provided me with information that helped me stave off the Bresnovs, at least for a while. They also agreed to protect the Hale name and give my father and the company immunity. In return I agreed to work with them, to use our connection with the Bresnovs to further their investigation."

"Holy shit." This shit was crazy.

He looked up at me for the first time in several minutes, remembering. "Lydia, that's who I was meeting with that night I was going to Amsterdam—a member of MI6."

"A government official."

"I didn't lie."

"I know. I trusted you."

Dylan nodded at this somberly.

"So you're still working with them?"

"The Bresnovs?"

I nodded.

"We made them investors on the official record, much to their chagrin, so it's much harder for them to use us to do anything illegal. And my father's supposedly been trying to bring the company back into good form legally. But they knock on my door every so often, reminding me or my father in subtle and not-so-subtle ways that they are just biding their time, waiting to get what they feel they're due."

"God," I said, not really knowing what else to say. "So until they're apprehended for other things, you're just holding them off."

"Precisely. Only tonight I learned there's more. My father didn't tell me everything two years ago, but he did this afternoon. I couldn't understand why he wouldn't just sell the company—if he sold, he'd still be rich, and since the Bresnovs are investors on public record, they'd get a cut. It would be out of our hands. And it's not as though he's ever actually cared about the business itself. Yet he was so bloody stubborn about keeping it in the family. I couldn't figure it out. Now I know why."

"Why?"

Dylan sighed and closed his eyes with resignation. "The Bresnovs' second condition was that my father make Humboldt Park an asset of HS."

"So Hale Shipping owns Humboldt Park?"

He nodded.

"Why would they do that?"

"Because they knew we wouldn't sell if it meant losing the estate. And if we can't sell, we have to keep helping them. They've been biding their time, but they're ready to cash in on my father's end of the bargain. They want him to get back to helping them launder money, and now they want a cut of HS profits too."

I was just trying absorb this. It seemed so far-fetched. So crazy. But everything now made sense. As long as the company stayed in the family, so did Humboldt Park. It had not been just anger or spite in Geoffrey's voice that day when he talked to Dylan. It had been desperation.

"So that's why your dad's wanted you so involved lately? He wants you to take over?" Dylan nodded in affirmation.

"In his mind he's been grooming me, trying to get me on board."

"But, Dylan, your father's only in his sixties. You don't have to take over now. We have time to figure this out. To get you out of it. You said you're working with British intelligence. We can figure this out together, Dylan."

We were both quiet for a moment. I was standing, as I had been for several minutes, in the center of the room, my arms wrapped around my torso, the gown I was wearing suddenly feeling heavy and yet not enough. I wished we were home, in private. There were so many questions, so many details. But I could see, even before he spoke, that another thing was happening here.

"Lydia, I'm not dragging you through this," he said, so decided. "Not when I can't be trusted to keep you safe. I was sure that it was the Bresnovs trying to put pressure on me...Fuck, Lydia. I was so distracted by that possibility, I didn't even see Tristan coming. I can't keep up. I should have had more security on you. I should have distributed my team better. I should have kept a closer eye on HS...All I wanted was to protect you from this." He threw his hands up, indicating that the whole world was a danger to me. "I can handle giving up architecture. I can handle taking this on. But I wouldn't be able to handle losing you. If anything happened to you—"

I felt my blood cooling. It was like I could feel him removing himself from my heart, pulling us apart, convincing himself that he had to pull away. All I wanted to say was *But I love you*, because shouldn't that be enough? Shouldn't that say it all? But I couldn't seem to get the words out.

"I never wanted to burden you with my life, my family, a father who would bribe his son's girlfriend to leave him, the need for a bodyguard, the presence of the criminals trying to take my family down, for fuck's sake. I've seen before what this does to people." Grace. He was talking about Grace. But we were different. We had to be.

"And then tonight. Tristan...The worst part is that in my gut, I knew it. I knew we should have stayed a secret. I should have just enjoyed you as long as I could and then let you go. Or I should have just controlled myself from the beginning. I was being selfish. I—"

No. He couldn't do this.

"Stop!" I said, finally finding my words.

"Lydia. Even you must see that everything I feared has come to fruition. You think I haven't felt your anxiety over the past few months? Your doubts, your fears about my stress and what I wasn't sharing with you? About what I *was* sharing? About the media, the photos? You think I couldn't feel how, even slowly, the mess that is my life was breaking us down?"

"But you weren't being open with me! And you're not giving us a chance. If you'd just—"

"No, Lydia. I can't do it all. It's time to face reality—duty has come calling, and tonight has made one thing perfectly clear: You're not safe in a relationship with me. I can't give you what you deserve. The truth is that you were always going to be out of my reach. I just couldn't help myself. I needed you. You're the fucking love of my life, and all I've learned is that I was a fool for ever thinking that mattered."

A tear glided down my cheek. No wracking sobs, just quiet defeat. It turned out it wasn't *me* who was flailing. It wasn't *me* who was screwing this up. I was fighting. I was clawing at the walls, digging my fingers in, determined to hold on to this, because I knew it was worth it. But he wasn't clawing at the walls. He didn't know we were worth it. He couldn't. He was giving up. I couldn't be strong enough for both of us. This wasn't my life I was trying to reckon with. It was his, and only he could save it.

I took a deep breath, this time calming *myself* down. I had a choice, and really there was only one thing to do. I took a deep breath and began talking, the words like ice as they rolled off my lips, because I knew where they were taking me. "Dylan, I could keep fighting you. Fighting *for* you. For us. I could stay here in this room in Buckingham Palace and try to convince you that we'll always be stronger together than alone. I could try to force you to see that. Because you're wrong. I *know* you're wrong. I look at you and I see something you don't—I see a future you deserve. One where you're not alone. One where you're the incredible architect, the good man you are, *and* the Duke of

Abingdon. I have faith in you—you can figure this out." He was looking at me and his head was shaking, almost imperceptibly, but there it was. "The only problem is, of course, it doesn't work if I'm the only one who believes that. Believes in this." I gestured to the space between us. Then I closed my eyes, and another tear fell. I knew I was about to let the best thing in my life die in Buckingham Palace. "So okay," I said, crying steadily but hunting for my resolve.

He looked up, slightly shocked that I was giving in. "You deserve more than this. Than me."

Deserving more than him was an impossibility. It wasn't about deserving a person. It was about deserving what we *had*, and I knew in my gut I'd never find what we had with anyone else. Although I guess in one way he was right—I did deserve someone who could see me through the muck, who would fight for me. So I tamped down every screaming retort, every begging plea for him to open his eyes and see what he was throwing away, and I nodded. "You deserve more too."

Dylan looked up at me, standing before him. I was wearing the most gorgeous couture gown I'd probably ever wear. I'd been styled by a team of experts. I had started that evening looking more beautiful than I'd ever look again, and I was ending it with the feeling that for the second time that year I was losing the most important man in my life.

Dylan rose from his seat and started to approach me, but I couldn't let him touch me. If he touched me, I'd lose all composure, all ability to do what he needed me to do.

So before he could get to me, I turned and walked away.

Chapter 26

I walked back into the hallway, and I saw a gaggle of giggling girls scurrying from the bathroom back towards the ballroom, happy on Champagne. We'd missed the toasts, the party, but these people hadn't. We'd all been in the same gorgeous palace, but they'd toasted to love, and I'd left any hope of love behind. There would be no beginning. This was an end.

I ducked into the ladies' room and took stock. I quietly wiped the smudged makeup from under my eyes. Patted my cheeks with cold water. Adjusted my dress. And forced a smile—did I look like I'd just been having a grand old time? Not even close, but no one would notice.

Dylan had the tag for my coat, and honestly I didn't have the energy to explain and try to get it back without it. And I certainly wasn't going to go back to Dylan and ask for the tag. I just needed to get out of there. I slipped out the door into the cold night. There was the odd driver standing by his car, a guard standing by the door, but otherwise it was quiet. The photographers who'd been approved were all inside, and the party still had an hour or so to go. So no one noticed me as I went down the steps and over the gravel. I didn't even feel the chill in the air, not yet, anyway.

Leaving the palace grounds on foot felt odd and wrong, like you should only be able to enter or leave by horse-drawn carriage or custom-made Mercedes-Benz. But there I was in my luxury shoes and rumpled ballerina gown, walking out the gates towards Hyde Park. Of course I should have called a cab or gotten on the Tube. It was freezing cold. I had no business walking through the park in the dark late at night, dressed as I was. But I couldn't. I just couldn't be bothered to take my phone from my clutch—it was a miracle I'd still been holding it when I left the palace to begin with.

So I just kept walking. Waiting. For what I wasn't sure, but it just felt like the night had a mind of its own. Like I was the night's captive. Like I didn't have the power to lessen the misery of it.

When I arrived at my doorstep forty-five minutes later, Will was there on my stoop, his hands deep in his coat pockets to keep them warm. He rushed at me.

"Good god, Lydia, you're freezing!" He took my keys and ushered me inside.

"What are you doing here?" I asked quietly as I gratefully stepped into my house. The warm air rushed my skin and made it sting. I was so cold.

Will winced. "I'm making sure you got home well. Dylan asked…Look, Lydia, he's—" I put up my hand to stop him, just as he wrapped a blanket from the couch around me.

"It's okay, Will. Thanks for looking out for me. Earlier, I mean. And now, I guess." I went to the refrigerator and poured one enormous glass of wine, drinking it until it was gone. I looked at Will to offer him some, but he shook his head. "I think I need to be alone."

He nodded and came over to me. He hugged me hard. Really hard. The tulle crinkled around my chest and waist. "You're the best thing that ever happened to him. I hope you know that," he said into my hair.

"Will, don't. I can't." I couldn't hear right now about how he loved me. I knew that he did. Just not enough. Will backed away, and I headed for the stairs before he had even left the house.

I had enough wherewithal to remove the gown and shoes, but then I just crawled beneath my covers. I didn't cry. I couldn't. It wasn't like the last time Dylan and I were over. This was too big. I couldn't let the tears in, or I'd never emerge again. I just closed my eyes and willed myself to sleep.

* * *

Saturday I stayed inside all day. More accurately, I stayed in my bed all day. I'm not even sure what I did. My phone rang in the morning, and I saw it was Emily. I couldn't answer. I didn't know if she had any idea what had happened, but I couldn't talk to her. I texted back, saying I wasn't feeling well. No calls from Dylan. I guessed we were on the same page, then—this was really over. This wasn't like last time when he'd called incessantly and tried to win me back. This was it.

Sunday was much the same. At around two that afternoon a messenger delivered my coat in a garment bag. I laid it on the sofa and went back to my room.

Finally, around midnight, I did something I didn't have the energy to do but knew needed to be done. I called Daphne. If

I didn't call her, it wouldn't be real, and if I was going to get through this at all, I needed to make it real. Because the shitty thing was that it *was* real, no matter how much I wanted to deny it.

"Oh my god, Lydia." She sniffled. Daphne appeared able to cry over my breakup even though I couldn't. "It just feels so wrong. I mean, after Greece? And he'd started opening up to you. I thought you guys were meant to be."

"Well, apparently we're not. Maybe this was always supposed to be the year of tragedy in my life. Maybe this is just the gods' way of showing me rock bottom early, so I can enjoy life more in the future or something?" Wow. I was really bad at cheering myself up.

"I'm sorry for pushing you to go for it with him."

"What? Daphne, in no universe is this your fault."

"Well, I feel like I should have done more to protect you—"

I screamed into the phone. Literally screamed. "Why does everyone feel like they have to protect me?!"

"Because we love you!" I didn't say anything. She sounded almost fed up, as though that answer should have been obvious to me. "Sorry," she added. "Look, Lydia, your dad was never able to be your protector, but he wanted to be. It's what we do for people we love. You're so used to taking care of yourself you don't understand that it's not about anyone thinking you're weak. It's what we do. You do it for me all the time—we take care of the people we love. You're going to have to learn to accept that at some point. I know you'll get through this. You're stronger than anyone I know, you've waded through more and accomplished more on your own than anyone, but this? This thing where we take care of each other? The way you wanted to take care of Dylan, help him navigate all of his stressful stuff? That's where the rubber meets the road in terms of relationships. He wanted to do that for you too, but he felt like he was failing."

I sniffled. A tear had almost escaped, but I pulled it right back where it belonged. "Where the rubber meets the road? Are you reading refrigerator magnets again?"

Daphne huffed a small laugh. "See? You'll be okay."

"Daphne, I'm really tired. I think I should go to sleep." I couldn't talk anymore. I felt shaky and cold and sad.

"Okay, lady, I'll see you in a few days, right? I get in Thursday morning—Thanksgiving. Good timing, right?"

"Right." I sighed. "Oh god, your flight. I mean, I don't think Dylan would cancel the plane or anything, but I guess you should check with Thomas? I should do it for you—"

"Stop. I'll take care of it," she said. Daphne sighed deeply on the other end. "I love you," she said, and I hung up the phone.

*   *   *

Monday morning, Frank was waiting outside my door in the Jag. I went to the window, figuring he didn't know that Dylan and I had broken up, so I told him.

"You're off the hook, Frank. Talk to your boss, but you're free of me."

"He told me. He also told me to drive you to work."

I shook my head. "Not his call anymore."

He looked at me sadly. I must have seemed pretty pathetic to him. "What about as a friend, Lydia. Can I drive you as a friend?"

"No, Frank. I need to get back to myself. Plus, we both know there's no risk anymore. But thank you." He nodded at me, resigned, and I walked towards the Tube.

The next three days at work were a blur. Not a busy blur. A sick blur—I'd developed the cold from hell after foolishly walking home that night after the engagement party, and I was currently living off Lemsip and Kleenex. And a numb blur—each moment the same as the one before and the one that followed. I went through the motions. I must have mumbled to Fiona that Dylan and I had broken up, because everyone seemed to know, but I didn't remember telling them.

Somehow I managed to get the dress back to the studio and the coat back to Selfridges. Somehow I managed to respond to emails and check on the training of the store employees. Somehow I managed to send Frank an L.L.Bean flannel shirt as a thank-you gift—I figured he needed to be in his natural lumberjack habitat. Somehow I managed to turn my eyes from the front-page headlines that Dylan and I had broken up—had he leaked that information himself, I wondered, put the final nail in the coffin? And somehow I managed not to crack. All those weeks of practicing for the press, willing myself to hide my emotions out in public, were finally paying off. The great irony: Dylan and I broke up, and I became a master at putting on the perfect show.

The fact that my office was isolated in the back of the store had originally been a downside—I didn't want to spend any days huddled in the back of a retail space alone—but now I was grateful for the solitude. Fiona and Josh tried to talk to me. Even Hannah wanted in on the making-sure-Lydia-held-it-together party. I still didn't cry, but I also didn't talk. I drank my lattes and ate just enough lunch not to worry anyone, even though all food tasted like sandpaper. I kept the business going. I did my job. I was a good girl, then I came home, stared into space, and went to sleep.

* * *

Thursday morning was Thanksgiving Day. Daphne would be arriving at my door any minute—her flight had gotten in at six in the morning, and it was already eight. Apparently, she was still flying in on Dylan's plane, which meant he was either feeling guilty or just extremely polite. Probably the latter. And Fiona and Josh surely knew to come to my house instead of Dylan's if they were going to come at all. I'd asked Hannah for the day off weeks earlier, and now I regretted it. Wouldn't it be easier to just go to work and pretend none of this was happening? This whole day was going to interrupt the good thing I had going. The good, albeit very fake, thing I had going.

At eight thirty the doorbell rang, and I stumbled down in my leggings and sweatshirt but was shocked to find Lloyd and Molly at the door, holding a box and grocery bags.

"Hello, dear," said Molly with a sad smile. "All of your groceries for today were at the house, and well…" She paused, flustered.

"We thought you'd need them here," Lloyd finished.

I must have looked terrible. I still hadn't said anything, and Lloyd and Molly exchanged concerned looks.

"Oh. Um. Wow. Thank you for bringing all this," I finally said and opened the door. I took a bag from Lloyd's hand and let them follow me to the kitchen. "This was so unnecessary. Thank you."

Just seeing them was making my eyes sting, and I knew I'd start crying if I let them stay or if I spoke to them for too long. But Molly must have been able to see I was on the brink, because she pulled me into the most un-British hug. I weakly hugged her back.

When she let me go, I wiped a tear from my cheek and looked back to them.

"You know, he's not well." Oh god. I couldn't hear about Dylan.

"I'm…I'm sorry to hear that," I said, pleading with myself to maintain control.

"He's been at Humboldt Park for the last day or so. His Grace had a heart attack on Tuesday." My eyes flashed up. Oh god. Poor Dylan. I couldn't hear this. This was the last thing Dylan needed. I was struggling to hold on to my own sanity, and believing that Dylan was doing well, was somehow happier and less stressed without me, was one of the very important ingredients in my *this-was-all-for-the-best* recipe. I gulped and used whatever energy I had to stay together.

"Is Geoffrey okay?" I asked, not even realizing I'd called him Geoffrey out loud.

Molly sighed. "I'm sure he'll recover, dear. I just thought you'd want to know."

I nodded my head. "Thank you both. Um…Please tell the Hales that I'm thinking about them." Lloyd and Molly looked at each other again, surely questioning my saying "Hales" instead of Dylan specifically. But I couldn't, wouldn't get into a situation where I was communicating with him through his staff.

Not five minutes after they left, Daphne arrived.

I pulled on my jeans and tall brown boots and grabbed my wallet, and we walked to get some coffee. I was three blocks from the house before I realized I was wearing my beautiful black coat from Dylan. And it wasn't until I went to pay for the coffee that I realized I was still wearing my bracelet. I'd been wearing it for five days and never even noticed.

"Whoa, what is that?" Daphne asked, pointing at my wrist.

I shrugged my shoulders. "He gave it to me on Saturday night. I just... I just can't take it off yet."

She put her hands on my arms, turned me, and gave me the first real hug I'd let her give me since she'd gotten there. The barista must have thought we were loons—this hug was clearly the work of two American girls. And there, in that upscale coffee shop buried at the bottom of Portobello Road, my tears started flowing.

Daphne grabbed our coffees and urged me to the back of the shop. We turned our chairs towards the back of the shop, and she just let me cry while she rubbed my back.

I cried because I felt so powerless. I cried because I was exhausted by keeping up a good front, by pretending I wasn't dying inside. I cried for Dylan and what he was losing, for the life he was choosing, for the limits he was putting on himself. And I cried out of the sheer frustration that he wouldn't *fight* for this.

Eventually I was able to pull it together enough to head home. Thankfully I had sunglasses in my coat pocket—the aviators Dylan had bought me in Greece—and we left the coffee shop. I kept my head down, remembering the photos I'd seen of Caroline from years earlier and suddenly recalling how sad she'd looked. I wondered if that was how I looked now.

We made it back to the house, and Daphne took over. Thank god she was there. She chopped and cooked and basted. She shredded herbs and even pulled out a bag of Pepperidge Farm stuffing from her luggage, which actually made me laugh.

I was devastated, there was no way around it, but a part of myself had cracked through the despair now that Daphne was here.

Fiona and Josh would arrive at six, so I had no idea who was at my door when the bell rang at four thirty.

Will.

He was standing before me with two white boxes tied with string. "Here, for your treacherous holiday," he said with a sheepish smile. I looked at the boxes, confused. "Apple and pecan. The Internet said those were the traditional options. They also mentioned pumpkin, but pumpkins aren't exactly plentiful over here, and Emily said it sounded foul." He shrugged apologetically.

"You made me pies?" I asked, smiling, and Will nodded.

"Do you want to stay?" I asked before realizing what I was saying. My heart was all of a sudden breaking in two again. I loved Will, but he was Dylan's friend. I'd have to let him go.

He shook his head. "I wish I could, sweetheart, but I'm needed elsewhere. I know…Look, I know it's probably hard right now. But I do adore you. I hope you'll come by the restaurant soon."

I nodded, knowing full well I wouldn't. "Thank you for the pies, Will. And…see you around?"

* * *

The five of us sat around my little farm table. Fiona and Josh had come right on time and on the sidewalk had run into Michael, who, clueless as to the change in plans, had been headed to Dylan's. I couldn't imagine what would have happened had he shown up there. I had completely forgotten I'd even invited him. He sweetly had brought Champagne, and Fiona and Josh had filled him in before they got to my door.

The turkey, thanks to Daphne, was perfection, although she'd had to literally pluck feathers out of it before cooking it. Apparently Molly had bought the absolute freshest bird she could find. Fiona and Josh brought sides, and really it was only because of the culinary perfection of Will's pies—who knew that a born and bred Brit would make the best apple pie I'd ever tasted?—that the meal was at all a success. In terms of food, anyway.

In all other respects, the Thanksgiving dinner was my bleakest in my twenty-four years, but I suppose that gave me cause to be more thankful than ever for my friends. It was my first without my dad, and my grief over him was oddly a welcome reprieve from my grief over Dylan. I finally let down my guard in front of Fiona and Josh and let them see how crushed I'd been.

"He's a bloody pathetic pile of bollocks if you ask me," announced Fiona supportively at one point. Michael looked slightly shocked, as though he hadn't quite realized what he was walking into.

"The thing is, Fee, I don't think he is...Okay, well, maybe a little. But you have no idea how hard this is for him," I pressed quietly.

"Oh puh-lease," she said. "He's the bloody 'Most Shaggable Bachelor of London.' I'm sure he's doing just fine."

"Fee," said Josh, scolding. "Really? You saw how that man was with her. You think this was easy for him? Plus, it's not as though Lydia put up a fight."

"Are you kidding? Lydia fought incredibly hard for him!" Daphne was coming to my defense. "She just knew when to leave a losing battle. This is just one of those tragic life things. He'll realize in time just how stupid he was not to fight harder for her, but by then Lydia will be living a fabulous life elsewhere with someone else."

Michael had the decency to keep quiet. I couldn't imagine that future. Not yet, anyway.

"Guys, please," I begged. "I'm not ready for this. Can we talk about something else?"

There was silence around the table as we all moved the crumbs of pie around on our plates with our forks.

"Well," said Fiona, "we could talk about the opening party for the store. Hannah said that Kate Moss might make an appearance?" she offered glumly, knowing I couldn't muster much excitement at the moment.

Just then someone's phone buzzed, and Josh reached into his man bag. "Have you got a telly?" he asked me, his face suddenly pale, and I nodded. "BBC News."

We turned on the TV only to see an old portrait photo of Dylan's father, dressed in full regalia. And the words listed under his photo startled me.

Geoffrey Hale, 16th Duke of Abingdon, Dies of Heart Failure, Age 61

Holy shit.

"Oh my god," I said. "Lloyd and Molly said he'd had a heart attack a few days ago but thought he'd be okay. Oh my god. Poor Dylan."

As if on cue, the screen showed live video of Dylan and his mother leaving the hospital and getting into a car. He looked horrible. He'd shaved, which didn't surprise me—his sense of duty and obligation in these matters was what would pull him through—but his face was cold, empty.

I told everyone I needed to be alone. Daphne followed the others to the pub down the street. There was something about this that was too overwhelming. This was what Dylan had been afraid of—this day when the world would come crashing down on him, when the responsibilities and choices about how to be the head of his family would be thrust upon him. We'd thought he had years before this happened, but he'd only had days. Why did it have to happen now? Why should he have to deal with this? I was overcome with sadness, not because there was any love lost over Geoffrey but because my heart was breaking for Dylan on top of my heartbreak *about* Dylan. And I also knew that any chance of him realizing that life wasn't so bad, that it wasn't that stressful, that there really was room in it for me, was gone. Even if there was a tiny spark somewhere inside that didn't want to believe it, most of me knew it was true.

It was really over.

Dylan

Chapter 27

Holy shit.

The bastard was gone. My father was gone. The bugger had gone and *died* on me. I wasn't fucking ready for this.

My mother was crying quietly in the seat next to me as we pulled away from the hospital in my father's car, his chauffeur behind the wheel. She wasn't making a sound. I only knew she was crying by the frequent wiping away of tears. I'd never actually *seen* her cry, and I wished I knew how to comfort her. She must have actually loved the bastard. I knew I shouldn't think that about him right after he died, but I couldn't help it. I put my hand over hers and squeezed.

"He wasn't always that way, you know," she said to me, and I stilled. My mother had essentially never spoken to me, not in any real, honest way. A confession like this was tantamount to her telling me she was really a man. "I know you think he was always horrible, but he wasn't. Not always. I really did fall in love with him when I was young. He was so handsome then, so charming. He would bring me these flowers—these white tea roses that grew by the west garden." She stopped, choking on her tears, and I could see her chin start to quiver. She stopped talking for a while, reining in her sadness, and the silence settled between us like dead weight, heavy and lifeless.

Then she turned to me. "You know you'll have to say something." She meant a statement of some kind. She was right. I would, but I wasn't bloody ready to even think about it yet. I just nodded once and squeezed her hand again.

"And you'll get Emily?" she asked.

"Lloyd is picking her up and bringing her to Humboldt. I'll take care of it, Mother." She nodded and let go a sob. My father had been dead only a few hours, and already I was stepping into his shoes.

It was amazing how quickly one's world could crumble. My father's death was going to turn my life wrong-side out, but that wasn't even the worst of it. Only five days ago I'd thrown the best thing in my life away, and I had no idea if I would ever recover from that, let alone this.

It was completely fucked, but instead of thinking of my father, I was thinking of her. Today was her Thanksgiving. I was supposed to be watching her play hostess, hold her hand during her first Thanksgiving without her father. I was supposed to be warding off that goddamn neighbor of hers, Michael. I was supposed to be *with* her. And instead, everything had gone to shite.

But what else could I have done? The whole disaster oozed with my own lack of self-control, my own selfish idiocy. I had let it go too far, and I'd had to let her go. It killed me that it involved hurting her, but better to hurt her now rather than later.

The real problem was that I had slipped up and let someone in at all, let her see me, the real me. Even worse, I'd exposed her to the cold gore that was my life, and just as I had known it would, it had cracked her and cracked me. Being with her had broken down my defenses, my frigid walls, the habits that let me ignore the pull of what I couldn't have and navigate through the world. She'd exposed me, and now I was fucked.

It had been more than five days since I'd heard her voice or touched her, and those five days had been different from the five before: torture, because this time I knew I'd never touch her again. That night at Buckingham Palace kept reeling through my head, on bloody repeat. I kept reliving it every time I closed my eyes.

Seeing Tristan's hands on her made me want to kill someone. Thinking about how devastated she'd looked as I'd ended things. Thinking about how devastated I'd felt when she'd let me. I was ill thinking about it. I was violent with frustration. I was angry. I wanted a different life, one that centered around her instead of a huge estate and a title. One that didn't involve chasing after a goddamn Russian mob family with MI6. And in a flash, with my father's death, my life became the opposite. Wrong-side out.

After she'd left that room, left me, I'd sat in that press office in Buckingham Palace for three hours before Caroline found me. Will must have told her where I'd gone, after he went off looking for Lydia. Knowing the position I was in, she'd waited until the photographers had all left before fetching me, urging me to go home. It was sweet of her to protect me, and thank god she had—I had blood on my shirt and looked bloody awful, but I probably would have deserved it if the event had been splashed across the papers the next day. *Dylan Hale back to his brawling ways.* How I hadn't been able to hide my temper. How I'd put my girlfriend in danger.

Tristan sodding Bailey. How had I missed that? I'd been blind.

He'd been interrogated of course, taken in. I'd had security go after him and then retrieve the photos and footage as soon as possible, and it had all been destroyed. He'd used Hale Shipping resources to hire some private investigator and some blacklisted paparazzi to follow us and get the photos. The Humboldt video had involved a stealthy trip to my room while visiting my father one weekend—a tiny video camera tacked behind one of my rowing trophies. The thought that he'd seen us during those moments made me want to both vomit and murder the fucker. The whole thing had me feeling more protective of Lydia than ever.

In the days after the engagement party, I'd stationed Abbott outside her house to make sure she was okay, but she hadn't left again until Monday morning and then wouldn't let him give her a ride. My stubborn girl. He'd said she looked sick, which wasn't a surprise given that the foolish girl had fucking *walked* home from the party in that dress. I wanted to spank her for that. Spank her and then wrap her in my arms and never let her go.

Apparently she'd gone to and from work and appeared fine, apart from her cold. She'd been seen buying groceries and having lunch with her friends. She'd been seen out for coffee and taking the Tube. She *appeared* fine, but I had this pit in my stomach. I knew that the press were following her, looking for photos of us. Someone had leaked our breakup—if I found out who, I'd strangle them personally—and she was doing just as she'd learned to do, never showing a crack.

That night, when the *Evening Standard* posted a picture of her and Daphne walking through Notting Hill, I realized that had changed. Lydia had been wearing her black coat and the sunglasses I'd bought her in Athens. I couldn't see her eyes, but I knew from the flush on her cheeks and the turn of her mouth and the worried look on Daphne's face that she was anything but fine. Even without seeing her eyes, I knew she'd been crying. The tabloids couldn't really claim that she was upset based on that photo alone, but I *knew* her. I could see her defeat. I'd done that to her. And the worst part was that I hadn't wanted to. And she'd *let* me. *Had* it been too hard for her? Did she really want nothing to do with my life and what came with it? She'd protested, but then she'd let me go. Then again, I'd pushed her away so fiercely.

Fuck me. What the fuck had I done?

Those were the thoughts that ran on repeat in my mind all afternoon, through the family dinner, through soothing my tearful sister, through climbing the stairs of the estate house, which now belonged to me, the day finally over.

I now lay staring at the ceiling in my bedroom at Humboldt. The last time I'd been in this bed, Lydia had been in my arms, her weight on my chest, and I'd been stroking her back. And we'd been violated. I looked around and saw the offending rowing trophy on the shelf, the books from school, the crap that fills a person's bedroom over a childhood. I'd be expected to move into the master suite, but *Christ*, I wasn't ready for that. Maybe I'd just renovate.

At that moment my phone rang. I stared into the big brown eyes in the picture on my phone, one I'd taken just as she was waking up. You couldn't tell from the photo, but I knew she was naked in the picture, and it made me instantly hard. Fuck, I wanted to answer. I wanted to talk to her, to tell her to come to me. But that would be selfish. I let the call go to voicemail and gripped the poor device so tightly to my chest I was probably in danger of breaking it.

Finally I went to my voicemail and listened.

Um. Hi, Dylan. It's me. It's Lydia. I heard about your father, and I just wanted to say… There was silence for a moment, and I could hear her voice crack as she began to speak again. *I've been there. I know you weren't close, and I know that today is about more than losing your dad, but I imagine none of that matters. Not entirely. He was still your father. An anchor in this world. A signpost, even if he was a bad one. Anyway, I wish…I…I'm thinking about you, okay? Goodbye, Dylan.*

I couldn't remember the last time I'd cried. As a child perhaps. But I didn't remember it feeling like this. I didn't remember that tears were so warm or could come so quickly. On any other day I probably could have survived the loss of my horrible father without so much bloody emotion, but Lydia, even from afar, even kicked out of my life as she had been, even over a sodding voicemail, wouldn't let me get away with that. She knew me too well to let me pretend that I didn't feel anything, that this day wouldn't be the most complicated of my life.

And if she knew all that, she also knew that I loved her. Which meant she also knew I was a coward.

When I came downstairs to the kitchen the next morning, Emily and Mrs. Barnes sat with coffees in their hands. I hadn't slept at all. If I managed to get Lydia off my mind even for a moment, I was left staring down the barrel of being the Duke of Abingdon, of having Humboldt Park, Hale Shipping, and my entire family's legacy under my charge. Something I hadn't even begun to come to terms with.

"Your Grace." Mrs. Barnes had said it quietly, but I still winced.

No. Please no. I was not ready for the formal titles, for these conversations. It wasn't her fault. She was just being proper, doing her job. I was technically master of this house now. Ready or not. Here I fucking come.

I kissed Emily on the cheek and touched Mrs. Barnes on the shoulder.

Suddenly Emily was up and out of her seat, pointing her finger at me violently. "You. Me. The library. Now." God, she could be downright scary. When had she grown up and become so bossy? I guess it ran in the family.

"What?" I asked, my voice cracking and groggy.

"I need to talk to you."

"Where's Mum?" Maybe I could distract her from whatever bee was in her bonnet.

"Busy despairing over being the dowager, something about how she feels old," she said, but then she snapped her fingers at me. "Hey. Don't distract me. We need to talk. Library."

"Can't we just do it here? Clearly the two of you have been chatting anyway. Just say what you have to say." I sighed and filled a mug with coffee.

"Fine. You're an idiot. This whole breaking-up-with-Lydia nonsense is a flaming pile of bollocks, and I"—she paused to look at Mrs. Barnes—"*we* think you need to get your sorry arse to London to get her back."

I stared at the two women, dumbstruck.

"I—"

"No," she continued. "Stop being a complete and utter prat, and get. Her. Back. I know you, Dylan, and you have the mother of all shit storms heading your way—"

"Emily!"

"Oh, please. Shut it. I use foul language."

"I don't think—"

"Exactly. You're not thinking. How the hell are you going to be the duke you're supposed to be without her?"

"The duke…?" The duke I was supposed to be? Meaning, the

duke *I* was supposed to be. Not my father. Not my grandfather. But me.

In one phrase, my sister had just wedged a sliver of hope into the *shit storm*, as she'd called it. Was she right? Was there another way to do this? If being the duke didn't mean having to run Hale Shipping, if it didn't mean having to follow the archaic rules my father lived by, if it didn't mean having to give her up…After a moment I realized I hadn't spoken. I was staring at the coffee cup in my hand. "I think I need a walk."

"As long as that walk is towards London—" But Mrs. Barnes put her arm on Emily's indicating she'd said enough. Christ, my sister was like a pit bull. Not to be reckoned with apparently.

"Emily, let's say for a second this made any sense, and I'm not saying it does. What makes you think she'd take me back? I couldn't protect her from everything that's hard about this. And I pushed her away. Being with me was nothing but hell."

"First of all, since when does *the* Dylan Hale take no for an answer? And somehow she didn't exactly look 'hell bound' when you were together. For some insane reason she loved you and seemed to be figuring it out. That girl is tough as nails, if you hadn't noticed. Plus, she doesn't exactly look happy now," she said, shoving yesterday's paper towards me across the table. Lydia's picture, her gaze behind those sunglasses, looked up at me.

"Dylan, dear." Mrs. Barnes placed her warm aged hand on my forearm to quietly get my attention. And it didn't escape my notice that she had called me *Dylan*. "Choosing someone to be with…well, it's about who you want with you when times are hard, who you want to hold your hand when you're in the trenches. Remember that." She looked so herself in that moment, so kind, and while I knew she cared for me, this was the first time she'd ever stepped outside her role so fully. Christ, this must have looked like a real emergency for these two to pounce on me. As if I didn't already know.

I sighed before walking out the kitchen door into the frosted garden—I needed to be outside.

All day Friday I was in the gardens. I walked farther into the park than I had since I was a child. I avoided my mother, saw her only once that evening—sitting prim and proper in front of the fire, staring into the flames—and I paused only briefly before heading up to bed. I also avoided Emily, which was harder, since she seemed to be lying in wait, ready to pounce, to talk, to insist. What she didn't know was that I'd heard her. And really what she'd done was to pull away the blinders, to shove my face into what I hoped to god I would have realized on my own eventually: This was my time, and if I started out this new phase by ignoring what I knew in my gut was right, then what hope did I have for the future? Start as you mean to go on—wasn't that what they said?

That night was a combination of excitement and calm that should've been impossible but I now realize is symptomatic of a good decision.

Being with her might be the most selfish thing I'd ever do, but the simple fact was, I couldn't do any of this without her.

Chapter 28

It was seven in the morning on Saturday when I finally rang her doorbell, and I couldn't remember being this nervous about anything in my life. Or more certain.

I'd driven myself over well before dawn and had been sitting in the car, waiting for it to be a reasonable hour to wake her. Daphne had left the day before, which I only knew because it had been on my plane. I needed Lydia alone. I needed her now. Seven was reasonable, wasn't it? It would have to be.

When she opened the door, she looked so perfect. All I could think was *Mine*.

Christ, I'd missed her. She was wearing those black leggings that made her legs look a thousand miles long and a dress shirt. *My* dress shirt. Her dark hair was askew, hanging around her shoulders. Her new fringe framed her face perfectly, making those innocent brown eyes pop.

"Dylan," she said, and she gulped in that way she always did when she was bracing herself, when she felt like something big was coming. She was right. It was.

"Damsel. Can I come in?" I gripped the doorframe on both sides, wanting to lean in all the way.

"I…" she started, and then her expression changed, remembering. "Oh god, Dylan, your dad. I…" She had a look of both sympathy and fear on her face, and the fear part slayed me.

"Lydia. It's like the bleeding Arctic out here. I don't want you to get sick again. Can I please come in?"

"How'd you know I was sick?" she asked, wrapping her arms around her chest to shield it from the cold, but then she quickly rolled her eyes. She knew me well enough not to be surprised that I'd had my eyes on her. She swung open the door and let me in.

She looked smaller. I looked closely and saw what the week had done to her, what the last several weeks had done. She looked thinner and like she wished her long bangs were still there to protect her. She wanted to hide from me. Well, no fucking way. I needed her to see me.

"Baby," I said, putting my hands on her arms. Fuck, how was I supposed to even do this? I inhaled deeply and went for it. "I've been an idiot." She looked up at me, questioning. "You were right." There was no way to do this except to dive in. "You said I deserved more from my life, and you were right. I want more. I *want* you."

Her eyes were softer now, a little of that fear slipping away.

"Please forgive me for pushing you away, Lydia. I was absolutely mad, and I behaved dreadfully. I felt like I was losing my hold on everything, and then I saw you getting hurt and I felt fucking insane that I couldn't stop it. That it had happened at all. I've never felt more powerless. I felt like I'd failed you, and I thought the only way I could stop that wretched feeling was to let you go." I was just getting going, but I needed her with me. I brushed her cheek with my fingers. "But that's bollocks, isn't it?"

She gave the tiniest hint of a nod, and I took the chance to run my hand down her arm and take her tiny hand in my own. "The only way to stop it is to let you *in*. You tried to tell me, and I didn't hear you. I'm sorry. I'm so sorry. I know I made it hard for you to be with me. I pushed you. I asked you to trust so much without giving nearly enough in return. I know that."

She was crying now, and I pulled her to me. I felt my shirt dampen with her tears, and I would have given everything to know why she was crying.

"Please, damsel, please. It will be okay. I fucking love you so much."

She wriggled her head free from my arms and looked up at me with so much affection, and I was flooded with relief.

"I know I need to open up to you, be honest, let you take care of me—I want that. I *need* that. But, baby, you *must* trust me, let me do the same. I need to feel like you're safe—you have to let me do that for you, but we can figure it out together. You're so strong, strong enough to handle all the crap that my life entails. I know that—but we have to do this *together*." She was nodding through her tears, and I was brushing them away with my thumbs as well as I could, kissing her cheeks, tasting the tears on my lips.

"I've missed you, Dylan, but I'm terrified that if I let you in you'll leave me behind again. You don't understand. I felt *safe* with you, and then I felt abandoned. You wouldn't open up to me, and it was like you couldn't even see me with everything going on. I'm scared. You're the first person I've ever loved, and I've already lost my own father, and now..."

She started to tremble slightly. She was trying to hold herself together.

"Shh," I cooed, "I *know*. But, Lydia, I'm not going anywhere.

I'm not going to let you out of my fucking sight. Don't you understand? It's *because* of everything that's happening, that's about to happen. I need you, and whether you want to admit it or not, you need me too. That's how it's *supposed* to be. I'm stronger with you by my side. You're it for me, baby. You're *all* I've been able to think about since the party. I won't ever make that mistake again."

She nodded hesitantly, wiping her tears away. Shit. I looked down and saw her pert nipples peeking through the thin fabric of the white shirt. This was so the wrong time to be getting a hard-on, but Christ. Those tits. Fucking made for me. I stifled a groan and pulled her closer to me.

"You're mine, baby. You always have been. I don't want one of those zombies from Caroline's circle. No Botox. I want you. I want your hankering for croissants in the morning. I want your insistence on taking the Underground. I want you sitting on the kitchen counter as though there aren't six perfectly good chairs in the room. I want you collecting hair bands on your wrist as though we don't live around the corner from the chemist." I snapped one on her wrist, and her laughter unleashed another wave of relief. Thank fucking Christ she was with me. "You. I just want you. I need *you*. Don't change a thing," I said and brushed her fringe with my fingers. "This can stay, though—you look bloody gorgeous." She smiled broadly and buried her face back in my shirt.

We stood there for what might have been ten minutes, just holding each other. I could actually feel the fear, the reserve, the self-protection leaving her body. She melted into me, just as I needed her to. After an eternity, she stood on her tiptoes and nuzzled into my collar.

"What took you so long to figure all this out?" she asked.

"I'm a bit daft, aren't I?"

"A bit." Her chin rested against my chest as she looked up at me.

God, I needed more of her. All of her. I slipped my palms around her torso, my signal for her to jump into my arms, and she did, wrapping those perfect lithe little legs around my waist. But she buried her face back in my neck, like she wasn't quite ready to see me after everything I'd said. It was too fresh, too real. I walked over to the couch in her lounge and sank into it, holding her against me so she was straddling me, her thighs tightly gripping my own. I ran my hands up her back and into her silky hair. Goddammit, this woman was going to be the end of me. I wanted to sink into her and stay there for a week. But I couldn't go there yet. I wasn't done.

"Baby. Lydia," I whispered in her ear. "I need you to look at me." She raised her head and fluttered her eyes at me, still red from crying but full of the innocence and strength that I couldn't resist.

"Do you trust me?" I asked her, and she nodded.

"My father died, Lydia."

"I know, Dylan. I'm so sorry." She held my hand against her face and turned her lips into my palm, kissing it.

"Baby, do you understand what that means?" She looked at me, unsure. "I'm the seventeenth Duke of Abingdon. I've dreaded this day my whole life. Seen it as the day the grim reaper would come for everything I held dear—my business, my freedom. The day I'd be locked in my own tower of sorts. I know it sounds dramatic, but I grew up looking at my father and seeing no hope there. He was cruel and lazy, and the idea of filling his heinous shoes has never exactly appealed to me."

"Oh, Dylan, I know, but—" I put my finger against her soft lips.

"Let me finish. I don't see it that way anymore. Running

Humboldt Park is a business. Hale Shipping is the company that supports it, supports my family. Both of those are my responsibility now. Being the duke the way my father was is not who I am, but I can figure this out. I believe in it. *And* I can keep Hale Design and keep you. I haven't the foggiest idea *how*, mind you, but I know I can do it. *We* can do it."

She smiled at me in a way that somehow conveyed more confidence in me than my father had over his whole lifetime.

"I need you there with me," I said steadily, wanting to make sure she was with me.

I held her face in my hands and looked into those dark eyes. "Lydia, will you marry me?"

Her jaw dropped, opening her mouth to me in a way that was sickeningly sexy. *Fuck. Please let her say yes.*

I stroked her cheek.

Nothing.

"Baby?"

"Marry you." It wasn't a question. It was like she was trying on the idea.

I smiled back at her. "Yes, baby. Marry me. I know it's asking a lot. Undoubtedly. There will be god-awful garden parties with Her Majesty. You'll occasionally have to stand for hours in heels during ceremonies that involve horses wearing ludicrous hats. There will be my mother to contend with, of course, and you'd be taking on the horrible paparazzi for eternity. So obviously there's no earthly reason you should accept me, but please do, baby. Do this with me."

She was smiling but still hadn't given me an answer.

"Shall I get down on one knee and ask properly?" I asked, and she nodded eagerly. For the first time in the last hour I felt she was truly, fully back with me.

I couldn't believe I was doing this, but she absolutely deserved a proper proposal. I didn't have a ring, because I was an absolute prat, but she did deserve me on my knees. I slid her off of me, and she landed kneeling on the couch, her ass perched on her heels, her palms on her thighs, her body excited for this. And I knelt before her on the floor, nervous as fucking hell.

"Damsel?" I asked, and she nodded. "I haven't got a ring at the moment, and you've got loads of reasons to turn me down, but please take pity on this poor bugger before you and agree to be my bride? I'll be grateful for all eternity." She laughed for a moment and another tear escaped—a happy one, I hoped. "How was that?" I asked.

She flattened her hand and seesawed it back and forth, indicating I'd done a mediocre job.

I took a deep breath. "Okay, how about this? Baby, I know exactly where to bite, spank, and lick you to make you come in approximately forty-five seconds. May I have the privilege of doing so for the rest of your life?"

"Dylan!" She laughed loudly and slapped my hand away from her leg, where it had been inching towards her center.

"No?" I smiled at her. "Okay then."

I sighed audibly, grabbed both of her hands in mine, and kissed them. The thoughts that had been running through my head for the previous eighteen hours came pouring out. "Lydia, I was raised in a home full of obligation and self-sacrifice, tradition and cold grandeur, where love was scarce and fickle. I thought the best I could hope for in this life would be flickers of feigned intimacy. That I'd have to settle for the hollow pride of fulfilling those obligations alone. Then you came along. And you started filling in the cracks. You made joy the *norm*—it was rather un-British of you, actually...You dared me to imagine

that instead of barren gestures and pomp and circumstance, my
lot in life could actually be worth something. You made me want
more. And now, I'm sorry to tell you, I can't live without it. And,
my sweet girl, you've made me believe I can give it in return,
made me *want* to give it in return. I want to thrill at your suc-
cesses, embolden you when you're tentative, tend to you, make
this life beautiful for you. I want us to build something together
that neither of us would ever be able to achieve on our own. I
want to be the man your father wished he'd been able to meet.
Lydia, I love you. Please, please be my wife."

She slid off the couch and onto my lap, where I caught her,
and she threw her arms around my neck and buried her face in
my shoulder. I kissed her head, and suddenly I could feel her lips
everywhere.

"Yes," she said and kissed my neck. Then she pulled back to
look at me. "You know you still have a lot of making up to do,
right?"

"Yes," I said and quickly dove for her neck with my lips.

"And you understand I love my job, right? That I'm never going to be one of those wives who sits around needlepointing by
the fire while her husband goes off to work?"

"Yes," I said again and pulled her shirt to the side so I could
kiss her shoulder.

She put her hands to my face, forcing me to look at her. A
move I'd pulled on her a hundred times, but it was her turn.

"Dylan?" Her eyebrow was raised.

"Yes and yes."

"Then yes," she said, and her lips landed firmly on my own.
I wrapped my arms clear around her and felt her words against
my own breath. "I love you."

"I love you too, damsel."

It wasn't ten seconds after she'd said yes that I had her shirt—my shirt—off over her head and my hands on those perfect tits. Her nipples were already hard, and I knew if I put my hand down those lethal little leggings I'd find her wet and ready for me.

We downright devoured each other. Her lips were on mine. Her hands were in my hair. And for a moment, that was delightful. Our mutual indulgence in what we'd just decided. But it had been too long, too many days, and more than anything, I needed to know my damsel was mine.

I took her hands out of my hair and swiftly planted them at her back. "There we go, my sweet girl. Let's get you to bed, shall we?"

She looked at me hungrily and sank into my hold, not resisting in the slightest. She nodded, and I stood, lifting her into my arms as I went. I walked her straight to her bed in that tiny room, and even in the moment, I relished that this wouldn't be her room for long.

"I guess this means I'm moving in with you," she panted, reading my mind.

"You are," I said. "But this will do for now." I rolled her onto to her front and yanked the leggings down her legs. The sight of her bare ass pleased me immensely—she'd followed my rules even in my absence. The little minx had known I'd be back. Or hoped. I slapped her pale ass, and she jumped. "Good girl."

I ran my fingers gently up her inner leg, and she started to shiver in anticipation—I'd never get over how responsive she was to my touch. And I couldn't contain my sigh of satisfaction when I sank my fingers into her and found her slick and wanting. I looked at her face, that hair landing softly on her shoulders, those eyes at half-mast, wanton, waiting. Stunning.

This woman was going to be my *wife*.

A hundred different things floated through my mind in a flash. Things I could do to her in that moment. To reclaim her. I could sink back into that tight ass. I could bind her hands to the headboard and see her helpless before me. I could spank her silly until she came undone in my hand. And I would. I would do all of those things. But right now, for the first time in my life, I just wanted to make love to her.

I shed my clothes and began laying kisses up the backs of her legs. "Wife," I chanted between kisses. "You're going to be my wife."

I turned her over, so I could look into those brown eyes, and I took her. I took her slowly, purposefully. I held her wrists in my hands by her head. I owned her, but of course she owned me too. "Husband," she said amidst her perfect groans of pleasure, the groans I'd missed like I'd missed a limb.

She came, and her fierce spasms around me made me come too. I had a feeling that no matter how much sex she and I had over the course of our lives—and I intended to have a lot—I'd remember this time.

We spread over each other in postcoital disarray, limbs over limbs under her duvet, and I finally took in the room. Empty takeaway cartons on the floor. Bags from Tesco and Boots strewn about. An enormous box of tiny Cadbury candies surrounded by wrappers.

"Tough week?" I asked her, stroking her arm.

"Probably not as tough as yours," she said.

"I'm sorry for pushing you away, damsel."

"I'm sorry for letting you," she said.

"I didn't give you much of a choice."

She stroked my chest, running her fingers through the hair there. "Dylan?"

"Mmm?" I said, my eyes closed, fighting off the urge to fall asleep.

"Would it be okay with you if…" I gave her a moment, but she didn't seem to want to finish the thought.

"What is it, Lydia?"

"Can we keep our engagement to ourselves for a bit?"

"*You* want our relationship to be a secret?"

"I do. Just for now. I want to keep this. I know that as soon as we go public, it will feel like it's not ours anymore, and right now? Right now I want this all to ourselves. And I think we need to take this part slowly, or slower. Everything has moved so fast."

I thought about it. I wanted her at my side. I wanted the strength I got from being with her. I wanted us to be impenetrable, and I knew that coming out with it would be part of that. But I also saw what she was saying. She blamed going public with our relationship for everything that had happened. And she wasn't wrong. She couldn't see that getting engaged, getting *publicly* engaged, would actually protect us from that attention, allow us to build a wall between our life and the public eye. But I didn't need to push her on this. She needed this secret. And I could give it to her. For now.

"That's what you really want?" I asked.

"It is."

"You mean I won't get to put a ring on this finger?" I took her ring finger and slid it into my mouth, sucking it, kissing it.

"Oh, I'm sorry. Do you *have* a ring?" she asked, giving me one of her evil eyes. Cheeky girl. I slapped her pert little rear for that one, and she jolted and giggled against me. I loved that giggle.

"Touché." I sighed. "You'll get your ring, I promise." I couldn't wait to get the ring for her from the family vault. I knew just the one I wanted to see on that finger. "Yes, baby. We can keep this to ourselves for now. But you should know that if no one knows you're my fiancée I won't be able to protect you from the press the way I'd like, and I won't be able to bring you with me to certain things, as was the case Saturday night."

"I understand," she said, rolling on top of me and tucking her hands under my torso. "I just want some time."

"Then you shall have it," I said, running my fingers up her back and down again to her ass. She fell asleep on me, like a blanket, and I began to imagine what was in store for her in a way that was impossible for her to do for herself. This delightful girl lying on top of me was going to be a duchess, and she had no idea what that meant.

Chapter 29

Four days later I stood between my sister and mother at the grave of my father.

I'd said my piece, reassuring the staff of Humboldt Park and the members of the royal family alike that we would remember my father fondly (mostly a lie) and that I would proudly take on the role of seventeenth Duke of Abingdon (mostly true). And I'd given a version of the same speech earlier that day for television cameras. Now I looked across the oblong hole in the ground, across that morbid gulf, and saw Lydia on the other side.

I couldn't ignore the symbolism. As it was, an abyss of social status and tradition separated us, at least to the public eye. But I also couldn't ignore *her*. In the black cashmere coat she'd let me buy for her, her hair pulled back in a conservative knot, looking respectful, when I knew my father hadn't given her an ounce of the respect she deserved. But there she stood, looking regal, elegant, and I felt so *relieved*, calmed by her presence. No one else noticed, but I saw her twist the simple platinum band around her right middle finger. The tiny diamonds barely noticeable at first glance.

We'd found the ring at the same estate jewelers where I'd bought her the earrings less than three months ago. It hadn't been expensive and was far more subtle than the ring I would eventually put on her ring finger, but she had insisted it be something she could have presumably bought for herself, something no one would suspect was an engagement ring. But I knew. She knew. And as she rolled it around her slender finger, her eyes met mine. She was right that releasing this news, as I would do at some point, would unleash a tidal wave of events over which we'd have little control. My mother would lose her mind and undoubtedly try to make our lives miserable. On top of that, there was still Hale Shipping to be dealt with and the bloody Bresnov business—that was hotter on my ass than I ever wanted it to be. And there would always be Tristan Baileys and neighbor Michaels—men who wanted nothing more than to take her away from me, for whatever reason.

But none of that mattered. All the Michaels out there could tuck their sorry tails between their legs and go home. Because that gorgeous girl across from me, that smart-as-hell, funny, ambitious, delightful damsel was going to be *my wife*. And the world would learn what I already had: Throw a disaster our way, and see just how much stronger we are together.

About the Author

Parker Swift grew up in Providence, Rhode Island, and then grew up again in New York, London, and Minneapolis, and currently lives in Connecticut. She has spent most of her adult life examining romantic relationships in an academic lab as a professor of social psychology. Now she's exploring the romantic lives of her fictional characters in the pages of her books. When she's not writing, she spends her time with her bearded nautical husband and being told not to sing along to pop music in the car by her two sons.

Learn more at:

Twitter: @the_ParkerSwift

Facebook.com/ParkerSwiftAuthor

Instagram: @Parker.Swift

Don't miss the thrilling next installment of
Dylan and Lydia's story!

Parker Swift's Royal Scandal series
continues!

Royal Treatment

Available for pre-order now

www.ingramcontent.com/pod-product-compliance
Ingram Content Group UK Ltd.
Pitfield, Milton Keynes, MK11 3LW, UK
UKHW022258280225
455674UK00001B/88